CHANGE AT
JAMAICA

CHANGE AT JAMAICA

A NOVEL

MARSHALL MESSER

BMA Press

Press

BMA Press
P.O. Box 545, Monterey, MA 01245

Copyright 2013 by Marshall Messer

ISBN 978-1-930589-32-2

Printed in the United States of America
10   9   8   7   6   5   4   3   2

Book design by Meighan Cavanaugh

This is a work of fiction. Names, characters, places, and incidents either are the product of the author's imagination or are used fictitiously.

And you, my father, there on the sad height,
Curse, bless, me now with your fierce tears, I pray.

—Dylan Thomas

All life is six to five against.

—Damon Runyon

BELMONT

The Captain and Genie always went to the track together. It was a Saturday ritual they had. For a while I tagged along. At the time I was renting a furnished room in the dreary apartment of a divorced cab driver on the Upper West Side. Lipschitz, his name was, which was perfect because he would start cursing from the moment he woke up. What a piece of work he was, always carping about his ex-wife. I could understand why she divorced him, but I could never figure out why she married him in the first place. As his part of the settlement, Lipschitz inherited the lease on their dilapidated railroad flat. The extra rooms he rented to various schnooks and losers who called the place "the Penthouse" as though it were a swanky residence. True, it happened to be on the top floor, but if you asked me it was just a flophouse for social misfits.

Alvin Lipschitz. What a character. He'd converted the living room and dining room into bedrooms so there wasn't even a common area where you could socialize or watch TV. Guys would congregate in the tiny kitchen, with its grimy, claustrophobic view of the airshaft, complaining bitterly about jobs, bosses, women, kids and ex-spouses, or else they'd loiter in the long, narrow hallway like stranded commuters on a subway platform.

Lipschitz had a minifleet of two Checkers, each of them held together with spit and scotch tape. The door handle was always popping off, the trunk was twisted fast with a coat hanger, and the meter had to be smacked just right to get it to start. What did I know? In no time I was driving a cab five days a week on top of working for my father. After what I was used to, it was like a sharp stick in the eye. I was new to the city, uprooted from the familiar routines of college life, working these grueling twelve-hour shifts and flopping in this dark, depressing apartment. The only thing I lived for was those Saturday afternoons at the track.

Saturday mornings I'd buy the *Racing Form,* sit in a luncheonette on Broadway. and handicap over hotcakes or eggs. Then I'd hop on the subway and take the train out to Belmont. If they were racing at Aqueduct, we'd meet there. One thing about the track, it was the only place I could get along with the Captain. I was in hot water again and things were pretty rocky between us. Five months earlier, at the end of the fall semester of my senior year, I had flunked out of college.

Saturday, June ninth, instead of participating in graduation exercises with my class in upstate New York, I was on Long Island betting on ponies. I could tell you I was painfully in touch with the magnitude of my failure—that I was racked by guilt, mortified with shame, tortured by regret—but that would be a lie. Any uncomfortable feelings I had I managed all too easily to repress beneath the pangs of elation I felt whenever it occurred to me that on this momentous day for my classmates I was playing hooky.

I remember thinking, *Guilt is such a stupid emotion.* Here I was at Belmont Park, my favorite place in the world, for the running of the Belmont Stakes, the biggest race of the year. I felt as if I'd been invited to an exclusive party, me and seventy thousand other lucky guests for whom the long lines and the crowds were scant inconvenience for a shot at seeing the first Triple Crown winner in twenty-five years. More than a mere spectator, I could well be an eyewitness to racing history. What was I supposed to do, feel bad?

So I'm at Belmont, right, and I'm feeling like I've died and gone to racing heaven. Nothing bothers me. Not the crowds. Not the abominable weather. Not the snail-paced wagering lines in the clubhouse swollen with penny-ante bettors. Not the twenty-minute traffic jam at the concession counter or the ten-minute wait for the men's room. Not even the clubhouse dress code that requires gentlemen be properly attired. So what if we're packed in like the subway at rush hour—regulars and first-timers in their summer sportcoats, WASPS from the New York Racing Association in their boring blazers and khakis—our smiles congealed and foreheads glazed as we slowly, courteously, immaculately roast to death?

The only sport jacket I own is of tan corduroy, so in this relentless heat I'm a walking sponge. Patches of sweat clot the cotton work shirt to my armpits. Trickles of sweat saturate the small of my back. Beads of sweat sprout on my forehead and every now and then plop onto the *Racing Form*, speckling the past performance charts. What do I care?

Nothing bothers me because I'm winning.

I got lucky in the fourth with a two-dollar exacta. That's what they call an exotic wager—a bet in which you specify two horses to finish first and second. So my 16-1 shot beat out the favorite by a head. My winning ticket paid a tidy hundred and forty-three smackers.

Alone in my father's reserved seats, I should be doping out the next race, which he and my uncle have already gone to the pari-mutuel windows to bet. But now that my pockets have been inflated with the track's money, I feel wonderfully buoyant, like I'm floating in a hot-air balloon. On the blacktop fronting the grandstand, along a corridor between the rail and the permanent seats, people mill about, the men in T-shirts and shorts, the women in sundresses or cutoffs and halter tops. Just looking at them makes me feel cooler. Beyond the rail, within the brown strip of racing oval and the inner turf courses, are the manicured grounds of the infield. A dozen Canada geese in a descending skein glide in and land beside a kidney-shaped pond dotted with picturesque islets about the size of those on which people are marooned in a *New Yorker* cartoon. The sky is hazy, and a tepid breeze offers no relief from the heat. Wiping my brow with the sleeve of my sport jacket, I return to handicapping.

The seventh race showcases a stellar field of three-year-olds that would easily make it the feature event on any weekday card. I study each horse's past performance chart, which lists its most recent races. The array of times, facts and figures represents the efforts and potential of a flesh-and-blood animal, although it's not always easy to keep this crucial idea in mind. As the Captain never tires of saying, each chart tells a story about a horse's fortunes that allows the perceptive handicapper to gauge whether the horse is well-conditioned and racing fit. Horses tend to round into winning form, hold that form for several races, then for various reasons lose their competitive edge. In a small field, it can be fairly easy to isolate the horses that are "live." When ten or twelve thoroughbreds are entered in a race, it's a lot more complicated to suss out the ones that are ready to run or "well-meant." My Uncle Gene hates it. With so many horses, he says, it's like betting on dice with legs.

I can't seem to get a handle on the race. A slew of entries vie for my attention, including the favorite, Forego, who ran fourth in the Kentucky Derby, eleven lengths behind Secretariat. At one hundred eleven pounds, he has as they say the "feather"—he's toting the lowest weight. And his three bullet works over the Belmont track mean that Forego trained faster on those days than all other horses who exercised at the same distance. But at 6-5 his odds are hardly attractive, so I'm looking for a way to beat him.

My deliberations are interrupted by the familiar trumpet flourish, which heralds the arrival of the field from the paddock. As the horses amble onto the track, the crowd stirs and applause ripples through the stands.

The 1 horse, Paternity, who is nuzzling his stable pony, doesn't interest me. Paternity may have finished in the money in each of his eight starts, but he likes to do his running in the slop, and today's sun-baked strip won't be to his liking. Nor can I get behind the 2 horse, a sprinter named Black Balled, who's stretching out to a mile and a sixteenth for the first time. Forego, the favorite, is next, and he's followed by Angle Light, who stunned the racing world in April when he beat Secretariat. Since then, however, he's fallen completely out of form, twenty lengths up the track in the Derby and fourteen back in the Withers.

As the field parades lazily before the grandstand, the 8 horse rears and the jockey fights to settle him down. Tugging from side to side, the horse caracoles in a ragged circle, bares his teeth, kicks at the dirt, lurches frantically toward the rail, then pulls at the reins, arching his neck downward as if to inspect the bandages on his forelegs. The rank entry is Indian Sign, at 52-1 the longest shot in the field. The jock gives the colt his head and the animal bolts away, a soupy lather oozing between his hind legs. The fractious colt gallops off, blazes down the long Belmont stretch and breezes around the clubhouse turn, his race prematurely run; forget about him.

I scan back to the post parade, training my binoculars on the 10, a nicely dappled bay, up on his toes and looking fit. A glance at the program, it's Illberightback, a son of Lucky Debonair, who won the Derby in '65. The 10 has back-to-back wins, both against older horses, a good sign. Won his last race here at Belmont, just four-fifths of a second off the track record. Bullet five-furlong work on May 31st. 20-1 in the morning line, but 13-1 on the board and dropping. Definitely a live one. I gather up *Racing Form*, program and field glasses and elbow my way up the crowded aisle toward the betting lines.

The shortest line I can find is strung out past the oak-paneled columns on the clubhouse floor, almost to the glass doors that lead to the reserved seats. Six minutes to post, but we're hardly moving. I check the odds board: Illberightback is 12-1. I decide to bet ten to win and ten to place. If I lose, I'll still be up a C-note, but now I'm playing for bragging rights. I've won more than my uncle Gene a few times, and I always lose less than he does, but just once I'd like to win more than the Captain. I sort through my pocket change for my lucky coin, a quarter-sized English groat my father gave me for my eighteenth birthday. Minted in Shakespeare's day, it's worn thin as a silver wafer, but you can still make out the date, 1590. I like the slick feel of it between my fingers and rub it for luck as the line babysteps forward.

Five minutes to post.

We move up several feet, but then the line stalls and I keep looking at my watch like an expectant father. I'm going to get shut out here for sure unless I can find someone I know. Quitting the line, I scan the betting queues for a wiry guy with a pencil-thin mustache, a receding hairline and close-cropped brown hair surrounding a bald spot the size of a beer coaster. Even in this crowd, Uncle Gene should not be hard to locate, not with the eye-popping outfit he's sporting. Today he's decked out in a plaid madras number—purple, chartreuse and pink—over a toxic-yellow polo made of some fashionable, unnatural fiber. Bingo! I spot his gaudy sport jacket six back from the pari-mutuel clerk.

"Genie, I been looking for you. Can I sneak in here and make a bet?"

"Sure, Eddie, if we don't get closed out." He's wearing a disgusted scowl and punching his fist into an open palm. "Can you believe this? Almost half a motherfuckin hour." I get in line, ignoring the hostile glare of the Larchmont type behind us, a dignified, silver-haired gentleman in blue blazer and green-and-yellow plaid slacks. "Come on!" Gene shouts, "move it up, for Chrissake. I swear this is the slowest fuckin line I've ever seen." A bettor peels away from the window and we shuffle a couple of steps closer. "About time," he says.

"Excuse me," says the plaid slacks, "I really must insist—"

Gene turns on the man. "You got a problem, pal?" The silver-haired gentleman holds the stare a moment, then breaks off and buries his eyes in his program. "That's right, buddy," Gene says, "mind your own business. What a fuckin madhouse," he says to me. "I can't believe you found me in this mess."

"Must be my lucky day." The line creeps a few feet forward.

"It sure ain't mine," he says. "I had that 10-1 shot in the second. It lost by a fuckin head."

"That's tough," I commiserate.

"Then in the fourth," he says, "I back a favorite and I get beat out by that 16-1 shot. I don't care what you say, you can't tell me that horse figured."

"Oh, I don't know, Genie, I thought it was finally rounding into—"

"16-1! You know when that horse figures? When the Dodgers move back to Brooklyn." He emits a short, bitter laugh, like a snort.

"Some days nothing goes right, eh, Uncle?"

"Can you imagine?" he says. "Me betting a favorite like the Captain?"

"What's the world coming to?"

"Ah, I'm disgusted. I play the chalk, a longshot comes in. I play a longshot, the favorite gets up to beat me." They say you can make a small fortune at the track so long as you start out with a large one. The adage would apply perfectly to Uncle Gene if only he were rich.

"You'll get 'em this race, Genie."

"Ah, forget about me. How are you doing today, good?"

"Yeah, I'm up for once."

"That's right. You hit that big exacta. Me, I'm down two bills."

"I hope you paid the rent this month."

"Very funny," he says. "How's the Captain doing, good?" We called my father the Captain because of his military rank, captain of artillery, and because he was by nature a martinet, but we never said it to his face. He'd have taken it as an insult, because it was technically untrue. When he retired from the service, he had been promoted to the rank of major.

"Did you ever notice, Genie, you always think everyone is doing fine but you?"

Gene shrugs. "What can I say?"

"The Captain is down more than you are."

"Finally," he says, "some good news."

"Say, where is my old man?"

"Fifty-dollar window. Where else?"

"That figures."

"So tell me," he says, "is your father behaving himself, or did he tear you a new asshole?"

"All I can say is, Gene, it's a good thing I'm winning. You know how he loves a winner." With a minute to post, only two bettors are ahead of us. "What do you think of the 10 in this race?" I show him my *Racing Form*.

"It probably has a shot, but I'm going with Adaptive Ace."

I check the board reflexively. My horse continues to drop, a good sign: It's now 11-1. Gene's pick, the 6 horse, is a huge long-shot. "For godsake, Gene, it's 41-1. Are you nuts?"

"So what? I think he's being overlooked." I point out that the horse finished eighth in the Jersey Derby, twelve lengths out of it. "Throw it out," says Gene. "It was too long and he didn't like the slop. But he won at a mile and a sixteenth a month ago, and the race before that he was third to Stop the Music."

"I think the heat is getting to you."

"I got a feeling about this one. It's a huge overlay, and I like that they're throwing on blinkers for the first time."

We reach the windows just before post time. I had decided to bet ten to win and ten to place, but facing the clerk something comes over me and I hear myself betting twice as much as I intended, but on Gene's horse, Adaptive Ace. My front pocket bulges with folded bills, wads of notes amassed from cashing my winning exacta ticket and from breaking tens and twenties on earlier bets. Behind me, impatient bettors are shouting, "Move it up." "Come on, already." "Let's go!" I count out forty bucks while the guy in the plaid slacks sighs in frustration. The clerk punches out four green-bordered, ten-dollar tickets and wishes me a perfunctory "Good luck" as the bell rings to close out the betting.

"Move your *tuchis*," says Gene, "I don't want to miss this." We hurry to watch the race. It's too crowded to return in time to the Captain's box so we join the loiterers who have no seats and the other late bettors, already two deep, behind the waist-high partition that divides the reserved seating section from the clubhouse floor.

"Illberightback is in. Waiting for Pontoise." The track announcer is identifying the horses as they load into the gate. "They're all in line."

Among the crush of people pressing up behind the railing, it's hard to get a clear angle of vision. Standing on tiptoe, I manage to aim my binoculars to avoid craned heads, wide-brimmed hats, and field glasses braced high by jutting arms and elbows, but before I can focus, the blurry doors of the gate spring open with a ring and a roar and the horses surge forward.

From way outside a horse shoots to the lead, its jockey in white silks with cherry-colored sleeves. I bring the number on the saddle-cloth into focus; it's the 8, Indian Sign, the rank colt I had categorically dismissed. After a quarter mile, Indian Sign is still breezing up the backstretch, half a length in front of Angle Light, another surprise.

"Cheap speed," says Gene. "He won't last." Sure enough, within ten seconds, Angle Light ranges up to collar Indian Sign, then edges ahead at the half-mile pole. The horse beat Secretariat in April. At 8-1, will he score another upset today? Four lengths back, Forego is a well-placed fifth, a head in front of Illberight-back as they round the sweeping Belmont turn. Gustines has Forego well in hand, holding back the favorite and rating him. Jockeys don't actually sit on the saddle as they ride but balance above it, bracing their thighs and knees against the thorough-bred's shoulders. Standing in the stirrups, Gustines leans forward in the standard "monkey crouch" over the withers and neck of the massive bay gelding, his seat high off the saddle, with plenty of horse left to call on. It's several more lengths to the rear of the pack, where Adaptive Ace has been shuffled back.

Someone shouts, "There goes Forego," and with a sudden, riveting rush on the far turn, the favorite sprints effortlessly to the lead, takes command at the head of the stretch and draws away steadily from the field.

Forego gallops down the lane, five, six, seven lengths in front. Gene says, "Look at that sonofabitch go." But I'm watching Ill-berightback, the horse I didn't bet on, follow Forego's path into the stretch and drive steadily past horses into second place. He's clear by two lengths in mid-stretch, and I'm castigating myself because I didn't trust my intuition.

But then Adaptive Ace, the 6 horse, closes rapidly, along with the 9, and they draw abreast of Illberightback with half a furlong to the finish. They're bunched tightly, 6 on the rail, 10 in between, the 9 outside, whips flailing, hooves pounding, necks striving, the 9 nosing ahead, the 6 rallying, the 10 gamely digging in.

"Come on, 6," I growl. "Bring it home, baby! You can do it." The horse seems to respond to my urging, refusing to give in, wedged against the rail, yet surging toward the finish. Even so, it's too close to call as the three horses hit the wire in a blur of bobbing heads.

"Photo for place," booms the track announcer. "Hold all tickets." On the toteboard the PHOTO sign is illuminated. Forego's number 4 is positioned at the top of the board where the order of finish is listed. The rest is blank. It takes as little as thirty seconds to furnish the stewards with a projection of the photo, but they may study it for five minutes before making a decision. We wait impatiently as the crowd disperses.

"So you bet the 6," says Gene.

"You talked me into it."

"What do you think?" he says. "Triple dead heat?"

I laugh. Perhaps the most famous photograph in racing annals records the finish of the Carter Handicap in 1944. Brownie, Bossuet and Wait A Bit are tied for first, the tips of their nostrils touching a thin white line that represents an extension of the finish pole.

"That would be something, eh, Gene? Triple dead heat for place?"

"Fuck, yeah," he says. "It would be fuckin historic."

Forego trots back toward the finish line to sporadic then robust applause. A groom grasps the side of the halter and walks the big thoroughbred into the winner's circle. Gustines salutes the trainer with a wave of the whip and tosses it to the smiling groom.

The tote screen goes blank for a moment, then posts the order of finish: 4, 6, 10, 9. A collective gasp, then bursts of joyous shouting.

"6!" I shout. Gene smiles and shakes my hand.

A moment later the race is official. Forego pays $4 to win; Adaptive Ace returns $18.60 to place. And I have it ten times.

"What a price, Gene. How much did you have on him?"

"Twenty to win."

"Yeah, but how much to place?" Gene makes a circle of his thumb and forefinger and holds it to his eye as if it were a jeweler's loupe.

"Zippity-doo-dah."

"A longshot like that and you don't put a saver on it?"

He shrugs. "Hey, man, I only play to win."

"Bummer," I say, shaking my head.

We walk down the concrete steps to the second row and edge across to our seats. The Captain brightens when he sees us.

"Where you guys been?" he says. "Did you see that race?"

"Pretty exciting," I say. "You had Forego?"

"Yeah, I had him for a few bucks," he says. "Did you catch that final time? One forty and four-fifths. What do you think of that?"

"Not bad," says Gene.

"Not bad?" mocks the Captain. "It's a goddamn tick off the track record. Don't forget, he wasn't even pushed; he won by nine under a hand ride. Mark my words, that Forego is going to be some horse." The Captain takes a leather case from inside his sportcoat and removes a fat eight-inch cigar, a huge thing called a Sultan, which he places under his nose and sniffs approvingly. In the elaborate ritual that follows, he applies a silver clipper to the cigar, incising a small V-shaped depression in the tip. Holding the cigar away from his mouth, he strikes a three-inch match, the flame of which never actually touches the rolled tobacco revolving slowly in his fingertips. A second match to the scorched end ensures a dull ring of orange-red that erupts at the first puff into glowing intensity. "How'd you guys make out?" he asks, puffing aggressively.

"I had the 6 to place, Dad."

"You had that 40-1 shot? That's a hell of a price."

"What can I say, Dad? I'm having a good day."

"Nice going," he says, patting me on the back.

"Genie put me on to it, but he only bet it to win."

"Don't remind me."

"What are you, an idiot? You come up with a 40-1 shot and you don't back him up? How many times have I told you—"

"Will you stop with the lectures," says Gene.

The Captain shakes his head sadly. "What's the point?" he says. "You'll never learn."

"I should have Forego at even money? No thanks."

The Captain fans out an eyeful of five winning fifty-dollar tickets. "Read 'em and weep," he says.

"You're amazing, Dad."

"Mazel tov," says Gene without enthusiasm.

"How many times do I have to tell you, genius? It's better to have an even-money winner than a 40-1 loser." He puffs triumphantly on the cigar, looking pleased with himself, smoke rising in gossamer ribbons toward the scalloped Belmont roof. Then he laughs heartily, the chubby hand with the outsized cigar quivering. Flakes of ash sift down and the fingers, like plump Vienna sausages, casually brush them aside, off the capacious fuchsia-colored sportcoat and the abundant belly encased in powder-blue silk, off the white belt and the yellow linen slacks, off the pale skin exposed above the thin white socks, and off the socks themselves and the tasseled white loafers.

Gene sits down, whips open the *Form*, studies it a moment, then stares off toward the parking lot beyond the clubhouse turn where cars bake in the sun, their windows mirrors of seething light. Every now and then he grimaces and shakes his head.

My father doesn't seem to notice. He's busy whistling "Sidewalks of New York" as he peruses Forego's chart. I have to give the old man credit. It takes guts to bet big on a short-priced horse when you're already down a bundle, I don't care what my uncle says. Gene would have you believe that betting a favorite doesn't qualify as a sporting wager. But the chalk only wins a third of all races, so backing a horse that goes off at 3-5 is by no means a sure thing. A lot of guys go broke like that, but the Captain has a knack for doing it at the right time. I can't tell you how many Saturdays, hundreds of dollars in the red, he's salvaged the day by bridge-jumping on an odds-on favorite.

"So tell me, Dad, did you have a betting key?" My father

stresses that some races are more bettable than others, especially those that can be reduced to a single factor, which gives a bettor the edge he needs to win. It might be the horse's last outing, how it runs after a layoff, a recent training workout, or knowing if the sire was a good grass or mud horse.

"You want to know the key? All right, Eddie, I'll tell you, but pay attention so you learn something." The Captain points to the bottom of Forego's chart. "You see this bullet work, four furlongs in forty-five seconds flat? That's the key, right there. You want to know why?" Before I can reply, he's off and running. "First let me ask you a question. You ever see a faster training work than that? No you haven't. Sure, during a race you might see a talented sprinter go a quicker half mile. Usually it's a Grade One speedball like Tentam or Shecky Greene. But during a workout? Never. Now look at Secretariat's work on the same day. Same distance but a second and a half slower, and he's the best thoroughbred in training."

"You mean you expected him to win easily?"

"Are you kidding? Forego was a stickout in this race. The horse ran fourth in the Kentucky Derby."

"Yeah, Dad, but eleven lengths back."

"Doesn't matter. He beat nine other horses, and this was a much shorter race."

"But he'd never won at more than seven furlongs, and he was 6-1 in the morning line. And in the Withers—"

"As usual, Eddie, you don't know what you're talking about. The race here, once the favorite was scratched, he had no competition."

"But how did you know he would get the distance?" I ask.

"He was bred for distance. You think they'd run him in the Kentucky Derby if he wasn't? His sire, Forli, was a terrific grass horse who was South American champion." He pronounces that last word as *champeen*. "There was a lot of ballyhoo seven or eight years ago when Charlie Whittingham brought him over. Remember that, Genie?"

Gene nods. "Leo's right, kid. Forli was a good one, but he only ran on the weeds. His first race in the States he set a track record at Santa Anita."

"At a mile and a sixteenth," adds the Captain, "the same distance as today's race. Then he broke down. It was big news at the time."

"How the heck am I supposed to know that?"

My father shrugs. "I guess you still got a few things to learn," he says. "The point is, Eddie, Forego had the class and the breeding, and he was ready to roll. This field was the perfect spot for him." He pauses briefly to puff on the Sultan. "I'll give you a tip," he says. "The first time Forego switches to grass, bet the house on him."

"I'll remember that," I say.

"Stick with me, kid," he says, patting my knee. "I'll show you how to beat this game." I believe it. My father not only knows breeding and history, he has the uncanny ability to predict how a race will develop. Nine times out of ten he knows which horse will go to the front, which ones will stalk from off the pace and which horses will come from behind. I could listen to him talk horses all day long, especially because when he's holding forth, he forgets to harp on what a disappointment I am to him.

"So listen," says the Captain, "did you hear the one about the guy who goes to the doctor complaining he's got aches and pains? The doctor runs some tests and tells the guy to come back a week later for the results. When the patient returns, the doctor says, 'I've got good news and bad news.' Guy says, 'Gimme the bad news first.' Doctor tells him, 'I'm terribly sorry but you have terminal cancer, it's inoperable, and you got three weeks to live.' Patient says, 'Jesus, doc, that's awful. What's the good news?' Doctor says, 'You see my receptionist, the gorgeous redhead with the great pair of tits? I'm fuckin her!'" The Captain lets loose a high-pitched, rapid-fire cackling. "That's a good one, huh? Abby Flynn told it to me. And you know what a character he is." Flynn is a betting clerk at the track. No one knows his real name, only his moniker, Abby, which apparently is short for "obsessed, obnoxious, and abnormal."

"Figures," says Gene.

Preparations are under way for the big race. A red watering truck rolls down the middle of the track, its long metal arm casting a spume of spray almost to the rail. Behind it, a fleet of green tractors inches past the grandstand in a parody of a stretch run, the one on the inside leading by a length. They are staggered equally from the rail out, so that their paths slightly overlap. Each tractor drags a flat iron pallet studded with teeth to harrow the track's surface into precise, well-groomed furrows.

The toteboard flashes the morning line odds for the Belmont Stakes and money quickly pours in on Secretariat. Having opened at 2-5, his odds keep dropping until the board reads 1-9. I've never seen that before and marvel aloud about the odds. The Captain explains that these are the lowest the board can register. The true odds are slightly lower; if you bet two dollars, you stand to win twenty cents. You have to wager ten dollars to win a buck.

The TV monitors spring to life, showing a rerun of the recent Preakness. Secretariat lies sixth and last passing the stands for the first time. Around the turn, he unleashes a blazing burst of tactical speed, sweeping past the competition to take the lead. The electrifying move, surprisingly early in such a long race, is stunning to watch, like Jackie Robinson stealing home in the World Series. Anyone who saw the race is destined to remember it.

"See that?" says the Captain. "That's why the horse can't lose."

"Lots of things can happen in a big race, Leo."

"Yeah, Dad. Look at all the hopefuls who won the Derby and the Preakness and bombed in the Belmont." The last and longest of the Triple Crown races, the mile-and-a-half Belmont Stakes has thwarted the ambitions of half of the sixteen horses who managed to win the first two legs.

"They weren't Secretariat."

"Just because the horse makes the cover of *Time* and *Newsweek*," I say, "doesn't mean he's going to win. Even Secretariat can have a bad day. He lost to Angle Light, didn't he?"

"Eddie's right," says Gene. "Three races in five weeks are a lot for a three-year-old, I don't care who he is. I wouldn't be surprised if Secretariat bounces today."

"Keep dreaming, genius. Secretariat's a stickout."

"You're forgetting something, Leo. Secretariat's a Bold Ruler colt, which means he can get a mile and a quarter, and then runs out of gas."

"As usual, Genie, you don't know what you're talking about.

Allow me to enlighten you. The key to Secretariat's breeding, at least for the purposes of stamina, is not in the Bold Ruler line but on the dam's side. And the sire of the dam happens to be Prince-quillo, who as I recall could run all day."

"He still has to deal with the heat," says Gene. The Captain eyeballs his brother over the top of his wire-rim glasses. "Well he does, Leo. It's humid today."

"Ah!" My father dismisses Gene with a wave of his hand. "What about you, Eddie, you got any other thoughts on this race?"

I pore over the *Form*, trying to find an angle that I've over-looked. I'd love to give the Captain a longshot. He'd never forget it. He might even cut me some slack and let up on me a little. I'm sure he'd still hock me, but that's better than being ignored. After Woodstock, he wouldn't even talk to me.

I have a sudden brainstorm. "Hey, I might take a flyer on Twice a Prince." At 20-1, Twice a Prince is the longest shot in the field.

"Why would you do that?" asks the Captain.

"He's had the most experience against older horses. And he had an excuse in the Derby. He was acting up before the race."

"Interesting," says my father. "At least you're thinking."

"And like you always say, Dad, 'pace makes the race.' If Secre-tariat and Sham hook up in a speed duel, the race sets up for the closers."

"You know, Eddie," he says, scanning the Form, "you might have something here."

"You really think the horse has a chance, Dad?"

"I think Twice a Prince could beat Sham. That's what I think."

"Not Secretariat? It would be a hell of an upset."

"Get it through your head," says the Captain. "Secretariat's a shoo-in. He'll win this in a walkover. And probably set a new stakes record while he's at it." Gene laughs his head off, but the Captain's prediction isn't an idle one. Secretariat won the Derby in record time, and he would have set a new mark in the Preakness had the official timer not malfunctioned. On top of that, the Belmont strip has been lightning fast of late. Four track records—at six furlongs, six and a half furlongs, seven furlongs, and one mile—have been smashed at Belmont over the last three weeks.

"New stakes record, my ass," says Gene. "Jesus, Leo, you think you know everything. What will you predict next, that he's going wire to wire?" The winner of the Belmont usually comes from just off the pace. It's unheard of to win the race all the way on the lead.

"I wouldn't be surprised."

"A hundred bucks says you're out of your fuckin mind."

"Save your money," says the Captain. "But you don't have to be a genius, genius, to know that Secretariat is head and shoulders the class of this race. You see him fly around that turn in the Preakness? You know how he did that? Because he's a natural lefty. He leads with that left and it pulls him around those turns."

"How do you come up with this stuff?" asks Gene.

"A natural lefty, Dad? Are you serious?"

"I'm telling you, he's a lefty, like me. You think I'm pulling your leg? Mark my words, that Secretariat is a special horse. He's got all the intangibles—the breeding, the speed, the heart, the effortless action—"

"The left-footed lead," I add. My uncle cracks up.

"Give us a break," says Gene. "First Forego, now Secretariat. You think maybe we can watch the race before we enshrine him in the Hall of Fame?"

"Go ahead, have your fun," says the Captain. "But when are you guys going to learn that there are two kinds of horses?" I know what's coming—a monologue I've heard many times before. "There are pigs and there are stickouts. The stickout wins every time. Why is that?" asks the Captain. "Because he has class." I catch Gene's attention, and roll my eyes. He smirks and shakes his head. "What's class? Two horses are running neck and neck down the stretch, they look each other—"

"In the eye!" I declaim, theatrically, imitating a pompous Shakespearean actor. *"And the pig folds in the face of the superior animal!* For godsake, Dad, we've heard this lecture a thousand times. How the horse with class digs down and has the heart to gut it out and pull away, blah blah blah." The Captain regards me with distaste, like I'm a housefly that has landed on his steak.

"Sure, Eddie, you've heard it before, but when are you going to learn it?" The Captain emphasizes every beat with a finger jab to my face. "When the hell will you look for the class of the race and not the horse with the highest speed ratings?" He is getting worked up and people are looking at us.

"Come on, Dad, I just won a hundred and eighty-six bucks on a 40-1 shot."

"Big deal! You picked the horse that came in second, nine lengths back. You didn't pick the winner."

"Silly me," I say. "And I thought the point of gambling was to win money."

"Let me put it in words you can understand. There are winners and there are also-rans. When the hell will you stop being an also-ran?"

"I don't believe this," I say, throwing up my hands.

"The kid is winning," says Gene. "Don't be a killjoy."

"Who are you, his lawyer? You representing him now?"

"Come on, Leo, knock it off."

"I'm curious, counselor," says the Captain, all genial sarcasm. "Tell me something. When the hell is he going to get down to business and stop pissing away his chances to make something of himself? When is he going to stop flunking out of college, can you tell me that? Does he want to drive a cab for the rest of his life like Uncle Sol? Tell him if he don't watch out, he may end up like you, riding up and down in elevators all day without a pot to piss in." Gene looks as if he's been slapped across the face. He glowers at his brother, oblivious to the stares we have attracted.

"What the hell is your problem, Leo?"

"My problem? I'll tell you my problem. I'll tell all of you my problem," he announces, addressing the people who are watching. "I can't get my son to wise up." He glances at me and shakes his head. "Kids! They're like pancakes. Sometimes you have to throw the first one out."

I stare at the *Racing Form*, too stunned to reply. The miniature type seems to be moving in and out of focus. I wonder if I need reading glasses. I rest my eyes for a few seconds and when I open them I have the strangest sensation: names, times and figures are so many inkblots that defy any attempt to invest them with meaning. In a long, disorienting moment, they seem to lift off the page and whirl around me like a tornado.

The toteboard flashes and resets, updating the amount bet on each horse and adjusting the odds; I scrutinize it intently. A dull throbbing extends from my temples to the back of my head. Every time the Captain puffs on his cigar, swirls of smoke drift past, fanning the ache and watering my eyes. Things are closing in on me. Like a horse with blinkers on, I have no peripheral vision. The crowd noise, the glaring sun, the scent of strong perfume, the brassy enthusiasm of a Dixieland band, the smell of hotdogs, the puffs of smoke, the sudden shouts and laughter meld into a sensory roar that leaves me small and distant, insulated from everything around me as if by layers of dense cotton.

The Captain announces he's going to cash, then visit the paddock to look at Secretariat. He sidesteps toward the aisle, moving his husky bulk ponderously. When he's gone, Gene and I sit in silence, ignoring the tumult of the crowd. The odor of my father's cigar smoke lingers, rancid as his remarks, in the heavy air.

The first time I went to the races, it seemed like everyone was smoking a cigar. That was at the old Jamaica Race Course. My dad bet two bucks for me on each race and told me to pick the horses by the sound of their names. The only one I remember is Timely Hitting, because he took a bad step down the stretch and splintered his cannon bone. The colt pulled up, his useless limb flopping like a wet mop. I started to sob, and my father ordered me to stop. "There's no crying at the track," he said. "Stop making a scene." But I only cried harder, so he dragged me out of there, pissed at having to leave early. I was eight years old, and he didn't take me back till I was thirteen.

"Your old man can be a real jerk," says Gene.

"Tell me about it. The best day I ever had at the track and he makes me feel like I'm losing."

"Fuck him, the prick. Now that he's raking it in he thinks his shit don't stink."

"Why does he have to embarrass me like that?"

"Because that's the way he is," says Gene. "Why are you so down in the dumps? Look at me. I don't have a pot to piss in."

I laugh. "Yeah, Gene, when are you going to stop being an also-ran?"

"Come on, kid, let's go for walk."

"You want to get a bet down?"

"Forget it," he says. "You can't make any money on this race."

We take the escalator down. Gene jabs an elbow into my side and gestures with his chin at a blonde in a spaghetti-strap sundress rising toward us on the escalator opposite.

"Check out the dairy on that farm," he whispers, draping a fraternal arm around my neck. "You know what Louie Armstrong said. The three best things in life all begin with the letter 'M'— music, money, and *mmm-mmm* pussy." I'm laughing so hard, I trip getting off the escalator. My uncle is so cool, you wouldn't guess he was only eleven years younger than my dad.

We enter the crowded rest room, filing toward the rearmost stalls. The last one opens, and Gene lurches into it, jumping the line, acting like he's wildly drunk and about to throw up. I follow him in and lock the door.

"It's okay," I say. "You're going to be okay, Morty."

Gene looks at me and mouths, "Morty?" Then he gets down to moaning and groaning. He sticks a finger into his wide-open mouth and dry heaves loudly toward the toilet. He keeps it up as he unzips his pants and urinates for almost a full minute. "Jesus," he announces, shaking off his dick, "I feel like shit." And in a whisper he cracks, "but I'm pissing like a racehorse."

"You feeling better, Morty?"

Gene chuckles quietly as he takes out a small nugget of hash, holds it over a plastic butane lighter until it crumbles, then fills the tiny bowl of a slim, silver pipe. He takes a hit, then another, inhaling deeply until he launches into a spasm of coughing. "Take it easy," I whisper, patting him on the back. "Breathe in more air to cool the smoke." He nods assent, hands me the pipe and looks on as I take a couple of tokes, demonstrating my flawless technique. I help him out of the stall, which reeks of the sweet, acrid smoke.

"Jesus, this place stinks," Gene says loudly. "Is somebody smoking drugs in here? Where the hell is a cop when you need one? I'm getting racetrack security up here immediately."

"Good idea, Morty. We should alert, forthwith, the local authorities."

Sniggering like schoolboys, we stumble past the line of people waiting for urinals. As we clear the men's room entrance, we erupt into giddy hysterics.

"Did you say 'forthwith?'" Gene asks.

I'm so weak I can only nod.

"Who the hell is Morty?"

"I made it up," I say, wiping tears from my eyes.

"Morty?"

"Stop," I plead. "I'm gonna pee in my pants."

He peers at me like I'm a laboratory specimen. "Are you on drugs or something? Damned college kids," he mutters, and takes off on a harangue about the youth of America not respecting its cherished institutions, all the while weaving through the crowded clubhouse to the nearest bar. We order some Schlitz, which tastes tepid and watery in the heat.

"Hey," Gene says, wiping his mustache of foam, "you hear

about the handicapper who has a heart attack after the first race? He has a 50-1 shot come in and it's too much for him. His buddy is standing over him when a cop comes up and asks, 'Is he alive?' 'Yeah,' he says, 'but only in the daily double.'"

"Cute."

"Speaking of cute," says Gene, as a redhead passes. He corkscrews his body to check her out. "Boy, did she give you the once over."

"Really?" I look after her as she disappears around a column.

"I can't figure out what women see in you," he says, gesturing with the beer cup. "Is it the blue eyes? The dark, curly hair? The air of brooding intensity?" He reaches out to feel the lapel of my sportcoat. "It can't be the *shmatte* you have on. How can you wear that sweat collector in this weather?"

"What's wrong with it?"

"I'll bring you over to my guy. Get you some decent threads."

"You mean like that plaid sportcoat? I doubt even Heywood Hale Broun would have the guts to wear something like that."

"Very funny," he says. "You know how light this is? It's part silk."

"I'd rather sweat."

"You've got no taste."

"And you've got enough for the both of us."

"Feel this," he says, showing off the neon-yellow fabric of his shirt. "Fifteen bucks. Never needs ironing." I touch the material, my hand leaping away as from red-hot metal.

"My God," I say, "it's radioactive. What do you call this stuff?"

"Qiana," he says proudly. "Meet the new miracle fiber. The next generation in polyester."

"Wear it well," I tell him. "If that's possible."

"You'll see. This stuff will be bigger than paisley. You'll have a closetful of these shirts by next summer."

"Qiana," I mouth the word seductively. "Answer me one question: Does this material breathe or just wheeze?"

"You'd be surprised how comfortable it is." We sip our beers. "You seen *Last Tango* yet?" I shake my head. "You won't believe the jugs on this Maria Schneider chick." He holds up his palms to show what he means.

"So you told me. How's Brando?"

"Incredible. He goes to check out a place to rent and she's there doing the same thing. They don't know each other from Adam, right? They take one look at each other and, boom, they start balling right on the bare floor."

"Yeah, I heard about that. The bit with the butter and everything."

"You'll love it," he says, draining his beer and ordering another. "Know what I saw yesterday? *The Devil in Miss Jones*. That's about a chick who's got no reason to live, right, so she commits suicide by slashing her wrists in the bathtub. So she goes to hell, see, because killing herself is a mortal sin even though it's the only thing in her life she's ever done bad. So now she's in hell and she figures, 'What the hell, I should be here for a reason.' She says to the Devil, 'Let me go back to earth till I can satisfy my lust.' Fuckin wild, right?"

"Far out."

"You don't know the half of it. First she goes to this sexual master who teaches her all about fucking and sucking—two guys at once, two girls and a guy and so on. At the end of the movie, she's back in hell, but now she's in a room with a guy who's a real homo. See, she's fingering herself like mad, but the guy completely ignores her. Deep, huh?"

"Yeah. Reminds me of *No Exit*."

"Well, I never saw that one, but if it's as hot as this flick, I'll check it out."

Every now and then my uncle's lack of a liberal arts education is glaringly apparent. His favorite subjects are movies, horses and sex, but not in that order. If you met him in a bar, you might wonder if he'd finished high school. He had, in fact, but just barely. Upon graduating, he had a slew of low-paying jobs, all of which he hated—forklift operator, used car salesman, elevator repairman. But he stuck with the last one and he was still repairing elevators when he picked up Aunt Cele at a Dodger game. After they married, her father, who worked in the comptroller's office, pulled some strings and got him a gig with the Department of Buildings as a "vertical transportation expert." For us laymen, that's an elevator inspector. He dug the job because the supers and the building owners all treated him with respect, like he was some kind of cop. The hours were decent, the pension was nice, and if the pay was low, the tips more than made up for it. But he wasn't so lucky in the marriage, which ended after three rocky years, when my cousin Randi was two.

We settle into our seats, a new lightness coming over me. My father's unkind remarks no longer sting, thanks to the pot. And now that I've given up trying to wrest winners from the confusing mass of information in the Racing Form, my headache seems to be ebbing. I can watch the Belmont purely from the perspective of a fan, unbiased by the prejudices of a betting interest. Down along the track apron, the number of railbirds seems to have doubled since the running of the seventh. People press in, wanting to be near the finish line, though it's impossible from there to get a clear view of the race. In the clubhouse nearly every seat is occupied. People are laughing, smoking, yawning, waiting, talking more loudly to be heard. I eavesdrop on a smorgasbord of superficial banter: that it's not the heat but the humidity; that the crowd might set a new record; that at these odds Secretariat isn't worth a wager. The brunette behind me—the one with the obvious nose job and the gold necklace that spells JAP—is upset that the dinner reservations are for seven, for God's sake, and she won't be able to go back to Bayside first to freshen up. I lean over to Gene and start to mimic her Queens accent when the bugler sounds the "Call to the Post" and heads turn to watch the lead outriders step their mounts onto the track.

The outriders are dressed in their formal attire, red hunting coats and black caps, signaling to the spectators that this is no ordinary post parade. But it is the entrance of the jockeys in their colorful silks that galvanizes the crowd. Applause erupts as Sham appears, his jock rigged out in green and gold. Secretariat follows with Ron Turcotte up, garbed in the blue and white blocks of Meadow Stables. An explosion of cheers is followed by a smattering of boos. I focus my binoculars on the favorite, admiring the velvety cinnamon coat and noting the markings I recognize from photographs: the star on the forehead—a white diamond that tapers to a thin stripe down the nose; and on three of the legs, the white stockings that rise halfway up the cannon bone. The colt steps lightly, unruffled by the noise. The rest of the field—Pvt. Smiles, My Gallant and Twice a Prince—parade to a brass-band rendition of "Sidewalks of New York." The jockeys perch like stick figures atop their mounts, which sashay by, all bobbing heads and swishing tails, out of sync with the music.

Carousing like a stumbling, sentimental drunk, Gene throws an arm around my shoulders, inviting me to join him in loud, boozy song. We're having a great, silly time rocking back and forth, singing "Me and Mamie O'Rourke," when I notice the Captain jostling his way across the packed row. He's dabbing a paper napkin at a wet stain on the shoulder of his sportcoat but I can't make out what he's saying until he's next to me. "Can you believe this?" he yells. "Fuckin pigeon shat on me in the paddock."

Gene laughs, we both do, like it's the punch line to the funniest joke we've ever heard. Gene actually sits down, he is laughing so hard. "What are you worried about?" he sputters. "It's probably good luck."

"I just bought the goddamn thing and it's ruined."

"It just a coat, Dad. Don't have a conniption." The Captain scowls and then scours his shoulder until the napkin disintegrates into white shreds.

"You get that dry-cleaned," says Gene, "it'll be good as new."

"Son of a bitch bastard."

"Did you get down on the race, Dad?"

"Yeah, I bet a few bucks."

"How was the paddock?"

The Captain's mood changes instantly. "Eddie, you never saw such a mob scene: lights, cameras, people pushing forward to get a view. And Secretariat prances around cool as a cucumber. Doesn't even break a sweat."

"But did he look like six million bucks?" Secretariat has recently been syndicated for that unprecedented sum. Were he to win the Triple Crown, he could conceivably earn a million dollars for each year he stands at stud.

"See for yourself." The Captain points his half-smoked cigar at Secretariat as the beautiful chestnut colt prances by. "Go get him, Red!" he shouts, swept up in the excitement. "Here," he says. "Maybe I was too hard on you." He presses into my hand a two-dollar win ticket on Secretariat. "Don't cash it. It'll be worth something one day."

In the minutes before post time, the clock moves forward in fits and starts. Time leaps ahead while the horses warm up, trotting easily up the long Belmont stretch and drifting back toward the finish line, then seems to pause as the colts linger before the starting gate, waiting to be loaded. Because the Belmont track is a mile and a half around, the race begins and ends in the same place, in front of the grandstand. The cheering follows Secretariat, gathering heat as he slips into his stall and the doors are shut behind, swelling as the other horses are led quickly in alongside, and peaking as the field is frozen briefly in the gate—held fast as in a photograph—while the spectators and the bettors, the outriders and the gatehands, the jockeys and their thousand-pound mounts, all of us anticipate the starter's impulse.

I pan twenty yards ahead to the finish pole, painted top-to-bottom in parti-colored bands of black, red, light blue and yellow. Next to it a track employee holds aloft a fluttering orange flag, which he will drop as the first horse passes, prompting the clockers to activate their stopwatches. "We're ready to go for this tremendous Belmont Stakes," reports the track announcer. "Everybody's in line." Dignitaries and photographers are strung out along the infield side of the rail, where a disc of brilliant light reflects off a camera's lens, followed by a great roar as the gates fling open, releasing the field in an exhalation of flesh and frenzy.

The start is good and the outside horses get away fast. Cordero guns My Gallant to the lead, and it's easy to follow the stable's colors—a red apple on a field of white—but Twice a Prince and Sham are right with him. Secretariat breaks fourth and moves up quickly on the rail. Sham grabs the lead at the sixteenth pole, and Secretariat collars him going into the turn.

We're already standing, but to get a better view I step onto my chair, bracing one foot on the seatback in front of me. From this precarious perch, I can tell Sham has opened up half a length on the favorite and eight lengths on the rest of the field. They duel around the turn and into the backstretch, striding easily, heads bobbing in rhythm, tails streaming like pennants. Outlined now against the high wall of hedge, Secretariat draws even with his rival and edges ahead. For several strides, Sham hangs at Secretariat's throatlatch before gradually giving ground. At the halfway mark, the red and white six-furlong pole, the big chestnut colt holds a widening two-length lead.

"What did I tell you?" brags Gene. "It's a speed duel. They'll both burn out." It's true. They have run three quarters of a mile in exceptionally fast time. By rights they should be backing up to the field, but contrary to all racing logic, Secretariat charges into the turn and steadily pulls away.

"Secretariat is blazing along," cries Chic Anderson, his booming voice expressing his surprise. "Secretariat is widening now. He is moving like a tremendous machine. Secretariat by twelve. Secretariat by fourteen lengths on the turn." The field catches

Sham and passes him, but Secretariat is all alone. He gallops into the stretch to wild screaming, discordant whistling and tumultuous noise, his lead expanding to eighteen, twenty-two, twenty-five lengths. At the wire, Secretariat is more than thirty lengths in front.

"I don't believe it," shouts Gene. He tries to tell me something, but it's drowned out. He mimes a whipping motion. "Turcotte never hit him once."

"Incredible," I yell. I've never seen anything like it. No one has. The final time shatters the stakes record by an astonishing two and a half seconds. If a horse can run five lengths in one second, Secretariat would have outdistanced the previous record holder, Gallant Man, by thirteen lengths. I turn to tell the Captain, but he's watching the rest of the race with rapt concentration.

"Come on, 5," pleads the Captain. "Gut it out, 5. Don't quit on me now." Two horses are driving all out toward the finish. The 5 is half a length in front, but the 4 is game. Their jockeys whip them on, but in deep stretch, the 4 hangs, neither gaining nor retreating. They cross the line like that, the 5 getting up for place.

"I got the exacta!" screams the Captain. "I got it! I got the exacta!" His face is flushed and he is brandishing an impressive deck of green-edged, ten-dollar tickets. "Holy shit! I don't believe it." He spreads out the betting slips to prove it. "I hit it. I hit the fuckin exacta." The 5 horse is Twice a Prince, the longshot I had touted him on.

"What did you have on it, Dad?"

"Two hundred bucks," says the Captain in a daze. "I got the exacta a hundred times." He sits down heavily, out of breath, the only person in our section not standing. His face is puffy, unnaturally pale, and he is sweating profusely in the withering heat and laboring to massage his chest.

"Jesus," says Gene, "you're white as a ghost."

"You okay, Dad?"

"Let me take your cigar, Leo." Gene gently pries apart the Captain's fat, tense fingers.

"Pill," he whispers, indicating his inside pocket. I find the vial, fish out a white nitroglycerin tablet and place it under his lifted tongue. Secretariat is being draped with a blanket of daisies and led into the winner's circle as thousands of people cheer with unbridled jubilation. It is the greatest racing performance anyone can remember, yet the three of us sit mutely, numb to the pandemonium, and I am not thinking about the Triple Crown or Secretariat or the record time or the astounding margin of victory. Neither am I thinking of the small fortune my father has won. While the Captain waits for the pace of his galloping heart to ease, I realize my own pulse is racing, prodded by a reverie as jolting as the sting of a whip. I've been taught to be protective of my father, ever vigilant of the symptoms that might precede a heart attack, and though part of me is relieved that he's all right, a breathtaking awareness predominates: I sense in my bones how free I might feel if my father would do me a favor and drop dead.

JAMAICA

Why, you may ask, would I wish my father dead? Was he so hateful, so odious, so monstrous, so malevolent? Nobody else seemed to think so. Everyone was crazy about him. He was loved by his wife, lionized by his late mother and adored by his relatives. His business partner trusted him, his competitors respected him, his friends were loyal to him and the neighbors felt fortunate to have him on the block. Every time it snowed he would order me to clean off Mrs. D'Addario's sidewalk, two doors down, and the elderly Sukenicks' across the street. Somehow he got all the credit. He gave generously to charities, participated in professional organizations and aided anyone in the family who needed it. His largesse was legendary. He contributed to his niece's college fund. He lent money to Uncle Sol for a new cab. He bailed out Cousin Bob's printing firm when it almost went belly up. And he set up Grandma Lou in a condo in Long Beach and paid for full-time care until she died.

When the coin business took off in the late Sixties, and the money really started to roll in, so did the emblems of status, which my family acquired at a dizzying rate: Renovated house, land-scaped patio, built-in swimming pool. Finished basement, pool table, central air-conditioning. Ride-on lawn mower, snow re-mover, Jacuzzi. Garbage disposal, dishwasher, remote-controlled color TV. From the top-of-the-line, fully loaded Caddy right down to the electric can opener, every last talisman of suburban success.

Then there were the vacations to exotic places—Spain, Israel, Hawaii, the Caribbean—each of which our Bell & Howell movie camera flawlessly recorded on reels of Super 8. As for me, I didn't have much to kick about while I was in school. Even when the Captain wasn't talking to me, he always paid my tuition and gave me enough pocket money so I didn't have to get a part-time job. Generous? My father was more than generous. He was generous to a fault.

And he wasn't only generous with money. Whenever some-body needed a favor, he habitually replied, "Don't worry. I'll take care of it." When Steve Shapiro, my high school friend, couldn't find a summer job, the Captain called a buddy at the Parks Department. When Gene wanted to buy a used Camaro, the Captain got his mechanic to check it out. When the Sukenicks couldn't get tickets to *The Sunshine Boys* for their 50th anniversary, the Captain phoned the manager of the Broadhurst Theatre and persuaded him to release a pair of house seats.

Before I had even finished my junior year, he'd begun engi-neering my admission to law school. He would get me in, he as-sured me. He knew all the right people. I told him I wasn't set on law school. I might want to take off a year to entertain my options.

"I've been thinking, Dad, maybe I should go into the coin business."

"And throw away your education? Over my dead body. You can do better than the coin business, Eddie. You can have a real profession."

"It's good enough for you."

"I quit school because of the war, and I still regret it. But you won't make that mistake." What he meant was, don't defy me. I had done just that by going to Woodstock, which resulted in a major rift we had only recently repaired. So I didn't argue. What would have been the point? Any effort to change his mind would have been futile. He never took no for an answer.

My life seemed to be a *fait accompli*. The future had come to assume the shape of a huge pillow settling inexorably over my face.

For the first time ever, I had a recurrent dream: I'm tripping on mescaline on the way to a Grateful Dead concert, crossing the suspension bridge that spans the giddy chasm of Fall Creek Gorge. Gazing down into the boulders and the gurgling water choked with autumn leaves, I experience an obvious drug-induced hallucination. I imagine a broken body sprawled face-down among the rocks—a momentary trick played by the obscure light on the detritus and glacial debris. Soon I am scrambling down a slope of loose scree to inspect further, and I discover it isn't a hallucination at all. When I turn the body over, I am confronted with the remains of my own decomposed face.

It didn't take me long to realize that I had to save myself from the airless future toward which I was quickly matriculating. But how was I to accomplish this feat? I couldn't admit to myself that

I actually wanted to flunk out. So I studied desultorily, smoked a lot of dope, cut classes and played endless games of pinball. For finals, I knew I'd have to cram, so I scored some Benzedrine and stayed up—two nights in a row. On the morning of my Social Theory of Industrial Society exam, I was so strung out, my brain refused to function. I read each question again and again, performing the futile catechism of repetition. Unable to divine what I was being asked, I opted for the kitchen sink approach and wrote down everything about the subject I could remember. I had a Psychology final the next day, so I popped another upper and tried to study. I never got to the test. I was found wandering around the Arts Quad at four in the morning. The security guard thought I was drunk. It seems I was babbling incoherently like a freshman after his first beer bash. I was taken to the clinic, where, dehydrated and exhausted, I needed a week to recover.

The funny thing was, I was still surprised when I got my failing transcript.

BY THE TIME the Captain feels better, the crowd has thinned considerably. We accompany him to collect his winnings across a clubhouse floor littered with losing tickets, discarded programs, tinted tout sheets, and stray pages of newspaper. A gray-haired old man in a rumpled beige raincoat is gathering betting slips, which he examines and stuffs into his pockets. "Cocksucker," he mutters, "I know it's here somewhere." He thrusts his arm into a trash receptacle and scavenges another pile of tickets to sort through.

The payout takes a while because the cashier has run out of

hundreds and wants to make up the difference in twenties. From the way the Captain chews him out, you wouldn't know how sick he was a few minutes earlier. The cashier, however, is unimpressed until the Captain starts pulling rank, insisting that Bob McElfresh come up to straighten things out. McElfresh, the Director of Mutuels, is an old friend of the Captain's. Either they served in the same outfit in North Africa or they grew up in Rockaway together or they were in the same class at Brooklyn Tech, I can't remember which, but somehow they know each other. Anyway, it's comical how quickly the guy changes his tune.

After counting his thirty-five hundred and twenty dollars, the Captain takes a crisp new C-note, crinkles it to make sure it's not stuck to another one, and slips it into the handkerchief pocket of my sportcoat.

"What's this for?"

"You earned it," he says. "You put me on to Twice a Prince."

"Come on, Dad. I don't need this."

He won't hear of taking it back. "Keep it, Eddie. It won't kill you."

There's no way out of it so I have to thank him.

"Who wants to go to Nino's?" he asks. "My treat." Nino's Pavilion, an Italian eatery in Valley Stream, is the Captain's favorite restaurant. Gene says he's got a hot date and begs off. I also decline, as politely as I can, reminding the Captain that I have to work Sunday, which means waking up at some ungodly hour for my five o'clock shift. Gene and I congratulate the Captain, shaking his hand and clapping him on the back.

"You're a genius, Dad."

"I know."

"You think you're all right to drive?"

"I'm fine," he says. "Just a momentary thing. It's finished."

"Because I'll go with you if you want me to."

He waves me off. "Go on. Get out of here."

"Okay. See you Monday."

"Right-O!"

"Say hi to Mom," I call after him. He doesn't turn around, just raises his palm briefly and keeps walking.

The Belmont Special is crowded but Gene and I find a couple of seats toward the rear of the train. The car, it seems, is not air-conditioned and the enclosed cabin is stifling. I take off my sport-coat, roll up my shirtsleeves, and hope that the cooling unit will kick in when the train starts moving. We do not have long to wait. An alarm bell rings for a good five seconds, the doors close and the car lurches forward. It crawls across a bridge that spans the Cross Island Parkway on which vehicles squirm bumper to bumper, tied up by the Belmont traffic. Before it hooks up with the main line to the city, the train snakes hesitantly to the northwest, past piles of debris—old rails, track clamps, heavy chain—rusting in the afternoon sun. The AC is definitely on the fritz. I had been looking forward to a comfortable ride back to town, but in no time I'm basting in my own sweat.

Gene retrieves from under the seat an abandoned *New York Times*, folds it in half and fans himself vigorously.

"So who is she?" I ask.

"Who's who?"

"The hot date."

"I don't have one. I made it up." He opens the paper and pages through the sports section.

I shoot Gene a look.

"No fuckin way I'm going to Nino's. You think I'm a glutton for punishment?"

"Eugene Sacks is turning down a free meal? Boy, this is a first."

"I've already had that meal. A couple a hundred times." Gene slips smoothly into a deft impersonation of the Captain: "The drinks are on me, folks. Everybody having a good time? Nino, bring that table another bottle of chianti. Hey, Genie," he slaps me on the back, "how's that veal parmigiana. Good, huh? You want something else? Anything you want, pal, just order it."

I laugh, but I'm thinking that my uncle has it easy compared to me. My father only forces food down Gene's throat. He's trying to force a law career down mine.

"I swear," he says, "sometimes he makes me want to puke."

"I know what you mean," I agree.

Gene resumes his reading of the sporting news and in a moment finds a new focus for his anger. "Son of a bitch," he swears, smacking the paper with the back of his hand. "Seaver lost to the Dodgers."

"Boy, you're really striking out today. How did the Yankees do?"

"Who cares?"

"They were still in first the last time I checked."

Gene gives me a look like I'm wasting his time. He raises the paper over his head, brings it close to his face and squints. "Let's see. They beat the Royals eight to one. They're a half game out."

"Mind if I look at that?"

"You're a pain in the ass," he says, handing me the rumpled paper.

"Yanks Belt Four Homers," I crow, reading the headline.

"We'll see who's on top at the end of the season."

I devour the highlights of the Yankee game, check the standings, then peruse the front page: Two trains crash in Mount Vernon, killing one and injuring more than a hundred; a mayoral candidate in Camden, an ex-con, is murdered on his New Jersey estate; Nixon delivers the commencement address at Florida Tech. This ought to be rich, I think, and keep reading: "Mr. Nixon, delivering the commencement address to a friendly but not enthusiastic audience of several thousand persons, did not mention the Watergate crisis that has buffeted his administration." No surprise there. So what does he say? What advice can he offer the class of '73, after all the half-truths and deceptions and stonewalling and dirty tricks? Let's see: "This is not the time for mouthing any pessimism about the future." Waist deep in the scandal of the century, the President urges us to stay positive. How reassuring.

Leafing back through the national news, my attention is drawn to an article entitled EHRLICHMAN AGAIN PLACES COVER-UP BLAME ON DEAN. I fold open the page and read the lead. "Boy, this is unbelievable," I say aloud.

"Ehrlichman resigned a month ago, and now he's trying to pin it all on Dean. They'll do anything to protect the President."

"You think Nixon knew about this Watergate shit?"

"Are you kidding me? You know that song they play when the president appears? They're going to rename it 'Jail to the Chief.'"

"Your father thinks he's innocent. He says he'd bet on it." My dad was an out-and-out Nixon man. A staunch Republican, he had supported the party ever since the local GOP gave *his* father a job in 1932. The way I saw it, the Captain's knee-jerk loyalty to any Republican administration tended to blind him to political reality.

"He's kidding himself about Nixon."

"I don't know much about it, kid, but Leo claims there's no way Nixon would have ordered the burglary. He says he's too smart for that." Gene tugs a neat white square of handkerchief from his back pocket and without unfolding it wipes his face and the back of his neck.

"Not only did he order the break-in," I assert, sounding more like my father than I care to, "he then went and protected those bozos after they screwed up. That's got to be an impeachable offense."

"What are you, an FBI agent? As far as I know, nobody's implicated him yet, unless you know something they haven't told the rest of us."

"I don't trust that shifty-eyed used-car salesman. Every time I see him giving a speech on TV I feel like he's lying through his teeth."

"All politicians lie. That's what they do."

"You ever hear of La Bruyère, the French moralist?"

"Who?"

"Some guy we studied in European history. He was a social critic who made clever observations, many of them as apt today as they were in the seventeenth century." I catch Gene's reflection in the train window, head cocked, eyeing me with unconcealed skepticism, but I prattle on. "He said, 'Even the best-intentioned of great men need a few scoundrels around them; there are some things you cannot ask an honest man to do.' If you ask me, that sums up Nixon in a nutshell. Except he's not well-intentioned, he's not great, and I wouldn't call him an honest man."

"Ah, they're all crooks. The Democrats are just as bad."

"Come on, Gene. They bugged Democratic National Headquarters. Don't you think that's extreme political conduct?"

"How the hell would I know? All I know is it's too fuckin hot." Gene fishes a tout sheet off the floor, examines it, says, "Shit," and crushes it into a ball. "Damn it," he says, flinging the golfball-sized wad into the aisle. "Why didn't I bet that longshot to place?"

"It's done with. Forget about it."

"I have to go for the big score."

"Come on, Gene. What's the point of beating yourself up?"

For a moment he is quiet, head bent forward, nestled against his palm. Then he slumps back against the seat and says, "God, what a dope."

The train rumbles through the seedy backyards of Queens. Gene broods in silent self-contempt. He picks at his cuticles, which are already cracked and bleeding. When he gets like this he's hard to be with.

We rush by rows of flat-roofed clapboard houses, boxy affairs in faded pink and tan and aqua. Some are less dilapidated than others, but none looks well-tended from the rear, their postage-stamp yards mostly sad scars of dirt. Every now and then a brick apartment building looms up next to the tracks. As these appear more frequently, the speed ebbs, slightly at first, then more deliberately.

"This train stops at Jamaica, Woodside and New York," announces the conductor. "Change at Jamaica for all other stations." We ease into the station, and a minute or so after the doors open

we're notified of a five-minute delay until the arrival of the Brooklyn train. We step into the humid air to stretch our legs. Maybe
it's the mention of Brooklyn, but on the spur of the moment I
decide to call my cousin Randi, Gene's daughter. She goes to Pratt
in Fort Greene, where she has just finished her freshman year.

"I have to make a phone call, Genie. I'll be back."

"I'll come with you," he says, and I can tell it will be impossible
to shake him. I dial the number, warning myself to be discreet.

"Hey, baby, how's it going?" I glance at Gene, who is standing
five feet away with his back to me.

"Who the fuck is this?" asks Randi, knowing full well who it is.

"Who would you like it to be?"

"Hey, hot stuff, where are you?"

"At Jamaica," I say, "with my Uncle Gene."

"How much did Daddy lose?"

"Enough."

"Give him a kiss for me."

"I better not."

"You know that was really obnoxious last night."

"I'm sorry. I don't know what came over me."

"I can't believe you put an ice cube in me."

"Neither can I. Although it seemed to melt pretty fast."

"I think I got frostbite."

"Oh, does my little sweetie have a booboo?"

"Yes, I do. You better come over and kiss it and make it better."

"I was thinking I might drop by. What are you doing for
dinner?"

"How about I suck your cock till your head caves in?"

"Oh, yeah," I say, as neutrally as possible, "that sounds good. I think I can get over there," I reply, as the Brooklyn-bound train crawls in.

"I'll be waiting," she says and hangs up.

"I'm going to Brooklyn, Gene. Change of plans."

"You can't fool me, you old muff diver. Who's this chick you're banging?"

"Some girl I picked up in my cab." I know this will appeal to him. He's always asking me if I've made it with any of my passengers.

"Good body?"

"Great body."

"Great body, huh? Think she might be into a little three-way action?"

"I'm not sure how comfortable she would be with that idea."

"Well, feel her out on the subject," he says, elbowing me in the side.

"You're sick," I say. "You got any other words of wisdom?"

"Sure: Find 'em, feed 'em, fuck 'em and forget 'em."

"I love you, Gene, but you have the consciousness of a paramecium."

"Believe it or not, kid, women find me extremely sensitive." I don't know what to say to this, so I wave goodbye and walk toward the waiting train. "And don't be an idiot," he calls after me. "Wear a raincoat."

Not till several minutes later, as I am relaxing in the air-conditioned comfort of a window seat, do I realize that my uncle is admonishing me to use a condom. I have to admit it's sound advice. Of course, if he knew what I was really up to, he'd probably cut off my dick.

BROOKLYN

Last March, having heard from Gene that I had flunked out, Randi phoned to ask how things were going and to encourage me to "hang in there." If anyone in the family could appreciate where I was at, she could. Randi had been a handful growing up and downright impossible as an adolescent. After getting expelled from two public high schools and an alternative vocational school, she had been exiled to a facility for troubled teens in northern Westchester. It was there that she straightened herself out, finding salvation in creativity thanks to a tough but understanding art teacher. She painted, she sculpted, she etched, she photographed, she drew. So devoted did she become to her new calling that she was motivated to acquire her high school equivalency diploma, which she parlayed into admission to art school.

The phone call had ended with an invitation. "If you come to Brooklyn," she promised, "I'll give you dinner and get you stoned. Not necessarily in that order."

"Why not?" I said. We had been getting high together since

she was fifteen, but I was curious to see if she'd learned how to cook anything more complicated than scrambled eggs.

A week later, bearing a small potted cactus and a bottle of Mateus, I rode the subway to Brooklyn. A Canadian cold front had ushered in freezing temperatures after several days of mild weather that had tantalized the city with intimations of an early spring. People seemed to shrink into their coats. At massive Brooklyn Tech, before a triptych of Gothic brass doors, a man burrowed into a tattered sleeping bag and covered his head with an inverted cardboard V. As dusk resolved into dark, I hurried by Fort Greene Park and walked purposefully past the superettes and taverns on DeKalb Avenue.

Randi had warned me that the intercom didn't work and that I was to call from the corner—unless I preferred to climb up the fire escape and crawl in her window. I opted for the more dramatic entrance but soon realized that scaling the ladder with my hands full would not be easy. It took me half a dozen leaps to pull the ladder down, and I had to pause briefly in my attempts and crouch in the shadows when a squad car passed. Once I'd managed to ply the ladder into position, I tucked the bottle under my arm, cradled the base of the clay pot in my hand, and ascended awkwardly with my free arm, my feet feeling blindly for each rung. I flopped onto the second-floor platform like a fish, both gifts somehow intact, picked myself up, brushed off my jeans and peered between the accordion struts of a metal gate into a room that throbbed with energy and disorder, an impression underscored by the raucous chords of "Purple Haze" that rang from the stereo.

The interior was cluttered and colorful. Unframed reproductions of a Dali dreamscape and a Rembrandt self-portrait shared wall space with posters of rock stars. Mick Jagger pranced and preened; Jimi Hendrix kneeled over a guitar in flames. Pen-and-ink studies were tacked up between color wheels, postcards, fashion magazine ads and photos that were curling at the corners. The walls, where they could be seen, were painted aqua, and the pressed-tin ceiling burnt orange, like the color scheme of a Mexican restaurant. Dominating the middle of the room was a sturdy, square-legged table on which a carved woodblock of a finely detailed hand—middle finger extended—leaned against a gooseneck lamp. Cans of pens and paintbrushes crowded one corner, and in the center on a sheaf of newsprint a clay bust appeared to be a work in progress. Along the wall a bed doubled as a makeshift sofa, with oversized pillows tucked beneath an Indian-print spread. A turntable sat next to it on some wooden milk crates, which housed a collection of record albums cocked at an angle. Toward the rear, a fluorescent ceiling fixture illuminated the small kitchen area where Randi was bent over at the waist, checking something in the oven. Her jeans were so tight, she must have used a shoehorn to get them on.

I rapped on the glass above the security gate and she walked toward me laughing, her long dark hair dancing about her face. Her faded bellbottoms had been patched with quilting squares and she had knotted an unbuttoned work shirt over some kind of colorful hand-knitted top. There was hardly a trace of the gangly kid I had last encountered a year before at Aunt Cele's Passover Seder. She had become statuesque and the prominent features—

deep-set eyes, strong aquiline nose and wide, full mouth—that had seemed so obtrusive on the cramped canvas of her adolescent face had miraculously cohered into a riveting, dark-eyed symmetry.

"You look like a prowler," she barked, and at least she sounded like herself, her voice hoarse and raspy, even at seventeen, from years of smoking. "I don't know if I should let you in," she said, "or call the cops."

"Hey, I'm just following instructions." I gestured toward the metal guard. "Open this, will you. It's cold out here."

"Now where is that fucking key?" she wondered. She thought for a moment before rummaging through the metal cans on the desk and the jewelry box on the dresser. "It might be in the kitchen," she called above the din of pounding drums and screaming guitar, and went to look while I rubbed some warmth into my ears and wished I had taken my hat and gloves. Several minutes later she returned to the window empty-handed.

"Look," I said, "just meet me downstairs, okay?"

She raised the window several inches. "I'm sorry," she winced.

"Don't worry about it."

"I'm really sorry." And in the next breath, she cried, "Holy shit! It was in the fucking lock the whole time."

"Next time I'll use the front door," I said, scrambling through the window.

"I'm such a space cadet," she said, offering her cheek for a kiss. "God, your face is cold. You must be freezing."

"It's nothing," I said, "just a little frostbite. Here. I got something for you."

"Just what I need," she said, "a fucking hard-on." I looked down and noticed, to my dismay, that the cactus resembled an obscenely engorged penis: a thick, spiny, green column topped by a bright knob of pink.

"In the store, you know, it seemed kind of hardy and interesting. I mean, I wasn't even thinking about any, um, similarity."

"Oh, it's interesting, all right."

"Now I wish I had bought the ficus."

"Don't be silly," she said, lighting a Marlboro. "I love things that are cute and small. They remind me of my last boyfriend."

"Spare me the details." I looked around. Visually, the place was overwhelming. I didn't know what to take in first. "You want to give me the tour?"

"The tour?" she said. "Honey, this is all there is. It used to be part of a larger apartment but now it's just a studio." She did a quick little pirouette. "So what do you think?"

"I think it's colorful and cozy and charming."

"Not the place, asshole. What do you think of me?"

"You?" I said. "You've got a beautiful face and a filthy mouth."

"Go fuck yourself," she said.

I shook my head sadly. "You can take the girl out of reform school, but you can't take reform school out of the girl." She kicked at me. "Okay, you look terrific."

"Liar."

"You really do," I said, taking in her adorable figure. "You're all grown up. And your place is incredible. Like a struggling artist's garret."

"What's a garret?"

"A romantic word for tenement. What is that intoxicating aroma? I'm starved."

"Turpentine."

"Great. I just lost my appetite."

"It's a surprise. But it won't be ready for a few minutes."

Over a glass of wine she described the classes she was taking and showed me some of her projects. The bust she was working on was of an old woman, perhaps eighty.

"Can you guess who this is?"

"I don't know," I said, "it looks like Grandma Lou."

"Good guess," she laughed. "It's supposed to be me sixty years from now." I compared the molded face to my cousin's, looking from one to the other.

"It's getting there," I said, although the features seemed small and out of scale with the whole.

"Something's missing," said Randi. "I'm still working on it."

"I don't know if this will help," I said, "but don't your ears and your nose keep growing and, you know, protrude more as you get old?"

"Shit. You mean my nose will get even larger than it is now?"

"I'm afraid so."

"That's not a bad suggestion," she said, smacking me on the arm. "I'll see if it helps."

"So have you decided what you want to concentrate in?"

"Please!" she shouted and put her hands over her ears. "I'm, like, freaking out about that and I have to declare a major next year. I don't know what I like best. Right now I get to do all these different things and I'm really into it."

"You sure have a lot of influences," I said, glancing at the walls. Repetitions of Marilyn by Warhol contended with cutouts by Matisse, a photo of a pepper by Weston, a mustachioed Mona

Lisa by Duchamp, a collage of a living room by Hamilton, a fur-covered cup, saucer and spoon by Oppenheim, and two plaster cheeseburgers by Oldenburg. The most attention-grabbing image, however, and the one to which my gaze kept returning, was an X-rated reference to the comics by Lichtenstein in which Lois Lane gives Superman a blow-job: At the moment of orgasm, Superman ejaculates through the back of Lois Lane's head, splattering a grisly mist of blood, brains and cum. Though the style was cartoonish, my shameless loins found the image extremely stimulating.

"Isn't that a bit anti-feminist?" I asked, indicating with my chin.

"I don't know, I guess so."

"You guess so? I think it really degrades women," I said, surreptitiously adjusting my crotch to conceal my erection.

"Maybe," she conceded. "But it's pretty funny if you look at it as every man's fantasy. Anyway, it's here for a good reason."

"Like what? To remind you not to date guys with super-powers?"

"No. To keep my mother away. It makes her so nauseous, she never comes to visit. Which is fine with me."

"I bet your dad likes it."

"You know Gene. He says it's disgusting but he can't stop looking at it. You seem to have the same problem," she said, eyeing the bulge in my pants.

"I didn't realize your place was going to be so stimulating." I sat down at the desk and crossed my legs.

"You don't have to be embarrassed," she said, smiling.

"Can't we talk about something else?"

"Like what?"

"Like what is that weird smell?" I asked.

"I don't smell anything."

"Randi," I said, gesturing toward the kitchen, "I think your surprise is—"

"Oh, shit!" she yelled. "The pizza."

"Turn it off," I said, but it was too late. Tendrils of smoke scudded into the room and drifted toward the ceiling. I flung open the windows to the freezing night and grabbed a record album to use as a fan. Randi had tossed a smoldering cookie sheet onto the stovetop and with a butter knife was prodding the inedible disk of charred dough and cheese.

"Fuck," she stamped, "I ruined it."

"I wouldn't say it's ruined," I said. "It's just well done."

"Oh shut up."

"Look, we'll just scrape off the scorched part, like so..."

"And then what?" she said. "It's burnt to a crisp."

"And then we'll throw it out." She laughed in spite of herself before venting petulant tears of frustration.

"Shit fuck," she said. "I wanted to make you a really nice meal."

"Look, I'm not even that hungry," I lied. I led her over to the bed and told her to sit while I aired out the room, but she pulled me down next to her so I put my arm around her shoulders to comfort her.

"Forget about it," I said, patting her head. Her hair was redolent of cigarette smoke and herbal shampoo. "We'll make something else. You have any eggs?"

She nodded.

"I'll fix an omelet." She mumbled something. "I didn't catch that," I said. "You were sniffling too loud." She whacked me with the back of her hand.

"There's salad," she said, "in the fridge."

"Great. We got salad, eggs, wine, we're all set."

She glanced at the record on my lap. "Be careful with my *Iron Butterfly*. It's the first album I ever owned."

"What, this piece of dreck?" I said, fanning the air overhead. "Too bad it wasn't in the oven instead of the pizza."

"Hey, man, when I was twelve years old, this was definitely where it was at." She snatched away the album, unsleeved the record, and slipped it on the spindle. An elegant organ flourish segued into the thumping bass line of "In-A-Gadda-Da-Vida." In a couple of measures she had coaxed me off the couch and we were singing the silly, infectious lyrics and grooving to the mind-numbing beat: "In-A-Gadda-Da-Vida, honey, you know that I'm loving you . . ."

"You know what that means," I said, "In-A-Gadda-Da-Vida?" I was shouting above the music and Randi shouted back.

"I always thought it was, like, abracadabra, like he was putting some spell on this chick."

"That's not what I heard," I said, executing a quick turn. "I was told the original words were 'in the Garden of Eden,' but Doug Ingle, the lead singer, was so wasted in the recording studio it came out all slurred like this. But when they played it back, everybody loved it, so they kept it that way."

"Far out!" she said. "Where did you hear that?"

"Hey, I had to learn something at college." She laughed, twirled about, shook her cute little tush, and backed toward me. I moved behind her and we sashayed in unison, side to side. Then I turned her around and she nestled into me, slow dancing, her smoke-scented hair reminding me of a campfire in the woods, and we coasted like that for a while until somewhere between the self-indulgent guitar lead and the unimaginative drum solo, she drew back and we stopped: our eyes met, serious and unsmiling, with such a gaze of naked wanting that her lips parted, our mouths brushed, our tongues touched and retreated and sought again, and the kiss blossomed into a devouring frenzy of supple lips and dancing tongues that ended only when we were called back to ourselves by the loud and incessant skipping of the phonograph needle.

My God, I thought, I'm out of my mind making out with my kid cousin. Except she wasn't a kid anymore, and her excited eyes urged me to go on.

I kissed her gently on the lips, on the eyes, on the forehead, and neither of us spoke. I think we were afraid to ruin the moment. I know I was. Silently, we disentangled. Randi threw *Abbey Road* on the stereo, bopping to the familiar intro of "Come Together" while she lit up a joint, took a slow, lung-filling hit and offered it to me. I had the impulse to turn it down, mumble a quick apology and split, which might have been the best thing to do. The responsible thing. Get out of there while I still could with things as clear and uncomplicated as they used to be. But I didn't leave. Because she knelt then on the floor and leaned forward, asking me with her eyes if I wanted a toke, and as I stood over her, admiring the exposed contours of her neckline to where they tapered into the hypnotic confluence between her breasts, I could feel myself being drawn into a thrilling vortex of curiosity and temptation.

"Oh, what the hell," I said. I pulled on the joint and held it as the room seemed to expand exponentially, leaned my mouth down to hers, and exhaled deeply into her soft, willing lips. She moaned as our tongues caressed, and then again as I undid the knot on her shirt and let it fall off her shoulders, revealing a crocheted bra made of two multicolored god's-eyes that only briefly concealed her small, delectable breasts.

We undressed each other as though swimming underwater, writhing out of our clothes it seemed without the aid of hands or fingers until I lay next to her breathless and trembling, definitely trembling, as I sucked and nibbled and licked my way toward her pussy, and pressed my face between her legs and flicked my tongue at the moist folds of her cunt, which she so demurely lifted up to me.

And then even as my senses were disordered by the dusky aroma of her flesh, I suddenly pushed myself away and leapt off the couch.

"I can't do this," I said.

"It's okay," she said. She seemed to be more startled than upset.

"I thought I could, but I can't."

"I know men sometimes have these problems," she said, hugging one of the overly large pillows.

I stared at her. "What are you talking about? You think I'm impotent?"

"I don't know," she said. "I thought older guys sometimes—"

I laughed, it was that funny. I laughed and she cried.

"Come on, Randi. Don't be upset."

"Who's upset," she sobbed. "I'll just be a virgin for the rest of my life." And she confessed through her uneven breathing what I should have already known: That she loved me, and had always loved me, because I didn't put her down and never made her feel the way her parents did, like some kind of delinquent or freak. That there weren't any other boyfriends—well, boyfriends, maybe, but not lovers—and she wanted me to be the first because she knew I would be gentle and caring and not treat her like a jerk. And didn't I know she would do anything for me. Anything I wanted. Anything at all.

Images rippled through my mind—odalisques in ankle bracelets, veiled and recumbent, in harem tents whose gauzy folds billowed in the desert wind.

"Anything?"

She nodded solemnly.

"Would you . . ."

"Would I what?"

"Would you touch yourself for me?"

"Like this?" she whispered. The pillow tumbled to the floor and she stretched seductively, her head tilting back off the side of the bed, and her fingers tiptoed lightly over her breasts and pinched her large, erect nipples, while her other hand lovingly explored the shuddering recesses of her clit.

"Oh, yeah," I said, "just like that." I walked over to her and caressed her cheek with the palm of my hand, until she opened her eyes. She rolled over then and reached for my cock, which she welcomed into her mouth until I was fully aroused. Then I unfurled a condom, slid over her and worked my way carefully inside.

"This may hurt a bit."

"What's a little pain?" she said, and she grimaced with each sharp thrust until I felt myself sink deeper, and she cleaved to me and recovered, and again urged me on with her profligate hips, and gave herself over to the waves of sensation she had fantasized for so long.

That this hot little bitch, my cousin, this vixen with the foul mouth, was still a virgin was one of life's incredible ironies that wasn't lost upon me as I toiled above her, endeavoring to prolong our pleasure by recalling Riva Ridge, Canonero II, Dust Commander and other previous winners of the Kentucky Derby in reverse chronological order. But even this desperate ploy was only briefly effective, especially when I lowered my lips to her succulent nipples, suckling and tugging and slurping as I imagined myself galloping gamely around the turn and pounding wildly down the stretch, whipped on by the unruly strands of her auburn mane and my own incontinent desire. And on what did I fixate as I finished all too quickly in bucking, powerful spasms—pangs of hunger roiling the pit of an empty belly—but a nice, thick, juicy slab of steak, medium rare, and a steaming, foil-wrapped baked potato, slathered in molten butter.

MIDTOWN

On the Triborough after dawn, the city is completely obscured, dozing under a dark quilt of low-lying clouds. There's not much to see beyond the sulfuric glow of the bridge lights. My fare from LaGuardia wants to know where the skyline went. Sometimes nature reminds us, I tell him, that Manhattan is a coastal island surrounded by water. He says he has heard a rumor to that effect. The air is damp, but at least the fog keeps the mercury in the eighties. When it burns off by midmorning, we'll all be wilting like onions in a hot skillet.

I drop at the Stanhope, a small hotel opposite the Met, and cruise Fifth Avenue for an early bird. I'll work through the morning rush, until it's time to check in at the store. By then Gene will have made the airport pickups, and the Captain will tell me when to return for the afternoon run to Wall Street. A doorman flags me down at Sixty-eighth, where my fare, a dour executive my father's age, demands the Chase Manhattan Bank on Maiden Lane without so much as a "Good morning." Swinging east, I hop on the FDR Drive and head downtown to the bouncy harmonies of the Beach Boys. My passenger orders me, from behind his *Wall Street Journal*, to "eighty-six the rock noise and find some news." Instead of "Good Vibrations" I have to listen to the gore du jour: An item about a teenager murdered by gang members in the Bronx is followed by the story of a Newark woman and her boyfriend who are being held without bail, charged with the beating death of her two-year-old son. I tune out the broadcast and retreat into my thoughts, trying to recall a disturbing dream that has hovered all morning on the periphery of consciousness.

My father was in the kitchen repairing the bicycle pump. I strolled in to ask if it was fixed. "It ain't yours," he said. "It's mine." He said to get him a screwdriver, but I could only find a vegetable peeler. When I handed it to him, he looked at me like I was an idiot, shook his head and threw it at me. It sailed past my head and impaled itself in the fridge. He asked for a pair of pliers; I handed him a pair of scissors. He asked for a wrench; I handed him a spatula. Each time he shook his head and flung the implement in my direction. Finally, he slammed down the bicycle pump and said, "It can't be fixed. You happy now?" and stormed out of the house.

I crawl through the rush hour from fare to fare, going over the dream and getting nowhere. I don't need a shrink to tell me that my old man is impossible to satisfy; there has to be more to it. Maybe the imagery holds some clues. Why do I offer kitchen implements when my father wants tools? Do they represent my feelings of inadequacy in the face of my father's overbearing demeanor? Does the air pump have special meaning? The refrigerator? If only I hadn't waited for the ill-fated night before my Psychology final to begin Freud's *Interpretation of Dreams*. After a while, I give up. I suspect the dream has some deeper meaning, but my thoughts are stalled, bumper to bumper, tied up in a psychological traffic jam.

Around eleven, I drop a fare at the Americana, flip on my off-duty light, park the cab at a taxi stand on Sixth Avenue and walk over to Fifty-fifth Street. I buy coffees for the crew at the deli opposite the store: no sugar for my dad, light and sweet for Tiny, regular for me and black for Gene. Irving, the office peon, drinks tea. As the counterman fills my order, I admire the elegant front of Midtown Coin Company and its tasteful logo of gold pieces in different denominations, one of which is partially enlarged by the black-rimmed outline of a magnifying glass. The Captain appears behind it, checks his watch and scans the block. He looks anxious or pissed off about something, but that in itself is hardly unusual. The same drive that made him one of the top numismatists in the country also makes it impossible for him to relax.

My father stumbled into rare coins in 1956 while convalescing from the heart attack that led to his honorable discharge. Having fought in World War II and Korea, Captain Leo Sacks was aiming to become a twenty-year man until excess weight, a two-pack-a-day habit and the stress of trying to make ends meet on a captain's salary finally caught up with him. My earliest memory, as a matter of fact, is of my unshaven father in bathrobe and slippers padding out to greet me in the antiseptic hallway of St. Albans Naval Hospital in Queens. I was five years old and according to family legend I handed him a gift I had selected from a supermarket checkout display, a book about coin collecting with the catchy title *Pocketful of Miracles: What Your Loose Change Is Worth.*

Within a couple of years, his hobby had grown into a mail-order business that was taking over the dining room while a series of ventures—butcher shop proprietor, freelance graphic artist, a start-up trucking operation—all went bust. The Captain's track record in business was dismal, yet he managed to borrow, mortgage, finagle and cajole until he had scraped together enough money to open the South Shore Coin Company in a modest storefront on Merrick Avenue in Lynbrook. The trade was strictly nickel-and-dime, occasional collectors and kids working on blue cardboard albums of Lincoln pennies, Jefferson nickels and Roosevelt dimes. My mother says he complained to her, almost from the get-go, how Long Island was too small-time and penny ante for a guy with his ambition. He thought of himself as having the right stuff. He was a Jew who had survived Officer Candidate School to become a captain, which wasn't easy with the prevailing prejudice in the military. More than anything he wanted to be a winner, which to him meant being rich, envied and well-connected. He saw himself purveying top-shelf merchandise to serious collectors in a going concern that allowed him to rub shoulders with the most respected dealers in the coin business—a goal he would have expressed in much more colloquial style: "You'll see, Goldie. One of these days I'll be shmoozing with the big *machers* in Manhattan." To that end he worked hard, studied voraciously and bided his time, so that by 1963 he had made a name for himself as an expert in several issues, including Morgan dollars, Standing Liberty quarters and Mercury dimes. Moreover, he had established a reputation for honesty and fair-dealing that brought him to the favorable attention of the nabobs of the American Numismatic Association, especially the *landsmen*. Coin World featured him in a story on how to identify fraudulent coins; Stack's called him to get a second opinion on several specimens of dubious provenance; and the *Red Book*, the preeminent guide to United States coins, hired him as a consultant. The following year his connections nominated him for admission to the Professional Numismatists' Guild, the esteemed inner circle of the profession. He had respect, status, and friends in high places, and if he had not quite arrived, he was getting there. The Captain had only one problem: He had newfound cachet, but not enough cash.

This conundrum was solved, literally overnight, at a coin show in Akron when a harried desk clerk at an overbooked hotel asked him to share a room with another conventioneer. He was thrown together with Tony Maduro, all fifty-eight inches of him, and the rest was, as they say, history. Only Tony's mother called him by his given name; he was "Tiny" to everyone else. A librarian at Brooklyn College, he viewed coins as a casual sideline. His specialty was antique and Roman coins, which few Americans were collecting in the mid-1960s, and each specimen he owned was merely an excuse for him to elaborate at length upon the exploits of Julius Caesar, the methods used by the Crusaders to storm a walled city, or the sea battles of English privateers on the Spanish Main. Tiny was knowledgeable and good-natured, in addition to having funds he might be willing to invest, especially if the rate of return was above average. The Captain, meanwhile, was on the lookout for a partner with plenty of cash on hand, and he appreciated the untapped potential represented by Tiny's numismatic interests. Before the weekend was over, he had convinced his diminutive new friend to throw in with him and open an upscale coin shop in New York City.

Tiny, as it turned out, was worth a hundred thousand dollars, which had come to him on the wings of family tragedy. His older sister, Maria, had died a few years before when her Boeing 707, en route to Los Angeles from Idlewild, lifted reluctantly off the runway, banked steeply, and plunged into the turbid murk of Jamaica Bay. All ninety-five people aboard perished in what was, at the time, the worst aviation disaster in U.S. history. Maybe a friend had advised her, or perhaps she had had a premonition, but for whatever reason Maria had purchased flight insurance before she boarded, and being unmarried had made her brother the sole beneficiary. So Tiny, as fortune's well-heeled fool, had plenty of dough to invest, especially with someone who could liberate him from his thankless job at the library's research desk. But it was more than his bank account and his gratitude that made Tiny the perfect partner. Possessed of an innate tendency toward acquiescence, Tiny had no problem taking a back seat while the Captain called the shots.

From the beginning, Midtown Coin catered to a select clientele of dealers and collectors who sought to obtain numismatic items of superlative quality. The vast majority of U.S. coins on display bore the grades mint condition or gem proof or simply B.U., short for "brilliant uncirculated." As for foreign and ancient coins, the Captain insisted that Tiny purchase only the finest examples of these as well. Before long, a tag line was added to their business cards in an elegant font that proclaimed: *The Tiffany's of the coin business.*

My father had the small space at 39 West Fifty-fifth furnished like a private men's club: Wine-red carpeting of a noticeably plush nap set off the handsome walnut cabinets in which rare coins were displayed on velvet-lined trays that at the touch of a button revolved like a Ferris wheel. Art Deco wall sconces illuminated mahogany shelves, while gilt-framed prints of "olde" New York adorned what little wall space remained with quaint scenes of ice skaters in Central Park, ninepins on Bowling Green and Washington's farewell to his generals at Fraunces Tavern. Well-dressed customers would linger over highly polished glass and confer in respectful whispers, or mull over a purchase in a cozy armchair by a picture window that looked out on the ever-changing bustle of the street.

Things went well, but soon they would go better, for in 1967 Congress passed a bill that required the Treasury after one year to cease giving silver in exchange for paper Silver Certificates. Silver Certificates, unlike the newer Federal Reserve Notes, were backed by hard currency. Each read "payable to the bearer on demand" and could be exchanged at any bank for a dollar's worth of silver coin, no questions asked. Spurred by the deadline, speculators bought up Silver Certificates with such zeal that the intrinsic value of the silver was soon worth twenty-five percent more than the face value of the coins themselves. Thirteen hundred of these certificates could be presented directly to the Federal Reserve Bank and redeemed for a thousand-ounce bar of silver, .999 fine, weighing about sixty pounds, bearing the stamp of the U.S. Assay Office and shaped like a small, dense, shiny loaf of bread.

Midtown Coin, which became the largest buyer of paper money in the country, had its Silver Certificates conveyed daily to the Irving Trust Company on Wall Street, which facilitated the exchange to silver bars. An official weighmaster weighed each ingot and converted the total into a certificate of deposit. The ultimate goal of these transactions was to purchase on the commodity exchange a number of silver contracts, which were sold every few days as necessary to acquire funds to buy more Silver Certificates. The revenue that the contracts generated fluctuated with the market, but on average the firm realized a profit of four cents on each Silver Certificate it purchased. And there were plenty around the country to be had. During the turbulent year before the deadline, Midtown Coin was turning over a hundred thousand Silver Certificates a day at a daily profit of four thousand bucks.

Midtown needed a new partner for this venture, as Tiny's capital had been exhausted by the renovation of the store and the upgrade in stock. The Captain found Abe "Foxy" Rosenthal through his connections at the Professional Numismatists' Guild. Foxy was a New York legend, a mogul who had built a multimillion-dollar empire from scratch. Or, as he once described his story for a magazine article: "From the outhouse to the penthouse." Foxy wasn't himself in the P.N.G., but he liked to dabble in coins, especially the more rarified issues, such as commemorative and territorial gold, and as New York's funeral parlor king, who laid to rest many of the city's dear departed, he had plenty of discretionary income to invest.

This silent partnership flourished, and it was still going strong when the cutoff date for redeeming Silver Certificates arrived. Without missing a beat, speculators shifted their attention to acquiring silver coins, thousand-dollar bags of which could be directly applied to the purchase of commodity exchange contracts. Airport pickups of eighty thousand dollars were routine. As insured freight, the silver was shipped in thousand-dollar bags, each weighing fifty-seven pounds. Eighty bags of silver added almost five thousand pounds to the weight of the Captain's forest-green Cadillac DeVille, which rode just a few inches off the ground. The heavy-duty shocks had be changed every couple of months and even then an unseen pothole or a patch of rough pavement would produce an awful scraping of metal where the chrome bottom of the rear bumper made cacophonous contact with the road.

By 1973 silver was still trickling in, though not at quite so heady a volume. Gene's daily pickups from the air cargo docks at Kennedy Airport totaled twenty to forty bags, or "pieces," shipped from Albuquerque, New Orleans, Chicago, Syracuse and twenty other cities. The silver was driven directly to the Manhattan store, where each bag had to be counted, spot-checked and repacked in its white canvas pouch, then secured with a new lead seal for the journey downtown.

I press the buzzer at the front door and wait for someone to admit me. Recessed into the wall of the vestibule, like a diorama, is a small velvet-draped window box displaying commemorative gold and silver. I love examining the likenesses of famous American figures on these coins: Washington and Lafayette, Daniel Boone, Generals Grant and Jackson and Lee. After a minute, I buzz again and rap twice on the glass. The rent-a-guard finally lets me in.

Though I have entered the store hundreds of times, I am never quite prepared for the whirlwind of noise and activity. Irving, the hapless assistant, is manning the counting machine that has long replaced one of the leather armchairs. He dumps a bag of four thousand quarters into the metal bowl and clamps the canvas sack onto the exit chute. When engaged, the motor revolves a metal plate that propels the coins past the counting wheel, rapid fire, like a machine gun. At the rear of the room, a teletype machine erupts into staccato communication, posting the latest quotes and queries on rare coins, rolls and proof sets. The Captain paces along the right wall, behind the handsome bank of showcases, barking into a receiver: "I wish I knew, Lenny. He's out somewhere playing with his yuggie. If you talk to that son of a bitch, you tell him for me he better get his ass over here."

Two lines ring simultaneously. Tiny answers courteously in his high-pitched, adenoidal voice, "Midtown Coin, good morning," places the caller on hold and fields the other line. He's at his usual perch by the front window, barely visible behind the glass-topped cabinet in whose red velvet trays repose exquisite examples of Greek tetradrachms, Roman silver owls, English gold angels and Spanish pieces of eight. My favorite, a Corinthian silver stater from 430 B.C., bears an image of a flying Pegasus with powerful, uplifted wings.

I first began working for my father the summer following my bar mitzvah. I was mostly a gopher. I'd go for coffee, go for stamps, go for office supplies. I loved returning to the tasteful serenity of the store. But that was before the silver craze, when what had been a haven of calm amid the hubbub of the city gave way to the adrenaline rush of continual speculation. Business was brusque, booming and boisterous. The summer days flew by with such force that by six o'clock I was wasted. My father, however, was exhilarated, and with good reason. Money was accumulating at such a furious pace that Midtown Coin might have been mistaken for a branch office of the U.S. Mint.

I continued to work summers until the big blow-up in 1969. I had just graduated high school and was doing airport pickups and other odd jobs. In the middle of August, the Captain drove my mom and Tiny down to Philly to attend the annual convention of the American Numismatic Association. I was supposed to keep commuting from Valley Stream, make the airport pickups, count and rebag the silver, then haul it down to Wall Street at the end of the day. The upcoming weekend, however, coincided with Woodstock. For weeks I'd been looking forward to "3 days of peace & music," but when Thursday afternoon rolled around, I realized if I did the downtown delivery, I'd never get back to the Island in time to meet my friends, who were driving up that evening to the Catskills. So I made an executive decision. I left eighty thousand dollars in the store, stacked in an imposing cairn of canvas bags. Then I drove home, packed up and split, leaving a brief note of farewell on the dining room table.

When I returned from Woodstock—the most intense and euphoric experience of my sweet, short life—I was so exhausted I slept for fifteen hours. As soon as I woke up, my mother informed me I was fired. The Captain was furious. How his son could willfully disregard his responsibility was beyond him. When we finally had it out, things got worse. "Why are you upset?" I said. "Nothing was stolen, was it?" I'm still not sure what incensed him more—the cluelessness of my remark or my complete lack of contrition—but the upshot was he wouldn't talk to me. For my entire freshman year. If I called, he wouldn't come to the phone. If I went home, he avoided me. All communication went through my mother. The big freeze finally thawed the following summer only because I worked my ass off and made dean's list. After that we got along for a couple of years. Until I flunked out.

"Who wants coffee?" I announce, sweeping aggressively into the pressure cooker of the showroom. "Here you go, Irving, tea with lemon." He digs into his pocket for change. "Forget it, it's on me."

"Always you remember," he says in a thick Yiddish accent. "Such a nice boy you are, Eddie."

Irving is fifty years old, but looks seventy. Sipping his tea, a faraway look softening his gaunt features, he reminds me of "Bontsche the Silent," a Yiddish story about a pious man who endures his terrible suffering in silence. When Bonstche dies, God rewards him with whatever his heart desires. What is the one thing for which Bontsche longs? A hot roll and butter.

Tiny stands up and motions me over. "You're a lifesaver, Ed." He puts his hand over the receiver and leans forward. "Your father's on the warpath. Gene hasn't come in yet with the delivery." I nod my thanks. When approaching the Captain, it helps to have a weatherman to know which way the wind blows.

"You heard about the big score, Tiny?"

"About twenty times. I feel like I was there."

I laugh. "Yeah, it was unbelievable. Thirty-one lengths. I doubt I'll ever see a race like that again."

The Captain slams the phone into the cradle and shouts, "That fuckin prick. Where the hell is he?"

"Relax," says Tiny. "Don't get your bowels in an uproar."

"I'll kill him," seethes my dad. "I swear I'll kill him."

"See what I mean," whispers Tiny. "Better gird your loins."

"Hi, Dad, here's your coffee." He grabs it without acknowledgment, pries off the plastic lid and gulps.

"Your schmuck of an uncle hasn't called."

"If he came in on the Van Wyck he might be a while. I heard a traffic report about an overturned tractor-trailer."

"I told him a thousand times to call if he's going to be late. You think he listens?" He sighs and seems to relax as the excuse for Gene's lateness registers. "By the way, your mother wants to know if you're coming out this weekend. What should I tell her?"

"Sure. I'll be there. What would you like for Father's Day?"

"You know what I want. A diploma."

"Stacks!" calls Tiny. "Line two."

"Would you settle for a cap and gown?" My father waves me away and picks up the phone. He listens attentively and nods, his face softening.

"I'd be happy to take a look," he purrs, offering his assistance in a practiced and deferential manner. "Send him over, Harry. Absolutely. Will do."

He glances at Irving, does a double take, and explodes. "What the hell are you doing, you putz?" Hunched over the bag he has just closed, Irving looks up questioningly, a slow old mule waiting to be whipped. "You can't leave that much play in the seal." The Captain storms over, opens his pocket knife, cuts off the offending fastener, lassoes a new one around the bulging sack and, holding taut the loop of twine, slides the lead seal snugly into place. "Gimme that," he snaps. Irving hands over the crimping implement, exposing his forearm with the infamous tattoo of small blue numbers. It occurs to me that Irving suffers Leo's abuse without complaint because it is nothing to the humiliation he endured in the camps. Still, I wish my father would treat him with more

respect. The Captain's jaw muscles twitch as he exerts pressure on
the limbs of the crimping tool, forcing the small rectangle of soft
lead into the shape of a metal "S." He picks up the hefty load and
heaves it atop the pyramid of a dozen or so completed bags, where
it lands with a thud.

"Are you out of your mind, Leo?" Tiny chides, in his comically
high voice. "Let Irving do his job, will you please?"

"Fine," says my father. "But if I don't do certain things around
here, they don't get done." He turns on Irving, not yet finished
with him. "Come here," he orders. "I got an errand for you. Take
this roll of '50 D nickels over to Benedetti. And don't dawdle."

"Right away, Mr. Sacks." Irving shambles out the door with
the package as my father watches with undisguised contempt.

"Unbelievable," he says to the guard. "I must have showed him
fifty times how to seal a bag. You think he listens?"

"Lester Merkin," shouts Tiny. "Line three." The teletype machine starts up again with a clatter.

"I should be getting back to work, Dad. I'll call you from the
road."

"You wait, Eddie." The fellow from Stacks enters, holding a
black umbrella like a walking stick. In his seersucker suit and bow
tie, the customer could be mistaken for a college professor. The
Captain is on the phone dickering about the price of Saint-
Gaudens twenty-dollar gold pieces. "What quantity are you looking for? The best I can do, Lester, is fifty-three per." Waving the
man over, my father takes the small white envelope he is proffered
and slides out a shiny Barber dollar. He holds the coin by the rim,
inspecting it through a loupe. "Get back to me," he says. "Right-O,"
and hangs up.

"They told me over at Stacks you might be interested in an 1895 Barber dollar that was minted in Philadelphia."

"I might," says Leo. He turns over the coin and examines the other side.

"I think you'll find that one to be in quite extraordinary condition."

"Well, it's certainly uncirculated." An uncirculated coin is one that has never been released by the U.S. Mint into general circulation. A proof coin, by comparison, is made especially for collectors and struck more than once to impart both sharpness of detail and a mirrorlike finish. It is impossible to confuse the shiny, imperfect quality of an uncirculated coin, which after being bagged tends to suffer nicks and scratches, with the highly polished surface of a proof specimen. "What do you think of that, Tiny? The gentleman would like to sell us an uncirculated '95 P."

"That's very interesting, Leo." The partners exchange a knowing glance.

"What is your considered opinion of its value?" asks the man.

"Well, let's see," says the Captain. "Retail, the coin goes for almost five thousand. That, of course, is what we get for it. I guess I would be willing to pay thirty-seven hundred."

"Indeed," says the man, who takes in the news by patting a hand across his head. His hair, which is very long on the side, has been flipped over to conceal his baldness. "You couldn't make it thirty-eight, could you?"

Leo looks at him and laughs. "You know, sir," he says, "it's an interesting thing about the '95 P. Fewer than nine hundred are known to exist, all in proof condition. There is, apparently, a record of twelve thousand having been minted, but I know of no one, until this very moment, who has actually seen an uncirculated one." The customer blinks several times, trying to take in what my father has just said.

"What exactly are you telling me?" he asks.

"I'm telling you that this coin in this condition could not have been minted in Philadelphia. This coin was minted in New Orleans with four hundred and fifty thousand others. I'm telling you, sir, that this is a '95 O with the mint mark removed." Coins issued in Philadelphia bear no mint mark at all; only the other branches of the U.S. Mint employ capital letter designations to identify the city of origin: O for New Orleans, D for Denver, and S for San Francisco are the most common. "See for yourself," says the Captain. "There's a ring of scratch marks where the 'O' has been obliterated."

"I don't see anything of the kind."

"You won't," says Leo. "Not with the naked eye. You have to look through this." Bolted to the display case is the spring-loaded extension arm of a black aluminum lamp. The Captain swings around the lamp head, a circular fluorescent bulb attached to a metal rim into which is set a powerful magnifying glass like a transparent shade. "You see the eagle's tail feathers?" The customer nods. "Look under there, just below the wreath," says the Captain, switching on the bulb. "By the way, may I ask you where you happened to get this coin?"

"This coin?" echoes the man in a vague, distant voice. "Well, you see, I represent the estate of a famous widow who wishes to remain anonymous."

"Is that so? I think you better tell her she's trying to sell a fake."

"I can't believe this," says the man. "Are you absolutely sure?"

"Without question," says the Captain. "I'd stake my reputation on it."

"This is most distressing." He slides the coin into its paper pouch, pockets it, hurriedly retrieves his umbrella and leaves. The moment the door closes, we all bust out laughing.

"Famous widow, my ass," says the Captain.

"Was it just my imagination," says Tiny, "or did he run out of here with his tail between his legs?"

"I don't get it," I say. "Was he the guy who doctored the mint mark?"

"Probably," says the Captain.

"But he seemed so shocked when you told him, Dad."

"An act," he says. "That guy was phony as a three-dollar bill."

"I think you're wrong, Dad. He didn't know the coin was fake."

"As usual, Eddie, you don't know what you're talking about."

"You know how often someone comes in here and tries to pull a fast one?" says Tiny. "Sometimes once a week. Go ahead, Leo, tell him about the phony dime."

"On Friday," says the Captain without missing a beat, "a guy comes in, wants to sell us a '16 D for five hundred bucks. So I look it over, and it's absolutely gorgeous—gem B.U. all the way—but there's just something about it that don't feel right."

"It looks fine to me," says Tiny. "It has the right date on the head and a mint mark on the tail."

"That's true," says the Captain. "It appears to be a legitimate coin, but the planchet seems a little thick. Sure enough, it's two dimes soldered together—the obverse, a '16 P, is mounted on another dime, probably a '17 D."

"That's unbelievable," I say.

"This stuff happens all the time," says Tiny, "but your father's not so easy to hoodwink as some of our fellow numismatists."

"That reminds me," says the Captain, "I better put the word out while I remember." He sits down at the teletype to compose a warning to other dealers about the fake Barber dollar.

"Gene," shouts Tiny. "Line one."

"About fuckin time," says the Captain, hurrying to the phone. Without so much as a hello, he picks it up and starts ranting: "Where the hell have you been? Is it too much to ask you to check in once in a while? You know, we're trying to run a business here." He listens for a few seconds and starts in again. "Who are you telling to calm down? Where are you? What are you doing at a police station? You got another ticket? You better not tell me you got another ticket. You what?" He sits down. "Oh, fuckin Christ." He hunches forward, still listening, rubbing his eyes with the tips of his stubby fingers. "All of it? The Camaro, too? Oh, for crying out loud. Where the hell did this happen?" He listens intently, shaking his head in disgust. "You'll what? You're damn right you'll make it up to me. Look, I'll be there in half an hour. Meanwhile, call your office. Lenny is looking for you."

The Captain instructs me to wheel the cab around as he pops a nitroglycerin pill under his tongue. Gene is at the 108th Precinct in Long Island City, not far from the Queensborough Bridge. In the Checker on the way over my father tells me what he knows. Gene was robbed on Borden Avenue when two vehicles sandwiched him off the road. They took his car, with eighteen bags of silver, and left him there, under the steel supports of the Long Island Expressway.

"But you have insurance, don't you?"

"Who's got insurance?" he remarks. "You got any idea what insurance costs?"

The news stops me cold. Eighteen thousand gone, with no chance of getting it back. My father curses Gene, whose poor judgment is forever landing him in hot water. Gene is supposed to take certain precautions when transporting silver, chief among them to vary his route from the airport every day. Periodically the Captain warns him to stick to well-traveled roads so he can't be isolated and cut off. Borden Avenue, a cabbie's back way of avoiding traffic to the Queens-Midtown Tunnel, is as bad a route as one can take. The desolate, pot-holed shortcut threads half a mile past massive stanchions and erector-set girders through an industrial district of brick warehouses, autobody repair shops and light-manufacturing plants. It's a perfect spot for a robbery.

The Checker clips across the outer roadway of the Fifty-ninth Street Bridge. I notice the fog has burned off, revealing a hazy sky over the East River on which a garbage scow crawls along, trailing a disorderly flock of seagulls.

"What a stink!" grouses the Captain, rolling up the window of the cab. "You know what really bothers me?" he fumes. "He mentioned to me last week what a time-saver Borden Avenue was and I distinctly told him to stay away from it." He fulminates, spouting insults and heaping scorn on his younger brother, whom he swears will pay in full for his stupidity.

"I hope he's okay, Dad."

"He won't be after I get finished with him."

They say blood is thicker than water, but I don't once hear him express a shred of concern for Gene. I glance over and he's staring straight ahead, jaw set, teeth clenched, and something in the downward cast of his mouth and the stolid, disapproving eyes reminds me of a coin on display in the vestibule window of the store, a silver commemorative half dollar from the year of my father's birth, stamped with the scowling profile of U.S. Grant.

VALLEY STREAM

When I was six my father surprised me with the notion that we actually dwelt on an island surrounded by water. Because we lived inland, I found the idea ridiculous and refused to believe him. Exasperated, the Captain produced a map and made me trace with my finger the narrow crab claw of land that jutted east from Manhattan and the slanting Atlantic coastline like a badly fractured limb. Years later I decided Long Island must have detached itself from the continent and drifted for millions of years into its oblique geographical position. I concluded this on scant empirical evidence—its relative position to the mainland seemed to suggest that it had once been beachfront property in Connecticut. But, as my father was fond of telling me, I didn't know what the hell I was talking about.

Forty thousand years ago, the area that would become Long Island was covered by the Illinoian glacier, a vast cake of ice. I learned this in a college geology course I took to satisfy the science requirement. The glacier, pushing southward, slowed until its leading edge was melting as fast as its forward momentum. The melting glacier deposited tons of boulders, gravel, sand and clay, creating an irregular landmass—a terminal moraine—over the southern half of the inchoate island. When the glacier receded, about twenty thousand years later, it settled into position along what would become Long Island's northern coast. Another moraine formed from the debris discarded by the glacier as it ebbed. Over time these immense piles of till coalesced into the island's south and north shores. Long Island evolved into its present shape on the unpromising rubble of a geologic garbage dump.

The present-day blight of so many thoroughfares sullied by chain stores, supermarkets, Chinese restaurants and other businesses can be traced, I suspect, to this ignoble genesis. On Hempstead Turnpike, Northern Boulevard or Sunrise Highway, one can cruise an interchangeable strip of banks and burger stands, delis and diners, supermarkets and gas stations, dry cleaners and five-and-dimes. Connecting these main arteries are many more unsightly avenues running north-south that delineate cookie-cutter developments in towns whose idyllic names conjure images of pastoral simplicity: Floral Park, Pinelawn, East Meadow, Brookhaven. Ride the Long Island Rail Road for any length of time and the place names of so many apparently picturesque locales will seep into your subconscious, thanks to the matter-of-fact delivery of the blue-suited conductors: "This train stops at Cold Spring Harbor, Greenlawn and Stony Brook. Change at Jamaica for Glen Cove, Deer Park, Sea Cliff."

I disembark at Valley Stream, where as you might have guessed no tree-covered hills rise up to form a verdant valley. If anything, the terrain is rather flat—a charmless topography of suburban sprawl marked by the Green Acres Shopping Mall, Sunrise Highway, and a dense grid of short streets lined with tidy middle-class homes and ending in four-way stop signs. There are, to be sure, a couple of parks with ballfields and duck ponds in walking distance from the depot, but as for a purling bucolic stream, there's only a sloped concrete drainage ditch lacerating the grassy, overgrown strip between the station and the roadway.

As usual, my mother is running late, a trait that drives the Captain crazy. He insists on military precision and Goldie ignores him, muddling along to an internal clock that's always twenty minutes slow. "Goldie time," we call it. He thinks being prompt is something she can control, a simple matter of discipline or willpower. But I don't see it that way, having long accepted my mother's chronic tardiness as an essential expression of her personality. She could no more be on time than she could drive untempted past a flea market, or fail to overcook the broccoli or refrain from opening as slowly as possible a cellophane-wrapped candy in a quiet movie theater. And, frankly, it's such a gorgeous afternoon I'm content to loiter by the station, watching the cars drive up to collect their waving passengers. Sooner or later my mother will arrive, we'll go home and enjoy a good meal, I'll give the Captain his gift, then take refuge in the finished basement and shoot pool.

Exactly twenty minutes later, Goldie pulls into the parking lot, chatty and apologetic. She was stuck at the beauty parlor, she explains, and then she had to duck into Woolworth's, which was having a closeout sale on Father's Day cards. Closeout sale, yard sale, rummage sale. That's my mother for you. No matter how much money we have, she'll never pass up a bargain. It drives the Captain crazy.

"Why must you buy that crap?" he says.

"Am I bothering you?" she replies. "Mind your own business."

When I was in third grade, my homework one night consisted of quizzing them on their favorite word that started with the letter B. My father said *bullion*; my mother said *bazaar*. At least they're consistent, my parents. They always run according to form.

"Nice hairdo, Ma." She could be auditioning for a local dinner-theater production of *Flower Drum Song*. Her brown hair has been whipped into an airy mass that reminds me of chocolate cotton candy. It sets off a vaguely Oriental face with high cheekbones that make her look younger than she is. A green and orange blouse sporting a bamboo pattern contributes to the effect. Like all her clothes, it's a bargain from a local sale.

"Thanks, honey. Sorry I'm late. My watch stopped."

"Why don't you get one that works?" I suggest. "Something that matches your jade bracelet." She glances at the expensive piece of jewelry on her other wrist. A birthday gift from the Captain.

"I know, I know." Out of nowhere she exclaims, "Ruined by cheap Chinese labor!"

"The watch was made in Japan, Ma."

"China, Japan, what's the difference? Look at this card," she beams. "Isn't it perfect?" I remove the stiff cardboard rectangle from its business-sized envelope. A pennant flutters across the sky proclaiming WORLD'S GREATEST DAD, who is personified by the cartoonish figure of a paunchy, cardigan-garbed shlub enjoying a much-deserved snooze in the backyard hammock. The inside reveals the groggy, just-awakened dad smiling tolerantly as he's

mobbed by the adoring wife and kids. A heart-warming senti-
ment follows:

For all the many things you do,
The kind words that you say,
We'd like to thank you with a hug
On this your special day.

"Perfect," I agree. "I can see why it took so long to pick out."
Either Goldie doesn't notice my sarcasm or she chooses to ignore it.

"Happy Father's Day," she says blithely.

"Thanks, Ma, but I don't have any children."

"Well, that's a relief. Because how could you possibly support
them on the take-home pay of a cabdriver?"

"Lots of people do it. You'd be surprised."

"So now you want to be a cabdriver for the rest of your life?"

"Give me a break, Ma. I didn't say that."

"You know, you come out once in a blue moon, you couldn't
get a haircut for the occasion?"

"Oh, please." The city-bound train from Far Rockaway eases
across a curved, elevated trestle and glides into the station. I wish
I were about to board it.

"I don't understand you," she says. "Are all the dungarees in
your closet ripped at the knee?"

"Will you stop?" I'm still holding the Father's Day card, which
resists as I try to replace it in the envelope, and I manage to inflict
a paper cut on the tip of my index finger. "Oh, Christ."

"Is it bleeding?" she asks.

"Can we go now?"

She shifts into drive and jams on the accelerator. The Riviera shoots through the parking lot, barges into the avenue and cuts across a lane of oncoming traffic. You know, it's a funny thing. When I drive a cab, I never wear a seatbelt, but when I'm with my mother, I can't get one on fast enough. I fumble with the buckle and tighten the strap. And since she drives more smoothly when she's not paying attention to the road, I try to distract her with conversation. "So, Mom," I venture cheerily, "how does he like it?"

"How does who like what?"

"Dad? His new chair?"

"Oh, Eddie, he's crazy about it. I only hope he'll get out of it when it's time to grill the steaks."

My mother agonized for weeks over which recliner to buy. She enlisted my aid, but I refused to get involved. "The eternal question," I called it. The Barcolounger versus the Stratolounger. One had thick, smooth cushions; the other offered upholstery that was deeply biscuit-tufted. One featured a hidden automatic headrest; the other had an extra-high back. One reclined with the use of a wooden handle; the other succumbed to steady backward pressure. One was available in crushed gold velvet; the other came in jet-black vinyl. After a month of listening to my mother perseverate endlessly on the relative merits of reclining chairs, I told her she was driving me nuts and that I didn't care which one she bought. Apparently she made the right decision.

I'd had my own problems deciding on a gift. My mother suggested an electric insect killer, a grotesque fixture for the patio that eliminates mosquitoes and other flying pests with a ruthless, audible zap. I rejected it along with an electric firestarter for the barbecue, a box of Sultans, a wristwatch fashioned from a silver dollar, and tickets to *Carousel* at the Jones Beach Theatre. I finally settled on a pair of compact, lightweight binoculars to replace the bulky old army field glasses that the Captain had been lugging to the track for as long as I could remember.

"Remind me to stop by Sally's for the cake," she says.

"Stop by Sally's for the cake."

"Why must you do that?" she scolds.

"It's Sunday, Mom. Sally's will be closed later."

"You're right," she concedes. "When you're right, you're right."

We drive down Merrick Road toward the bakeshop. The day is perfect—sunny, seventy-five degrees and low humidity—a welcome relief after the hot spell of the previous week.

"I saw Richie Birnbaum's mother at the beauty parlor," she says. "Guess who got into medical school?"

"That's nice, Ma."

"Refresh my memory," she says. "How many credits do you need to graduate?" We pass the Village Diner, my old high school hangout; Jahn's Ice Cream Parlor, where we celebrate special occasions; and the new store where one can exchange books of S&H Green Stamps for a tantalizing array of small appliances.

"Have you been to that redemption center?"

"Don't change the subject, Eddie."

"Who's changing the subject? I'm just wondering if you cashed in your Green Stamps. I can use a new clock radio." She rolls toward a red light and stands on the brake, the sudden halt pinning us back then propelling us forward. Goldie has never learned the knack of easing off the pedal at the last moment, so every stop packs the unpleasant bonus of an extra kick.

"I'm waiting." Normally my mother has the attention span of a three-year-old, but when it comes to the particulars of my education, she can be as annoying as a paper cut.

"I don't know," I sigh. "Nineteen, twenty. Something like that."

"And how many can you take in the fall?"

"Fifteen, I guess." I've promised my parents I will enroll at City College, but what I'd really love to do is table the whole business for another year. Keep driving a cab and living in the city. I'd sign up for an acting workshop. Take a watercolor class at the Art Students' League. Learn yoga, join a gym, find a poker game. I long to take an extended hiatus from the stress of academics.

"That's what we thought, your father and I, and it seems to us if you take two classes this summer, you can finish up your degree next semester. That way, you'll only lose six months, tops."

"I wouldn't say I'm losing time, Ma. On the contrary, I'm keeping careful track of it."

"Very funny, Eddie." The light changes and we dart forward. "So have you thought about summer school? It's the middle of June already."

I take a deep breath and depress the switch that opens the window. A warm breeze bathes my upturned face. "I was thinking I might hold off for the summer. Vic and Steve want me to go with them to Europe. It would be a great opportunity." My high school pals are planning to spend the summer abroad. "We hear you can buy a cheap car in England and drive it down to

Athens, where you can sell it to American GIs who are stationed there."

I didn't intend to blurt it out like this. I was hoping to reveal my plans at a more receptive moment, like after dinner on the quiet of the patio.

"Oh, your father will love this."

"That's a shame," I say. "I don't think we'll have room for a fourth."

"You know what I mean, smart aleck."

"It's my life, isn't it?"

"Yes, and you're doing a wonderful job screwing it up."

I WANDER INTO THE DEN, where the Captain is hunched forward on his new vinyl throne, aiming the remote control at the Zenith like Captain Kirk operating a phaser. *Click.* Lee Trevino blasts out of a sand trap. *Click.* Batman and Robin battle the Penguin's henchmen. POW! SOCK! BAM! *Click.* Edwin Newman quizzes Dr. Spock about drug use among teenagers. *Click.* Pat O'Brien pleads with Jimmy Cagney in prison.

"*Angels with Dirty Faces*, Dad. I love that one."

"I've seen it a hundred times," he says, leveling the remote at the screen. *Click.* Clad only in undershirt and boxer shorts, his skin looks abnormally pale against the jet-black upholstery, as if it has been dredged in flour.

"Whoa, Dad, nice chair."

"You like it?" he says, brushing crumbs off the padded armrest. "You ever see something like this?" He leans back to show it off.

The foot support jerks up his outstretched legs. "The action," he says, "is a little stiff."

"Impressive, Dad. You could fly the Starship Enterprise in that thing."

"Your mother really outdid herself this time."

"I hear she searched high and low," I say, "for just the right one." He looks like a middle-aged Babe Ruth on his day off, the massive trunk supported on spindly legs, which he crosses just now in carefree repose.

"Here. I got you something." He takes my gift and sniffs it.

"I know what this is," he says. "Cigars, right?"

"I can't fool you."

He tears off the wrapping, and his face registers subtle shades of adjustment from assumption to surprise. He lifts the under-sized binoculars out of the Styrofoam tray and trains them at the color TV, where I recognize the tinted visage of Senator Baker, vice chairman of the Watergate hearings, from his no-nonsense eyeglasses with the thick black Buddy Holly frames.

"Hey, Dad, there's your boy." He grunts. As the ranking Republican on the Watergate committee, Baker is in an unenviable bind. He must try to be impartial, yet do what he can to protect the President.

"Goldie," he calls, "come here, you have to see this."

"By the way, Dad, there are two focal knobs. The wheel in the middle is for your right eye; the one on the left eyepiece—"

"I know all about it, Eddie. I was using binoculars before you were born."

She hurries in, takes one look at the Captain and throws up her hands.

"Leo, I thought you would be dressed by now. Or do you plan to spend the whole day in your underwear?" Immediately she starts picking up the packaging and smoothing out the wrinkled gift wrap to use again later.

"Will you leave that alone. Look at these."

"What is that, a camera?"

"Binoculars," I say, "for the track."

"But they're so small." She takes them from my father and before she even looks through them exclaims, "My God, they're so light!"

"That's the point, Ma. Now he doesn't have to lug those heavy field glasses around."

"I can't get over how small they are."

"Don't touch the glass!" he snaps. "You want to ruin them?" He grabs them back and drapes the strap around his neck.

"Get dressed, Leo. It's almost two o'clock." My father ignores her.

"And I thought it was a box of cigars," he says, polishing the lenses with the hem of his undershirt.

"I almost gave them to you yesterday," I say, "at Belmont. The 5-1 shot you sussed out in the feature, now that was a sweet piece of handicapping."

"That filly Magazine? Cordero rode her beautiful, didn't he?" In a daring move, the jockey managed to sneak through on the rail and steal the race.

If my uncle were there, he would've had a heart attack, but Gene had business to take care of upstate. It was the first Saturday he'd missed since I started going with them, but I can't say I was surprised. Things at the store had been in turmoil all week.

Leo needled him constantly about the robbery, Gene protested, and when they argued, the Captain fired him. After the way Leo treated him, Gene was probably glad to get away.

"These look great, Eddie, I can't wait to try them out."

"Happy Father's Day."

"You know, you're all right," he says.

Pleased, I look away at the TV, still dominated by the head and shoulders of Howard Baker. He's being grilled about the recent testimony of Jeb Stuart Magruder, former deputy director of CREEP, the Committee for the Re-election of the President. Magruder had dropped a bomb on Thursday when he confessed that he and other high-ranking officials had plotted to bug Larry O'Brien's phone at Democratic National Committee headquarters and then tried to cover it up. Magruder fingered John Mitchell, the former attorney general, Bob Haldeman, then the President's chief of staff, and John Dean, the former White House counsel. But he didn't name Nixon.

"You know what today is, Dad? The first anniversary of the Watergate burglary. What do you think of that?"

"What do I think I of it? I think the fuckin Democrats are going to gnaw on this story like a bone."

"Why shouldn't they? Did you read Thursday's testimony? Magruder really spilled the beans."

"He didn't name the President."

"No, but he implicated everyone else."

"Nixon is innocent. They'll never get him."

"Let me get this straight, Dad. You're telling me the Attorney General of the United States, the White House counsel, and the

President's chief of staff planned and executed a burglary of Democratic national headquarters, then tried to cover it up, but the President knew nothing about it?"

"That's right. Why should he?"

"Oh, come on."

"Eddie, you don't know the first thing about politics. Their job is to insulate the President from these shenanigans. Don't forget, he's got a country to run. And he's doing a damn good job, by the way."

"Shenanigans, Dad? Try obstruction of justice. Try high crimes and misdemeanors."

"Don't get carried away with rhetoric. Four guys broke into an office building."

"Right. Four ex-CIA operatives. The guy I can't get over is Gordon Liddy. What a case he is. Do you know what he planned to do in San Diego at the Republican Convention? He wanted to kidnap the leaders of all these radical groups and detain them in Mexico until it was over."

"Liddy's an idiot."

"Yeah, but these other guys aren't. Mitchell, Dean, Haldeman. They're so afraid of O'Brien, they want to bug his phone so they can get something incriminating on him to force him to resign. Then when the plan goes south they try to cover it up. And the punch line is, all this illegal stuff, it was totally unnecessary. I mean, Nixon won in a landslide. And now they're all going to jail. It's laughable."

"Jail?" he scoffed. "Don't be naive."

"You think they'll get off with a fine?"

"A slap on the wrist. These guys have high-powered attorneys. If they do serve time, it'll be in some minimum-security country club."

"You think that's where Tricky Dick will end up? Or will they send him up the river to the Big House with Jimmy Cagney?"

The Captain sits forward to face me, collapsing the footrest with a violent *thwack*. "If I've told you once, I've told a thousand times," he explodes, "you don't use that phrase in this house. Nixon is innocent and he is still the President, and when you're in my presence you show him some respect or you can take the next train home. Understand?" He swipes the remote from the end table, clicks off the Zenith and storms out of the room.

I sit frozen for a minute, astonished that my innocuous remark could so quickly ignite my father's wrath. Everybody knows the Captain has a short fuse, but when he's raving and venting over something as petty as this, he looks ridiculous, like Ralph Kramden throwing a tantrum. I don't know how anyone can take him seriously. I keep a straight face, of course. I have to.

Down the block a lawnmower sputters and drones. I wonder if I should slip up to my bedroom and get stoned, sedate myself for the long afternoon. That would put me in a mellow, monosyllabic mood and keep me from locking horns over stupid stuff. I need to relax. I get off the sofa, ease onto the recliner and lean back. The action is stiff and I have to grab both armrests for purchase. The seat is warm, thanks to the Captain, and the chair is luxurious and comfortable. I point the remote at the blank set and bring it back to life. The Mets game is in the bottom of the first and Rusty Staub, the power-hitting outfielder, is batting with a man on. The

Padres' pitcher misses outside with a slider. Staub lines the next pitch, a fastball, up the middle, moving the runner to second. Milner is up and smacks a hard grounder to the right side. Staub runs by the second baseman, screening him from the ball, which skips off his glove into right field. Digging from second, Millan crosses the plate to give the home team a one-nothing lead. The Mets celebrate in the dugout as my mother bustles in.

"What's wrong with you?" she demands. "You should know better than to get your father upset."

"It doesn't take much."

"It's his day, remember, so be nice."

"Fine."

"And don't talk about politics."

"Whatever you say."

"That's a good boy," she says, patting my head. "Go start the coals."

"In a minute," I tell her.

"Now!" she says sharply. "Hop to it. Your father wants to eat soon."

I know that tone of voice well. The top sergeant is issuing orders that come straight from the commanding officer. I can either procrastinate and get chewed out, or do what I usually do in these situations, which is just what I'm told.

On the way to the back yard I stop in the bathroom to bandage my cut. The medicine cabinet, like Fibber McGee's closet, is an accident waiting to happen, crowded to overflowing with tubes and containers and jars. A vial of nitroglycerin tablets—my father's heart pills—totters on the edge and I push it back between a can of Right Guard and a bottle of Vitalis. I find the Band-Aids, apply one to the tip of my finger, and head off to the garage.

I haul out the bag of charcoal and dump onto the barbecue a pile of briquettes, which I arrange into a pyramid and douse with lighter fluid. The flames riot and ebb, fouling the air with the acrid odor of petroleum. I flop onto a lawn chair, away from the unpleasant smell. A robin hops in the grass by the rock garden where a fountain gurgles among well-tended beds of petunias, impatiens and marigolds. Smoke drifts in lazy plumes over the sparse clumps of forsythia along the fence, where only a month ago their blossoms had massed into a buttery tapestry. I close my eyes, letting the warm sun blanket my face, and doze—I'm not sure how long—until the screen door slams and my father exits, ass first, carrying a plate of thick steaks and a tray of condiments. The Captain is still wearing the binoculars, which now rest against a white apron that reads KNOW YOUR STEAK and is illustrated with raw slabs of prime beef labeled "porterhouse," "shell," "ribeye" and "filet mignon."

"You ever see steaks like this?" he says, plunging a fork into one and lifting it for my inspection. "You're in for a real treat."

The shell steaks look incredible—two inches thick and well marbled. He prepares the barbecue by spreading out the ash-covered coals and seasoning the circular grill with half an onion that has been impaled securely on the twin tines of a wooden-handled fork. The steaks, which he places lovingly on the metal grate, sear and sizzle, flames lapping at the dripping fat. "Your mother tells me you want to go to Europe," he says, carefully sprinkling garlic salt over the exposed surface of the beef.

"I'm thinking about it."

"When would that be?"

"Sometime in mid-July. About a month from now."

"And what about summer school?"

"I guess I'd skip it and start fresh in September." He picks up the onion powder and applies it with the same precision.

"I think you ought to reconsider."

"Oh, yeah? Why is that?"

"Because I told you to, that's why."

"I see."

"No, you don't. Now listen to me. I have some good news for you, Eddie. Some very good news. Foxy says—you know Foxy Rosenthal, right?"

"Your partner in the silver business."

"That's right. Our silent partner. Tiny and I have made a pile of money for him. A shitload." The Captain plunges the long-tined fork into the tip of a steak and flips it over. "Only Foxy is so loaded, he has to give a lot of it away. A million a year. And one of the places he gives it to is his *alma mater*—Columbia Law School. He says they're probably going to name a building after him." He looks over at me to let the idea sink in.

"Actually, Dad, I think the term *alma mater* only applies to the college you graduate from. It doesn't apply to graduate school."

"The point is, wise guy, one word from Foxy and you're in."

"Have you taken a look at my transcript lately? I don't have the grade point average for Columbia."

"That doesn't matter. Foxy says your board score is good enough and he can run interference for you. As soon as you complete your undergraduate degree, you'll get accepted. You understand what I'm telling you? Columbia Law School!" My father is grinning. He seems to be waiting for me to jump up and down in joyous celebration, but I'm too shocked to move.

"That's amazing," I say. "I can't believe it." The image of a bridge comes to mind—the pedestrian walkway spanning Fall Creek Gorge.

"How many times have I told you, Eddie? It's who you know that counts. Connections, kiddo. It's all about connections. And when you get out of Columbia, you can write your own ticket. Believe me."

"But, Dad, I was hoping to take it a little easier before I got back into the grind. I don't want to sound ungrateful, but couldn't this wait six months? I can relax a little, go to Europe and complete my course work by June."

"Are you out of your mind?" he shouts. "Fuck Europe!"

"All right, Dad, calm down." To my surprise, he takes a deep breath and sets off on another tack.

"You know how old Foxy is?" I shake my head. "Eighty-two. And not in the best of health. Who knows what's gonna be in a few years. But he can give you a leg up now, Eddie. That's why you have to jump on this while the iron's hot. Forget Europe. You can go to Europe next summer."

There seems to be nothing I can say to change his mind. Nothing that won't antagonize him. I drop onto the lawn chair and gaze at the grass.

My mother comes out laden with plates, utensils, serrated steak knives and colorful aluminum tumblers. She dumps them, clattering, onto the picnic table and one of the tumblers rolls off and strikes the flagstone. I retrieve it and hand it to her.

"Bring out the potato salad," she says, "and the iced tea."

When I return, the table is set, and the steaks have been plated. My father cuts into his meat and nods. He crams a large cube of beef into his mouth and smiles.

"Oh, man!" he says, chewing away. "Taste that, Eddie, you'll love it." The beef is charred almost black on the outside, succulent and reddish-pink in the center. The first bite is intense—crisp and buttery and mouth filling.

"Good, huh?"

"Delicious, Dad."

"This is the life, eh, kid?"

The Captain tucks away a thick slice of steak and I'm almost inclined to agree. When Babe Ruth was dying of throat cancer and reduced to eating soft-boiled eggs, a sportswriter asked him what he missed most about the good old days. It wasn't the home runs or the cigars or the World Series celebrations or even the sex. It was the steaks, he said. "To think of the steaks."

"How do you like your steak, Goldie?" Without waiting for her reply, he attacks his plate, sawing furiously at the juicy beef. His lips gleam with grease.

"Very tasty," she says. "Must you eat so fast, Leo?"

"Don't tell me how to eat, will you please?"

"You're wolfing it down like it's your last meal."

"Shut up."

"Don't tell me to shut up, you *hozzer!*"

My father stares down at his plate, fighting to control himself. He grips the side of the picnic table as if he might heave it over. The three of us sit frozen in the afternoon light, heads bowed, as though one of us were about to say grace. A bird flits into the yard, swoops over the table and alights on the ground, its bright red plumage outlined against the pale yellow carpet of fallen Forsythia petals. Lifting up its crested head, it opens its black-rimmed beak and calls as if trying to get our attention. At least that's what it sounds like, a slurred whistle descending in pitch, punctuated by two final notes, *whoit, whoit.*

"Hey, Dad. Check out that bird with your binoculars." My father studies it with the field glasses. Allowing his anger to subside, he praises the ease of focus and the brightness of the optics.

"I can't wait till I take these to the track," he says.

"How does that cardinal look up close?"

"What do I care?" he says. "I see them all the time."

"Not a bad life," I observe, "gallivanting around singing your heart out."

"Gallivanting around is one thing," says my mother, "but you have to get serious sooner or later."

"If you say so, Ma." One of my mother's specialties is making awkward, transparent shifts from one topic to another.

"I'm only saying you can't run around for your whole life."

"I know, Ma. I'm going to get my act together, I promise."

"Driving a cab," she says, "is not getting your act together. Going off to Europe is not getting your act together. I hope you're finally going to buckle down and take advantage of this incredible gift your father is giving you." Even though I'm stuffed, I return to my steak with newfound interest.

"Your mother's right," says the Captain. "You graduate Columbia Law School and, I'm telling you, you got it made."

My parents keep at me with a persistence that is mind-numbing. I nod politely and tune them out, concentrating on the cardinal as it stalks a cricket. Their voices buzz like insects.

My mother is saying, "Don't forget, Eddie, you have to register for summer courses next week." I feel like smacking her with a fly swatter.

"I don't even know if I want to be a lawyer."

"What are you talking about?" says the Captain. "You wanted to be a lawyer since you were a little kid."

"No, Dad. You wanted me to be a lawyer since I was a kid. I'm not sure what I want to be."

"You're full of shit," says my father. "You were born to be a lawyer."

"That's just a myth," I tell him, "something we all assume is true because we've repeated it for so long. But I keep having second thoughts, Dad. I really don't think it's for me."

"Don't give me this crap, Eddie. You're just afraid. You're going to law school and that's all there is to it."

"Why? Because you say so?"

"Believe me, I know what's best for you," he says, gesturing with his knife.

"Just because you have this in at Columbia doesn't mean I have to use it. I don't really deserve to go there."

"You'll go where I tell you to go."

"I'm supposed to follow you blindly? Is that it?"

"If you know what's good for you," he yells, rising from the wooden bench.

"Sit down," says my mother. "You're getting agitated."

"Sit down?" he says. "I'll sit down when he promises to go to Columbia."

"I'll think about it," I say.

"There's nothing to think about," he rants. "You want to be a loser your whole life?"

"It's my life!"

"I won't let you throw away your future."

"Jesus, will you leave me alone?"

"No, goddammit. No, no, no!" On the last negative he grabs the binoculars, lifts them as high as he can, the strap clearing his head, and flings them down. They bounce off the gray flagstone, shattering the lenses and denting the metal housing. An eyepiece ricochets off the underside of the picnic table while the focus wheel wobbles drunkenly toward the flowerbed bordering the patio, where it keels over on its side.

"Leo!" shouts my mother. "Are you crazy?"

I stare at my father, who stares back behind the congealed remains of his steak, and I think, *You asshole! You moron! You stupid idiot!* I imagine bashing his face with my clenched fists. I ought to tear into him and curse him the hell out. I bet that would raise his heart rate. Instead I hesitate, shocked into silence by his infantile behavior. I know what I'd like to say: *Take your law school, you sonofabitch, and shove it.* My head rages with expletives, but I am powerless to provoke him further. Though tears rush to my eyes, not a single retaliatory word escapes my lips.

The Captain is patting himself down, looking for his medication.

"Go get your father's pills," says Goldie.

I walk quickly into the house and straight to the bathroom, where I grab the appropriate vial from the medicine cabinet. The label reads, "100 tablets nitroglycerin, 0.4 mg. Take one sublingual as needed for chest pain." I ought to hide the bottle and tell them I can't find it. That would fix him. I pry off the lid and tap a pill into my palm. Instead of rushing back to the table, I look at it for a moment, then pop it under my tongue. It dissolves immediately, a bitter taste accompanied by a mild burning sensation. I sit down on the edge of the tub and wait for the rush to pass.

CHINATOWN

Gene swears the best Chinks is in Chinatown. The food is fresh, he says, the service prompt and the damage always low. He eats there three or four times a week so he should know. I can tell you this: He's as familiar with the narrow, winding streets as any Chinaman. I don't think there's a tea parlor, coffee house or noodle shop he hasn't tried. I mean, what do you want? Cantonese? Hunan? Szechuan? Just ask him. He'll tell you where to get the crispiest duck, the most succulent sea bass, the tastiest dim sum or the spiciest salt and pepper shrimp. Sometimes he drags me way down East Broadway to sample more exotic fare— Thai or Vietnamese or Cambodian—out where the only English words are on street signs, and it's possible to imagine we're no longer in Manhattan but some rundown quarter of Bangkok or Saigon or Phnom Penh.

We meet outside a faded saloon on Mercer Street. Gene leads the way, pushing through the frosted glass doors and stepping up to the ebony counter. Tacked to the scrollwork above the bar, a jury-rigged string of fifteen-watt bulbs casts a quaint if feeble glow. We take our beers to a table against the wall, which is dominated by ancient photos of boxers. Wherever you gaze above the dark-brown wainscoting, nicked and bruised from a century of sparring with Father Time, their baleful stares regard you with deadly detachment, as if, having just knocked you down, each champ were awaiting the referee's signal to wade in and finish you off.

I recognize maybe every third name, but Gene knows them all from the sports pages of his childhood or memories of radio broadcasts or fight nights at the old Garden. He points out Ray Robinson and Billy Conn, Kid Gavilan and Carmen Basilio.

"I once saw Basilio pummel a bum so bad, his nose was shaking hands with his ear."

"Jesus."

"Yeah, just beat the shit out of him," he says, brandishing his fist for emphasis. "Let me ask you something, Eddie. I'm thinking of growing a bushier mustache. Should I do it?" He combs his mustache with his thumb.

"I don't know. It's your face."

"Real Russian style, like Josef Stalin. Or Akim Tamiroff. What do you think?"

"I'm kind of used to the Errol Flynn look."

"Now there's a guy who got more ass than a toilet seat." My uncle idolized Flynn, whose sexual prowess was legendary. "I don't know, maybe I'll just keep it the way it is." Gene glances at me before sipping his beer. "Know where I went last night?" I shake my head. "A peepshow on Eighth Avenue."

"You're kidding."

"I can't help it, I get horny. What else is there to do? Go home and jerk off with a magazine?"

"Speaking of magazines, that's some fashion statement you're wearing." The pattern on his shirt is a motley collage of *Playboy* covers; in each rectangle a scantily clad bunny poses provocatively on a field of black, white, maroon, orange or blue.

"You like this?" he says. "It's a collector's item."

"I can see why. So what happened at the peepshow?"

"First I paid my quarter and went in."

"A quarter! That's all it cost?"

He looks at me like I'm a virgin. "I walk into the back, and the girl there is beautiful. She has the biggest ass I've ever seen. I tell her I wish I had a tape measure so I could measure it. She says, 'I'll tell you what it is, it's forty-one inches.' I go, 'Come over here and let me suck it.'"

"You did not."

"Swear to God." He's trying to get the attention of the waitress, but she's busy with other orders.

"And did you?"

"Did I what?"

"Suck it?"

"Are you crazy? I told her I better not put my head in there—you know, between her legs—because she might sit down and suffocate me."

"That's very suave of you."

"I said, 'Baby, just come over here and let me sniff it.'" Gene lifts the glass of beer to his nose and inhales lustily.

"You did?"

"Look at you, you're blushing. Come on now, don't get all embarrassed."

If I'm blushing, it's not from my uncle's sordid sex games but from the memory of last night's adventures with Randi on the tar beach of her apartment building roof.

"So how much did that cost you?"

"Nothing. Couple of bucks is all. They'll let you do anything. You can feel 'em up, suck their tits, whatever you like."

"What can I say, Gene? When I die I want your life to flash before my eyes."

"You want to go sometime?"

"Did she have nice breasts?"

"Yeah, sure, but that's not my thing. I'm strictly an ass man. I'm very anal. Although I'm oral too. And I like pussy. So what does that make me, genital?"

"It makes you a triple threat."

"That's good. I like that."

"I'm not surprised."

"You want to check it out?"

"A peepshow? Me? I don't know." What I'm really thinking is that it can't be as much fun as having an orgasm under the stars.

"Come on, kid. What do you got to lose?"

"I've never been to a pro."

"Well, who needs one when you get free love all the time. I know what you were doing at college. Making love, not war. Am I right?"

"What do you think college is, Gene, a four-year fuck-fest?"

"Well, isn't it?"

"Not quite."

"Come on," he nudges me, "what about all those promiscuous hippy chicks?"

"I got some bad news for you, man. Those X-rated movies you're watching, they're not fact, they're friction."

"You're a riot," he says.

"And you have the wrong idea about campus life. It's not *The Harrad Experiment*."

"Hey, look," says Gene, "I know this much. Women want sex. They want you to shoot your load till you're dry. Then when you're used up, they get rid of you."

"You know, Gene, you're about as liberated as a football coach."

"What can I say," he says, rising. "I'm old fashioned. Order me a Jack Daniels."

"I thought we were going to dinner."

"Just order me a shot, will you." Gene makes his way toward the ornately carved black wall cabinet that partitions the back room from the bar area. He passes through the doorway, under a sign in Gay Nineties lettering that directs patrons to the LADIES AND GENTS SITTING ROOM. I sip my beer and examine the pressed-tin ceiling, which is the same neglected coffee-with-cream color as the walls. It's uncomfortably warm and the only ceiling fan is a metaphor of futility; its two ancient blades rotate slowly as if exhausted by the heat.

That my Uncle Gene should assume I was some Casanova in college is laughable. I know he would be in stitches to learn I was a virgin until the summer after my sophomore year. Promiscuous coeds may have prowled the campus dorms, but I never seemed to meet any. My attempts to get laid for the first time resembled if anything the labors of Hercules. There was Gwen from the mixer who gave up on me after I broke her bra strap trying to unhook it. There was Janet of the incredibly soft lips who wanted someone with experience. There was Jackie the virgin from Vestal, New York, with whom I went to bed several times, but who was much too freaked out to put out. And there was the willing and wonderful Wendy from Wells College, who in her panting desire for my naked body managed to snag the uncooperative zipper of my stiff new jeans to the sensitive skin of my scrotum. That dalliance died in the emergency room under the prying eyes of the night nurse.

I finally got lucky over a summer weekend on Fire Island, when I woke in the middle of the night in a strange living room to find myself sharing a sofa convertible with a young woman I had never seen before. She woke up at the same time, smiled demurely, and excused herself to pee, stepping lightly in T-shirt and underwear over the snoring bodies of prostrate revelers. I brushed sand off the sheets, remade the covers, lay back and closed my eyes. When she returned, she complained she was cold and snuggled up to me. Holding led to caressing, then to kissing, then miraculously to muted, slow-motion lovemaking, so as not to disturb the inert forms around us. When I awoke in the morning, she was gone, but for the faint suggestion of perfume that scented her pillow. She left no note, no memento, no phone number, nothing tangible to remember her by, not even her name. Only the memory of our muffled exertions amid the sibilant rustling of sheets.

"Where's my drink?" asks Gene.

"It's too busy. The girl never came."

"Screw it," he says. "I got to make a call, then let's get out of here."

Gene heads for the phone while I dawdle by the front doors, perusing the photo of a crouching Rocky Graziano ready to pound away with either hand. THE ROCK is stenciled on his shorts. A few feet from the bar, I find myself eavesdropping on the earnest pick-up line of a guy who looks like Jesus's double in a black beret.

"Have you ever modeled before? Because you are perfect for an abstract study I'm doing of the female nude."

"If it's abstract," replies the young woman, whose heavily kohled eyes give her the startled appearance of a raccoon, "why would I have to take off my clothes?"

Gene taps me on the shoulder. "Come on, let's blow this popstand."

"Wait," I whisper, "I have to hear the rest of this conversation."

"You're killing me," he shouts, "I'm dying here," and pulls me by the arm through the narrow doors of the pub. We walk south toward Canal, our shoes beating a rhythmic tattoo on the cobblestones.

"So how you doing?" he says. "Good?"

"I could be better."

"What do you got to kick about?" he says. "I hear the Captain got you into law school. Boy, you should hear him talk. Columbia this, Columbia that. He's pretty pleased with himself."

"I don't know why. I haven't been accepted yet."

"That's not what I hear."

"Fine. Don't believe me." It's just like my father to broadcast something like this before it actually happens. He probably thinks if he tells enough people, it'll be impossible for me to back out.

"What kind of lawyer would you be?"

"I don't know, Gene. I haven't figured that out." We hang a left on Canal and westbound cars career toward us, headlights blazing. "So how was your day?" I ask.

"Interesting," he says. "I had an experience I never had before."

"What was that?"

"I had an emergency call in one of those projects in the West Sixties. The interlocks on the gate switch were jumped out so the cab was running with the door open."

"Would you mind repeating that in English?"

"There's a door to the cab," he says. "It's called a gate door, because on the old elevators they used to have a gate."

"Like in some of the old buildings."

"Right," he says. "So if the contacts are screwed up, the cab can run if the door is open. So I'm on the tenth floor and this kid, maybe four or five, goes by me on a tricycle. You know, with those big wheels. I don't even think about it. I got the hoistway door open—that's the outside door on each floor—and this one swings out, so it's resting against my *tuchus* while I'm looking down the shaft to see where the cab is. The next thing I know, I feel somebody leaning on the swingdoor, trying to push me into the shaft."

"What did you do?"

"I push back and when I get into the hallway I see the kid running away. I said, 'You little motherfucker.' The kid runs to his apartment and the next thing I know the mother comes out and wants to know if I cursed at her son. I said, 'Your little angel just tried to push me down the elevator shaft.' She says, 'I'm going to complain to the city about you.' I said, 'Be my guest.' Then she yells at me and slams the door."

"I guess the job has its ups and downs."

"Hey, that's my line," he says. Gene has often told me how much he loves being an elevator inspector. He couldn't have invented a better job. Lenny, his supervisor, is a decent guy, and basically he's his own boss so he gets to work by himself. I can dig it because that's what I like about driving a cab: There's a lot of freedom and you're not constantly under somebody's thumb. Which is a good thing when your boss is a real schmuck like Lipschitz.

Gene takes me to a restaurant on the Bowery, where he knows "the cat who runs the place." We stop at the front windows to regard the lobsters that huddle at the bottom of a large glass tank, and the sea bass that swim lazily in another. Sammy, the owner's thirty-year-old son, greets us warmly and leads us down the aisle to one of the booths along the wall.

Once we're seated, Sammy presents us with menus, which Gene waves away. He wants to know what's really fresh tonight. Sammy suggests the sea bass with ginger and scallions, the razor clams in black bean sauce or the special house T-bone with Chinese vegetables.

"The steak sounds good," says Gene. "How do you prepare it?"

"We grill the steak separately," says Sammy, "with secret Oriental spices, then cut it up and mix it with sautéed vegetables in a brown sauce. It's excellent." Sammy's English is perfect, without the slightest trace of an accent. His dark, slicked-back hair is shiny with Brillcreem, and in his sharkskin suit, white shirt and thin black tie, he projects the easy, smirking charm of a lounge lizard.

"Secret spices, huh? Like what?"

"That's proprietary information," says Sammy. "If I tell you, I have to kill you."

"I love this guy," says Gene. "We'll take the steak, medium rare, and the sea bass. Sound good to you, kid?"

"You're the boss, uncle."

"I wish. You want an appetizer, Eddie? Scallion pancakes maybe, or spare ribs?"

"I eat enough garbage driving a cab. How about something green?"

"Try the bok choy with garlic sauce," says Sammy. "You won't be disappointed."

"Beautiful," booms my uncle. "Sounds incredible. A couple of Heinekens and we're all set."

"Very good," says Sammy. "Let me guess. Playboy Club, right?"

Gene is stumped for a second. "Oh, you mean the shirt? Yeah."

"Rayon or silk?"

"Polyester and cotton. Sixty/forty. But soft like butter. Go ahead, feel." Sammy fingers the material.

"Nice," he says. "I have to get one of these."

"Some people," I remark, "consider it a collector's item."

"I'm not surprised," says Sammy. "The Heinies will be right up. Enjoy your meal."

"Funny guy, Sammy," says Gene.

"Yeah. He's a character all right."

"You like the place?"

"It's a little bright, but it's clean." Mirrors run the length of the dining room on each side, creating the illusion of a larger space so the restaurant, though long and narrow, does not feel cramped.

The beers arrive and the waiter pours them slowly into glass tumblers.

"So I gather you're back on speaking terms with the Captain."

"Sure," says Gene. "Why not?"

"Because he fired you?"

"He wasn't happy with the robbery, if that's what you mean. But I'm still on the payroll. I just have a different gig."

"Really? Doing what?"

Gene glances at the empty booth behind him, his bald spot gleaming under the bright lights. Then he leans toward me and lowers his voice.

"Hauling silver in from Canada."

"Isn't that illegal?"

"What can I do? They got eighteen Gs in the theft, which normally I wouldn't be responsible for. But Leo knows I screwed up. I kept going the same way and they caught on."

"But smuggling? Are you nuts?"

"Look, I have to pay them back. The good news is there's no risk."

"How do you know?" Gene shifts in his seat and looks at me, and I realize he's speaking from experience. "You've done this already."

"Yeah," he says. "I ran through it the first time last weekend. Saturday I drive four hundred miles, way up Interstate 81, to some little Canadian resort town on the St. Lawrence River. I can hardly pronounce it. All I know is, it rhymes with 'Rockaway.' I check into a motel and the next morning this guy meets me at a local inn." Gene describes in detail the guy, the town, the inn and especially the "Canuck breakfast special" of hot cakes, real maple syrup and thick-cut Canadian bacon, which they enjoyed on the open-air terrace overlooking the Thousand Islands. He pauses as the waiter approaches with bowls of rice and several domed, stainless-steel serving dishes, which are uncovered with a flourish to reveal the steaming sea bass, the bok choy and the steak with vegetables. Gene spears a slice and cuts into it. The meat is barely pink, closer to medium than medium rare. "No good," he says. "Too well done."

He calls to Sammy, who hurries over and in the process of apologizing, summons our waiter and hands him the dish while issuing instructions in Chinese. "And bring these gentlemen another round." He turns to us, smiling cordially. "Sorry about that. The beers are on the house."

"Thanks," says Gene. "The sea bass looks fantastic." He deftly manipulates the serving spoons to separate the firm white flesh from the bone.

"So you eat breakfast. Then what?"

"He sells me sixteen bags of Canadian silver."

"Where is this? In the parking lot?" It would be just like my uncle to do business in broad daylight.

"Come on," he says, "what's wrong with you? I follow him down to a quiet little spot on the riverbank. We're transferring the bags and I can see fishing boats trolling out among the islands. I'm telling you, it's absolutely beautiful. Some of the islands are so tiny," he says, "they're like little mounds with pine trees sprouting in all directions."

"And the guy is a coin dealer?"

"No. That's the beauty of it. He owns vending machines. He's got a slew of them, so he hires these women to pick through the coins, take out all the ones minted before 1964, and sort them into bags." Prior to 1964 the silver content of Canadian coins was 80 percent.

"You want some vegetables?"

"Yeah, let me have that." Gene dishes some bok choy over rice. "Man, I would love to do that sometime—go fishing up there. When I was a kid, Leo once took me up to Lake George. I was maybe thirteen at the time. This was 1945 and he had just returned from Germany. We drove the old Mercury up there, just the two of us. This was already a couple of years after Pop passed away."

"That must have been fun."

"Some of it was," he says, his eyes turning inward toward the past.

"So you got the shipment. Then what?"

"I take the bags, stow 'em under the rear seat and cross into the U.S." He shovels bok choy into his mouth with his chopsticks.

"Were you nervous?"

"Yeah, a little, but the silver only weighs, what? Eight hundred pounds? And with those heavy-duty shocks on the Camaro, you don't even notice. I'm telling you, it's a sweet deal. The border guards waved me right through."

"I thought your car was stolen when you got robbed."

"It was," he laughs, "but they recovered it out in Bay Ridge a couple of days later."

"Boy, are you lucky." Gene was crazy about his car, a black '67 Camaro that could go from zero to sixty in under six seconds.

"Believe me, I got this all figured out. There's no risk, and I can make fifteen hundred bucks a run. Eleven more trips and I'm paid up."

"I just hope you know what you're doing."

"Will you relax," he says. "Have some fish." We eat in silence until the waiter returns with the steak. It's flavorful, if too rare, and though I am willing to let it go, Gene is adamant. "I can't eat this!" He whistles to get Sammy's attention and beckons him with an impatient finger. Responding with less alacrity than before, the owner's son stares unhappily at the undercooked beef. "I don't know what the chef is smoking," says Gene, "but I want some of it." Sammy takes the dish and trudges back to the kitchen.

"So what did you do with the silver?"

"Oh, you'll love this. I drive six hours to Saratoga Springs to meet the weirdest-looking guy you ever saw. He's got a big gut, a weak chin and four bottom front teeth."

"You mean Tim Callahan?" I ask.

"You know him?"

"Sure I know him," I laugh. "He's the Saratoga guy who ships us silver. In fact, I stayed at his house once. Big mansion on Nelson Avenue, right next to the track." Last August he and his wife invited my parents and me up for Travers weekend, which is the culmination of the Saratoga meet. They made us a great meal— grilled steak, fresh-picked corn, peach melba—but the image I remember is Mr. Callahan trying to scrape corn off the cob with his lower incisors.

"So he's got a big house, so what? Basically he's a scumbag with a big ego who runs a smelting plant half an hour from town. You'll love this part: I follow him down a rutted dirt road deep into the woods to this makeshift foundry they have, which is nothing more than a glorified shack made out of corrugated tin. Metal stovepipe spewing out smoke. Couple of guys with rifles. Looks like a whiskey still."

"You witnessed this operation?"

"Yeah, but I was only there ten minutes. That's all I could take. It was too hot and noisy. And it smelled like hell."

"Hot, huh?"

"Are you kidding? It was like a hundred and twenty degrees. First thing I had to do was put on a welding mask. Everybody was wearing one. I felt like a medieval knight. And the scene in this place. Unbelievable. Men dumping coins into a red-hot furnace. Pouring streams of molten silver into ingot castings. Huge exhaust fans making all kinds of noise. They have to have their own generator because they're out in the middle of nowhere."

"What does Callahan do with the silver?"

"I didn't ask too many questions, but I think he sells it to a refiner, like Englehard. The silver still has a lot of impurities in it. That's what the Captain told me."

The waiter brings the steak dish for the third time.

"Déjà-vu," I say, "all over again."

"Now it comes!" says Gene. "I'm not even hungry no more."

"Me neither," I say, prodding a slice of steak with my fork. "Maybe I should take this home."

"Forget it," he says. "It'll be dried out by tomorrow."

Gene calls for the check, which comes on a plate of pineapple sections and fortune cookies. I crack one open, read and then re-read the message: *Mighty storm came. Great bird flying. Sun break through.*

"What do you make of this?" I ask, handing him the slip of paper.

Gene scowls at it and says, "This ain't a fortune. What kind of cockamamie fortune is this?"

"I kind of like it," I say. "Reminds me of a Japanese haiku."

"I don't know," says Gene. "This place is really going downhill." He bites his cookie in half, fishes the fortune out of his mouth and reads aloud: "'*Do not mistake temptation for opportunity.*' Now that's a fortune," he says. "I don't know what the hell it means, but at least I know a fortune when I get one."

I pick up the check and start adding in my head, but Gene snatches it away, checks it over and flags down the waiter. He refuses to be charged for the steak entrée. Sammy intercedes and wants to know what the problem is. He's chagrined to find the perfectly cooked steak untouched.

"What's the matter, guys?"

"We waited half an hour for the dish and we're no longer hungry."

"Take it to go," says Sammy. "We'll wrap it up."

"We're going to pass, man."

"But we cooked a whole new steak for you."

"Well if you cooked it right the first time," says Gene, rising from the booth, "this wouldn't have happened."

Sammy flinches as if he's been slapped.

"Look," I say, "I'll pay for the steak."

"No," says Gene, crossing his arms, "you're not paying for the damn steak because we didn't eat the damn steak."

"Fine," says Sammy. "Don't pay for it and don't come back again. You're not welcome."

"Fuck this place," says Gene, "and fuck you." He punctuates his profanity with the back of his hand, upending a glass full of water, which drenches the check and seeps fanlike across the white tablecloth. Pineapple sections float over the plate like unmoored buoys.

Gene storms out and I feel compelled to apologize for his behavior. I pay for everything, the steak included, dropping bills on the sopping table, overtipping to make amends. I catch up to my uncle at the corner of Bowery and Canal, where he is complaining loudly to himself, outraged at the way he's been treated.

"What nerve!" he says. "I hope you didn't pay for that crap."

"Calm down, will you." It's just like my uncle to beat the check and then bitch about the meal.

"Get a load of that guy, kicking us out like that. What a dick!"

"Well we did order the dish, you know."

"Let me ask you something. Is it so hard to cook a damn steak?"

"All right already. Forget about it."

"Fuck it," he says. "You want to go to the Shithouse?" The Shithouse is what we call the wreck of a coffeehouse around the corner on Bayard. But caffeine is the last thing I need. I have to be up at four in the morning and I'm ready to call it a night, which is something Gene has never learned to do.

"Then come have a beer with me. Come on, kid. I'll take you to Billy's, the best titty bar in New York."

I yawn. "Sounds tempting, but I have to get some sleep."

"Lucky you," he says. "I haven't slept good since the robbery." Gene looks at the Manhattan Bridge and sighs.

"Why? Was it that bad?"

"No, it was a blast. I love having some fat son-of-a-bitch stick a gun in my face and tell me he's going to blow my brains out."

"I'd like to hear about it."

"I'll have to tell you sometime."

"Goodnight," I say, offering my hand. "I'm going to hop on the subway."

He grasps my hand and shakes, but doesn't let go. A woman is walking a Chihuahua and he watches it till they pass. "I should have trusted my instincts, Eddie. I had a feeling I was being followed, but I wasn't sure. I was keeping an eye on this Dodge Dart, checking it out in the rearview mirror. I figured I could outrun it if I had to." He sighs again and releases his grip. "It was the other car I didn't expect, the blue Lincoln. He must have been waiting on Borden Avenue. He pulls out in front of me, slows down and stops right before the railroad track, making like his motor stalled out. I'm so concerned about the car on my tail, I almost run into him. Before I even realize what's going on, two guys have their guns out and are telling me to move over. We drive a couple of blocks off Borden Avenue to some deserted warehouse."

"How many guys were there?"

"Four of them. In ski masks. Three in the car behind me, and one in the Lincoln. He's the ringleader. A big fat fuck who can't even get out of the car. I guess I laughed out of nervousness. They handcuff me to this chainlink fence and the fat guy comes over and shoves a revolver in my cheek. 'Something funny, asshole?' he asks. Before I can reply he says, 'I don't like witnesses,' and pulls the trigger. I hear a loud click and my heart jumps. The chamber is empty. The other cocksuckers are cracking up like it's a big joke. The fat guy says, 'Nice car, Gene. You keep your mouth shut or we'll pay you another visit. *Capisce?*'"

"He knew your name?"

"Of course he knew my name. You don't pull off a robbery like that without planning."

"Is there any hope of catching these guys? I mean, you got a good look at them, didn't you?"

"Don't you listen, Ed? They know my name. They know where I live."

"I thought they said that just to scare you."

He laughs. "Do you have any idea how things work? Any idea at all? These guys are mob-connected. They're part of the Lucchese crime family that works the airport. I already know who they are. Their mugshots were in the book at the precinct. I can ID them tonight and tomorrow morning you'll find me at the bottom of Jamaica Bay."

Colorful phrases come to mind: *Cement galoshes. Concrete overcoat.* Once when I was eleven, I was home alone—my parents were at the movies—and the phone rang. I thought they were checking up on me, but instead this gruff voice whispered, "It's all set. We threw the body in the river." I was so terrified, I locked all the doors, turned on the lights and ran upstairs to hide in the back of a closet.

"I didn't tell you the worst thing," says Gene. "They're about to leave when the fat fuck belts me in the stomach so hard I double over. I would have collapsed, except my arm is still handcuffed to the fence. He puts his face right next to mine. So close I can smell his stinking cologne through his ski mask. 'By the way,' he says, 'your daughter Randi is very cute. For her sake, you better hope we don't get caught.' Then they get into the cars and take off. As soon as they're out of sight, I puke all over my shoes."

"Jesus, Gene."

"Yeah."

"That's heavy."

"How the fuck do I get into this shit?"

"What did the Captain say when you told him?"

He shrugs and looks away. "Nothing," he says.

"You didn't tell him, did you?"

"I didn't want to get into it. And, anyway, he was so pissed at me, I didn't want to talk to him." He examines a fingernail that's been bitten to the quick, and gnaws at it some more.

"So now what?"

"Now I need a fuckin drink," he says. "Let's go." He tugs me across Canal Street but in the middle the light changes and traffic barrels by, hemming us in. One drink, I suppose, isn't going to kill me. It might even help me sleep. I yawn and glance at my uncle, who is following the weaving progress of an ambulance, its siren screaming. His bald spot gleams from the glare of passing cars. He starts to tell me something—the name of a bar, I think. I look down to concentrate, but it's too noisy. His shoes haven't been shined in ages. I can't stop looking at them. Something tells me they're the same ones he vomited on during the robbery.

EAST SIDE, WEST SIDE

I get a postcard from Paris of Jim Morrison's grave. Candles, peace signs, photographs and flowers have transformed the headstone into a shrine. Eventually I decipher from the cramped, miniscule scrawl that Dave Ryman, my college roommate, has met a French girl while tripping on mescaline in Père Lachaise Cemetery. "Delphine is a free spirit," he writes, "adventurous and impulsive." He and his "Gauloise-smoking siren" are headed for Marrakesh, then to the Beaujolais region to pick grapes during the harvest.

Vic Castelli and Steve Shapiro, my old high school buddies, are about to fly to Holland, where they plan to buy a cheap car to drive around Europe. They met through me and learned to tolerate each other, but they make an odd pair. I first crossed paths with the soft-spoken Castelli in Calculus and soon we were hanging out together and playing chess. He doesn't go in much for carousing, but one sip of culture and he's drunk. He loves art, theater, classical music, even opera. His parents have a subscription to the Met so he knows as much about opera as I do about

horseracing. Once he took me to see Joan Sutherland in Doni-
zetti's *Lucia di Lammermoor*. I thought it would never end. When
Lucia finally went mad, I could hardly blame her.

Shapiro I've known since elementary school. Aggressive to the
point of being obnoxious, he's competitive about everything—
games, grades, girlfriends, even miniature golf. He was into student government in high school where he was a brilliant campaign
manager whose candidates never lost an election. He likes to
smoke cigars, play Ping-Pong and argue vehemently about politics. Give him a good action flick and he's happy; Castelli only
attends art films. Without me there to act as a buffer, I wonder
how long it will take for them to drive each other crazy.

Still, I'm aching to join them each time Steve calls me with
updates about their plans: a coffeehouse in Amsterdam where the
hashish is supposed to be primo; a *pensione* in Venice that's ridicu-
lously cheap; a beach in Mykonos where the girls sunbathe topless. It's the trip of a lifetime, he asserts, so I better get on the stick
and book a flight.

"What are you going to do, Sacks? Sit around all summer and
smell your farts?"

"It stinks, I agree, but it's the path of least resistance."

"*Carpe diem,* man. Gather some fucking rosebuds." The papers,
he informs me, are full of two-hundred-dollar airfares. "Mark
my words, man. If you blow us off you'll regret it for the rest of
your life."

"Only if I live that long."

"The rest of your life, asshole."

Shapiro is so sure he's doing me a favor, he calls me several
times a day, berating or cajoling in his aggressive manner.

One morning I'm awakened from a deep sleep by one of Lipschitz's boarders who says there's a phone call, and assuming it's Shapiro, I chew him out.

"Temper, temper," says a voice I can't quite place. "Is that any way to greet an old friend?"

"Castelli?"

"I'll get right to the point, Edward. I'd feel a lot safer with you along. You know something about cars and you're a professional driver." A physics major, the ultra-rational Castelli never raises his voice. He seeks to persuade through impeccable logic, and failing that, urgently whispered appeals.

"Give me a break, Vic. Shapiro knows more about cars than I do. He's the one who took an auto mechanics course, not me."

"You've seen Shapiro drive. He talks so much, he hardly looks at the road."

"I don't know, man. My parents want me to go to summer school."

"I thought you were taking a hiatus," he says.

"I called an audible at the line of scrimmage."

"You or the head coach?"

"You got that right. The Captain has been leaning on me to complete my degree."

"Is this wise, Edward? You practically had a nervous breakdown last fall."

"I don't know, Vic. I'm supposed to buckle down and get serious."

"Why don't you just reason with him?"

"With the Captain?"

"What are you afraid of? Just play up the mental health issue.

Because I merely wish to point out," he whispers urgently, "that such a trip would do wonders for your psychological well-being, which frankly, Edward, I worry about."

"I'd like to go, man, I really would."

"So do something about it. Be persuasive."

"Look, you know my father. It's easier to sell bacon to a rabbi than to get the Captain to change his mind."

"There's no harm in asking, is there? I hear the sunsets on Mykonos are amazing. Especially on the topless beach. But do what you have to. We'll understand."

Their persistence finally wears me down. After a week of their pleading and needling, I give in and buy a plane ticket.

Meanwhile, my father is bugging me nonstop not to blow my big chance.

"Foxy ain't gonna live forever, Eddie." To get him off my back, I sign up for summer courses, even though I know I'll have to drop them when I take off for Europe. Since I've already been accepted for fall admission to City College, I have no trouble telling myself that we all win. I get what I want and my parents eventually get what they want. When I call Goldie to tell her I'm back in school, she weeps. My father, she assures me through her sobs, will be so happy.

"And you're not going to get side-tracked this time, are you dear?"

"No, Ma."

"Because it's very important that you get your degree."

"I know, Ma."

"You have to work hard, Eddie, and go to every class."

"I will, Ma."

"I know I can count on you. Right, dear?"

"Sure, Ma. I have to go." Ten minutes later, when she finally hangs up, my teeth hurt from lying through them.

To attend classes, I switch to night shift. This is fine with Lipschitz, who never liked his night driver, Nelson Rodriguez. Nelson may be dependable, but he has one unforgivable trait: He's happily married. He works with a framed photo of his cute, smiling wife on the dash and just the sight of it puts Lipschitz in a foul mood. In fact, he is so glad to get rid of the guy, he offers me a break on the lease fee.

I stop working for Midtown Coin as I am no longer available for the afternoon silver run to Wall Street. The Captain doesn't mind, since I am now, as he puts it, "dedicating myself to a higher purpose." He gives me a grilling that is remarkably similar to the one I received from Goldie. I go through the motions of reassuring him with the same terse, transparent replies: *Sure, Dad. You're right, Dad. I certainly will, Dad.* Go ahead, I figure, tell the Captain what he wants to hear. A month from now I'll be in Amsterdam, relaxing in a coffee shop beside a quiet canal, so stoned on hash I won't be thinking about him.

The first few weeks of summer school stumble by in a sleep-deprived haze. My shift ends at five a.m. and I sleep fitfully until noon. I manage to get to both courses—Macroeconomics and The Proletarian Consciousness in Literature. The economics class, with its indifference curves and various models of how the money supply works, is a bore. But Lefty Lit is riveting. I'm appalled by the treatment of miners in *Germinal*, disgusted by the cynical practices of the meatpackers in *The Jungle* and outraged by the murder of a union man in *Waiting for Lefty*. The play is based on a cab drivers' strike, so it's easy to relate to the radicalized fire-brand who resolves in a stirring speech to fight against the system that keeps him down. The travails of these defiant protagonists are so engrossing that I intend to complete the reading on my own and purchase Dos Passos's *USA* trilogy to take to Europe.

When I'm not studying, I watch the Watergate coverage. In several days of testimony before the Senate committee, John Dean claims what many people have long suspected—that the cover-up was run by Ehrlichman and Haldeman, and that Nixon was in on it from the beginning. Dean seems to be telling the truth, but his allegations are uncorroborated. The White House counterattacks, tarring Dean with sole culpability and insisting that he is lying to save his skin. Two days later, Dean drops the bombshell about the "enemies list"—a file several inches thick containing the names of various people who represent a threat to the administration. Communists, terrorists and psychopaths, right? Guess again. The country, to its chagrin, discovers what Paul Newman, Steve McQueen, Pete Hamill and Dick Gregory have in common, along with hundreds of other politicians, newsmen, businessmen and entertainers. Joe Namath, for godsake, is on it. It's overwhelming to me, all this animosity unleashed like buckshot in so many directions. My own anger is trained, unwaveringly, on a single target. I can't imagine hundreds of names. On my enemies list there is only one.

That I don't have to see my father is the main reason I prefer hacking at night, but there are others. The driving is less harried than the day shift. After rush hour, the traffic thins and I can really cruise. The hours from eight to midnight, when I can hustle unhampered from one end of Manhattan to the other, are golden.

Around one, I line up at the clubs. Then I hit the after-hours joints. When they dry up, I cruise over to Houston in the wee hours to hang with some guys I met serendipitously my second day on the night shift. I needed some singles and they needed some rolling papers, which I was fortuitously able to produce after patting down the pockets of my jeans jacket.

I pull up at three a.m. behind a Ford Fairlaine, its hood un-latched and slightly ajar like my own cab to allow air to cool the engine in the summer heat. Moose is schmoozing as usual with Jack the Hack. *"As-salamu alaykum,"* I greet them, sliding into the back seat, where the pungent aroma of marijuana hangs heavy as smog.

"Wa-alaykum al-salaam," replies Moose. Moose is Mustafa Bastuni, an Israeli Arab who grew up in Jerusalem and moved here as a teenager after the Six-Day War. It took me a while to understand him, his accent was that garbled, as if he had taken speech lessons from Henry Kissinger.

"Hey, Money," says Jack. "What's up with this heat wave, man?" They dubbed me "Moneybags" after I told them about the silver business, but that was soon shortened to the simpler nickname. "Fuckin weather sucks, man. And on top of that, guess who goes OT?" Jack points at Moose with the joint he is holding and takes another hit. "Fuckin Spring Valley, man. On a slow night like to-night. Can you believe this lucky fuck?"

"Nice," I say. "How much?" Moose turns down the volume on George Jones.

"Thirty-four dollars," he says. "Best fare I've had in months."

"That's pretty sweet, Moose." On a good night I can clear fifty bucks after making my nut, which amounts to the leasing fee and a tank of gas, but on this slow post-holiday weekday night, I'll be lucky to net forty by the end of the shift. I take a toke and exhale, propelling a stream of smoke at the roof, where it fans outward like the mushroom cloud of a nuclear blast. "So where was this, at the airport?"

"Right off the street," he says. "Some executive at Thirty Rock."

"Know what I think," says Jack. "I think he was one of them working alcoholics, man. They got a lot them at Rockefeller Center."

"Don't you mean 'workaholic'?" says Moose, stripping the plastic from an air freshener in the shape of a Christmas tree and looping it over the tuning knob of the radio, where it joins several others, swaying in unison.

"Whatever," says Jack. "All I know is, I'd love to go out of town, man. It beats thirty-five fares a night at two bucks a pop."

"I caught one like that from LaGuardia," I say, "my third day on the job. I'm dropping at TWA and some woman flags me down on the departure ramp and wants to go to Cos Cob in Connecticut. Boom. Just like that. Forty bucks. I'd like to see one of those again." At the time I had no idea it was the perfect job. It's totally illegal, of course. You're supposed to refuse the fare and direct the customer down to the nearest hack stand, but no cabbie in his right mind would ever do that because it means giving up your shot at a big night to wait in the lot with the other loafers, bullshitting with the Haitians and the Russian Jews, drinking coffee until you're so hopped up it's impossible to relax. When you finally get dispatched, all pretense of fraternity ends. You jump in your cab and take off, and if no one says "Good-bye" or "Have a nice night," at least the Russians say "Make money," because there's no more fervent capitalist, I've learned, than a refugee from a Communist country.

Everyone is stoned and the lull in conversation is filled by George Jones on the eight-track working his way through the heartache of "She Thinks I Still Care."

"Hey, Moose, man, can't we listen to something else, man?" A casualty of the sixties, Jack loves to get stoned and listen to hard rock: Cream, Hendrix, Zeppelin. The louder the better. But music is the driver's prerogative, and Moose only listens to country, which he finds relaxing.

"When we sit in your car, my friend, the rock music is so loud it hurts my ears. But do I say anything?"

"Fuckin Arabs," says Jack to me. "What is it with them, man? They come over here and fall in love with the worst elements of our culture. Hillbilly music." He taps out a Camel from a pack he keeps in the pocket of his tie-dyed T-shirt, lights it and, waving away the smoke, peers at me over the front seat. "So will Nixon be impeached, man?" With his bushy blond beard tied in a ponytail, he looks like a psychedelic prophet whose work is to spread the gospel of sex, drugs and rock 'n' roll.

"The way things are going," I say, "I wouldn't be surprised."

"It will never happen," says Moose. "The Jews like him too much because he backs Israel."

"But he's got a lot of enemies," I say. "Like Joe Namath." Everyone I know loves Namath, whose fun-loving personality is backed by prodigious talent. A great quarterback, he can fire a frozen rope of a pass right on the money for a twenty-yard gain or heave the bomb in a perfect parabola to Don Maynard, fifty yards in the air. During my high school years, the Captain had season tickets to Jets games, and I got to watch Namath in his prime through the championship season of 1969. The idea of him as a political enemy is so absurd, I crack up.

"Know what I think, man?" Jack takes an enormous toke and holds it. "I think Nixon dropped a shitload on the Jets, man. That's what I think." I laugh as Jack exhales until I realize he's not kidding.

"You're serious, Jack?"

"Hey, man, power corrupts. I'm telling you, man, if they ever released a record of Nixon's football action, which is classified, see, because the President isn't supposed to choose sides, right? Well you would see, man, and you would be able to prove beyond a shadow of a doubt that Nixon punishes the teams he bets on that fail to cover the point spread. Sics the I.R.S. on 'em, man. Not just the players, man, but the owners, too. It's common knowledge in Vegas. I mean everybody there knows what's going on. It's only a matter of time, man, before all this stuff comes out." Jack shakes his head at the depths to which our highest elected official has fallen.

I glance at Moose, who is regarding Jack with a look usually reserved for a person who has just confided to you that he was once abducted by aliens. "Tricky Dick," I say, "has a lot to answer for."

"Right on," says Jack. "Hey, man, I wouldn't be surprised if Watergate is only the first round of Senate investigations,"

"What's next?" I wonder. "Football-gate?"

"Yeah," says Moose, laughing, "after Watergate, they're going to extradite him to Nevada to stand trial for his real crimes." Jack looks at each of us.

"Hey, man, I don't like it when people make fun of me."

"Don't get bent out of shape, Jack. It's just a joke."

"The thing of it is, man, I try to clue you guys in and this how you treat me."

"Don't be so serious, my friend," says Moose.

"Kiss my ass, man," he says, and opening the door he adds, "Hey, man, I don't need this shit."

"We're sorry, Jack," I call after him. "We apologize. Come back."

"And hang out with you shitheads? You can both drop dead for all I care." Jack storms off to his cab, guns the motor and pulls out. The more incensed he becomes, the funnier the situation strikes us, and as he passes, his hand raised in a middle-finger salute, we collapse in hysterics, gasping for air.

"I don't get it," I say. "I thought he was some kind of laid-back hippie type."

"He's not exactly the sharpest tool in the shed," says Moose, sounding now like a stoned Henry Kissinger. Every now and then, Moose uses an idiom that surprises me.

I get out of the car, climb into the front seat and settle in. This is the part of the job I like most—hanging with Moose in the middle of the night, sipping coffee and listening to one of his country music tapes. Moose is younger than I am but seems older. Part of it is the large build and the purposeful attitude, steady and phlegmatic. But it's more than that. He's so unlike me, already so serious about his future. After a year of college, he was restless to get to work, so he quit to get his hack license. He lives with his parents in Jackson Heights and saves most of his earnings for the cab he is planning to buy. After two years at the wheel, six nights a week, he is close to having the down-payment for the medallion, the flat metal ornament that cleaves asymmetrically to the hood of every cab like a large wet leaf, and which represents the hugely expensive permit to own and operate a taxi in the city of New York.

"So, how are you, my friend? Or as we say in Arabic, *keefak?*"

"At the moment I'd say I'm feeling no pain."

"I can see that. And how was your Independence Day?"

"I worked." Goldie had begged me to come for a cookout, but I made my apologies as visions of the Father's Day fiasco exploded in my head like fireworks.

"Guess who I talked to yesterday?" says Moose, browsing through his box of eight-track tapes. "A broker who says he can fix me up with a medallion for twenty-six thousand and the financing for the new yellow."

"Hey, Moose, that's great."

"Thank you, my friend. So how would you like to co-own a taxi?"

"What do you mean?"

"I mean go into business for ourselves. As partners."

"You're kidding, right?"

"No, Money, this I wouldn't joke about." There's a Merle Haggard cartridge in the tape player and Moose sings along without any apparent sense of irony: *"I'm proud to be an Okie from Muskogee. The place where even squares can have a ball . . ."*

"I don't understand, Moose. I thought you were all set to buy on your own."

"It's true," he says, "I can jump in right now with both feet. My father will co-sign the note and I can be on the road in two weeks. But Ghada and I plan to marry this summer and I have lots of expenses. I have to pay off my father-in-law and rent a place for us to live."

"Your future father-in-law?" Moose nods. "Ask him to wait a while. I'm sure he'd be willing to give you a break."

"No, my friend, I have to pay the bride price. You have, I think, a special word for this."

"Dowry?"

"Dowry. Yes." He shows me a wallet-sized photo of a plump, dark-haired girl in cap and gown smiling shyly for the camera. A mole in the shape of a fruit fly has alighted on her chin. "High school graduation," he beams. If he hadn't said anything, I would have guessed she was his sister, the resemblance is that strong.

"Very pretty," I lie.

"She wants to be a nurse."

"How long have you been engaged?"

"About ten years," he says, laughing his great, booming, infectious laugh. "The marriage was arranged when I was eleven."

"That's heavy, Moose. Being forced to marry someone. I know I would resent it."

"No one is forced to marry," he says. "That is a misconception. You can always say no if you don't like the person."

"I guess you like her then."

"Ghada? I grew up with her. Her father is my uncle."

"She's your first cousin?"

"Yes, of course. This is the most desirable choice."

"That's wild, man." I listen to Moose elaborate on the particulars of arranged marriage, and frankly I'm appalled. Balling your first cousin is one thing, but marrying her? It's nuts. I mean what if you had kids? They'd be completely inbred.

"In America they don't approve of this custom, but this is the way it is done in my culture. And Ghada and I have been living with the idea for so long, we act like we're already married. Except for the sex," he adds, poking me with his elbow.

"Good luck."

"Thank you, my friend." He kisses the photo before slipping it into his shirt pocket. "So what do you think about my offer?"

"I don't know, Moose—"

"I have a great idea. Listen to this. We get the medallion, then we join one of those radio groups, like Scull's Angels. You can take radio calls or pick up off the street. The name of the game, my friend, is versatility. You'll see. In a few years, we'll be able to buy another medallion." He looks as if he's just floated a million-dollar idea, and his coy smile suggests that he doesn't expect me to turn him down.

"Let me ask you something, Moose. Why me?"

"I've given this a lot of thought, my friend, and I think it would be good for you to take on some responsibility. In America people stay in school so long, it makes it harder for them to grow up. This is why I dropped out. Because I wanted to get on with my life. You see what I mean?"

"Yeah, I see what you mean." What I see, though, is that he doesn't really view me as an adult, and I'm a little ticked off at the guy's condescending attitude.

"So if you are like me," he says, "and you are tired of waiting, and you want to get on with your life . . ." He glances at me. "And from what you say about your father, he can probably lend you the money to get started."

"Ha!" I laugh abruptly, imagining the look on the Captain's face when I tell him I'll be giving up law school to hack with an Arab.

"What is so funny?"

"Moose, come on. I only know you three weeks."

"What is there to know? You're smart, I have a good feeling about you, and I'm sure we can work together. You know, my friend, there's an old Arabic proverb: 'Choose your neighbors before you choose your house.' So what I want to say to you is, I think you will make an excellent neighbor. Even if you are a Jew." He offers his hand across the front seat and I grasp it firmly, whatever negative feelings I have evaporating under his uninhibited smile.

"Thank you, Moose. For an Arab, you're all right." That this guy I hardly know wants to go into business with me is mind-boggling. My own father thinks I'm a jerk, an untrustworthy screw-up, and here's this person I don't know from Adam who has extended an offer based on little more than first impressions and intuition. My eyes well with tears and I look away to where a chainlink fence protects a deserted playground.

"So what do you say, my friend?"

"I say I'm flattered, man, I really am, but . . ." I think of the times I love driving, the unexpected moments of sudden beauty—cruising through Central Park after a snowfall or gliding along the shore on the Belt Parkway or being seduced by the city's skyline from the Throgs Neck Bridge or encountering a row of smudgepots in the fog sputtering like cartoon bombs on Cross

Bay Boulevard out by Broad Channel. But I just don't expect to want to own a cab anytime in this lifetime. I keep coming back to what a drag it would be to be imprisoned in the driver's seat for the rest of my life, my belly expanding until eventually it's lapping at the steering wheel.

"This is your future we are talking about."

"My parents are pushing me to finish college."

"Think about it," he says. He pulls out his receipt pad and prints his name neatly on the line that says FROM, and his phone number below it on the line that reads DESTINATION. He tears it off and presses it into my palm.

I have the munchies big time after leaving Moose and drive up Sixth Avenue past the darkened storefronts of Greenwich Village to an all-night doughnut shop. An abandoned copy of Thursday's *Post* lies on one of the padded stools at the counter. I take my cruller and coffee back to the cab and sit there reading yesterday's news. On the front page, wedged between a story on the arrest of a suspected leader of the Black Liberation Army and a piece about the mismanagement of radioactive waste by the Atomic Energy Commission, is a photo referring to the recent gravediggers' strike. A man toils away at a cemetery in Queens, digging his father's grave. Tombstones crowd behind him, as if jostling to get a better view, as he unloads a shovelful of dirt. Some guys, I think, have all the luck.

A skinny dude in a leather vest—like a British rock star with the longish hair to match—taps on my window and wants to know if I'm for hire. I motion him to hop in, which turns out to be a production. He has several large shopping bags full of clothing, which he has an awkward time situating on the spacious floor of the Checker. I cannot for the life of me figure out his problem until I realize that he hasn't folded up the jump seats. I lean over the front seat to help and he glares at me, hunching forward to protect his belongings. "Look," I say, "they fold up," and reach back slowly to collapse them as he eyes me with unconcealed mistrust.

"Eighty-second and York, Chief. Take the East Side Drive."

"Eight-two and York," I repeat. "Got it."

"So why ain't you fuckin moving?"

"Would you mind closing the door?" He slams it shut.

"G'head," he says, "you can go now." I put it in gear and step on the gas, the cab hesitating till the transmission kicks in and we lurch away from the curb. The windshield is powdered with dust, but washing it is hopeless. The dull edges of the wipers skim ineffectually over the curved glass, filming the surface with pale blue fluid when they ought to be squeegeeing it clean. A month ago I told Lipschitz I would change them myself, but he wants to get these special wiper blades that truckers use. I can't figure the guy out. Either he's a congenital procrastinator or he can't allow himself to take time away from his shift or he's too cheap to spend the money. It's the same thing with the brakes. For weeks they've been grabbing down near the floorboards and when I remind him, he swears up and down he'll get them changed but nothing happens. All I can say is, if the vehicle were my livelihood I would keep it in tiptop shape. But Lipschitz, he thinks the Checker ought to fix itself and then he whines when it doesn't work right.

"How about some air, Chief? I'm dying back here."

"Sorry, man, it's on the fritz."

"How the hell can you work without air conditioning?"

"You got me, man. My boss says he's going to get it fixed." Any year now. The passenger rolls the windows all the way open then falls back as if exhausted into the back seat. "Music?"

"What about it?" he says.

"You want some?"

"Whatever you want, Chief. I don't care." I check him out in the rearview mirror and he's rubbing his forehead like he's got a headache, his hands encased in leather driving gloves on this sultry summer night. Why, I wonder, do I always get the strange ones?

The radio reception has been iffy since the aerial was broken off, but I manage to tune in "Stairway to Heaven," humming along as I swing east on Twenty-third past the angular presence of the Flatiron Building, a shadowy stairway to heaven looming vertiginously above the intersection of Fifth and Broadway. I sail over to the East River, then shoot up the FDR and exit onto York as my passenger rustles through his shopping bags, muttering to himself and looking for God knows what.

"Where the fuck is that fuckin thing," he says. "Piece of shit, cocksucking motherfucker." The more frantic he becomes, the more profanity-laced his tirade. I assume he can't find his wallet or more likely he's broke, but whichever it is, I expect to get stiffed for the fare. "Goddamn it," he says, "this fuckin thing is empty."

"You got a problem back there?"

"Just drive and mind your fuckin business." At Eighty-second Street he tells me to "hang a rodge," and I turn into the quiet, tree-lined block as he scans the facades of the brownstones, searching for "this chick I know's pad." He checks out both sides of the street, and when we're halfway in tells me to pull over.

"Is this it?" I ask, my hand poised on the flag to stop the meter. A cab appears in my rearview mirror, its off-duty light illuminated in the pre-dawn darkness. It stops by a hydrant a few car lengths behind, the engine idling as driver and passenger converse.

"I cannot fuckin believe this," he says. He cranes his head out the window and curses the unfamiliar buildings. "Fuckin shit, man. This ain't fuckin right."

"So where would you like to go, sir?" I know for sure I'm going to get stiffed, and I just want to get the guy out of my cab as soon as possible.

"It must be on Eightieth. Try Eightieth, chief." I gun it to the corner, down East End to Seventy-ninth and up York again. "Man, you need some better shocks on this thing. These are shot."

"I'll tell my boss. I'm sure he'll fix them immediately." I make the first right, cruising slowly.

"Yeah, this is the place." The meter reads four dollars and forty cents. My passenger rummages through his bags for what must be a good minute while I wait for him to tell me he can't pay the fare. Finally, he hands me a crumpled ten spot and asks for five dollars back. I'm shocked. I thought I was going to get beat for sure. I open my cigar box to make change and when I look up to give it to him, I'm surprised by the comically short barrel of a snub-nosed .38.

"Turn around," he says. He puts the Saturday night special to the side of my head and in an angry, agitated voice says, "Hand over your money."

I stop breathing, then force myself to take long, slow breaths. No longer stoned, my mind vaults into a state of serene hyperclarity.

"Give me the fuckin money, I said, or I'll blow your fuckin brains out." I can smell his hair, wet and sweaty, as he leans toward me.

"I'll give you the money. Just calm down."

"Now, asshole."

"Listen," I tell him, "I'm going to hand you my cash, nice and easy." All the time I'm thinking, that's just what the guys who robbed Gene said: "Give me your money or I'll blow your fuckin brains out." What is it with these guys? Do they all say the same thing? Is there some course they take at crime school?

"Get out of the cab," he says.

"You're taking the cab?"

"Yeah, asshole, get the fuck out."

"Listen, the car is in drive, so I'm going to shift into park. Okay?"

"Turn off the engine."

"I'm turning off the engine. I'm handing you the keys. Now I'm going to open the door and get out." I tug on the door handle, which sticks, and when I pull hard it comes off in my hand. Great, I think, isn't this terrific? This piece of crap deathtrap is going to get me killed. And the funny thing is I'm not even operating the stupid thing. I fit the handle onto the threads of the stem and pull up gingerly, releasing the catch.

"Hey, Chief," he says, "Wait a second."

Here it comes. I close my eyes, expecting to get shot. My left arm is fully extended, bracing the partially opened door.

"That long song," he says. "Who sings that?"

"What song?"

"You know," he says, and makes a half-hearted effort full of off-key notes. At a loss, I try to focus on the last few sets the radio played, fearful of antagonizing my attacker with the wrong answer.

"You mean 'Stairway to Heaven'?"

"Yeah, that one."

Relieved, I answer, "Zeppelin."

"Led Zeppelin?"

"Yes, Led Zeppelin."

"You sure?"

"Of course I'm sure."

"What album is it on?"

"What album? I don't know, man." I wonder if this is some sadistic test for my life. "I think it's *Led Zeppelin IV*."

"*Led Zeppelin IV*, huh?"

"Yeah, there's a picture of an old man on the album cover. He's bent over at the waist and he's hauling something on his back. A load of faggots, I think."

"Faggots, like he's a homo?"

"Sticks. A load of sticks."

"Oh. Well, I never listened to it before," he says, and starts singing, "*Buy-uy-in a stair-air-way to hea-ven.*" His thin tenor voice weaves like a drunk driver around the melody, and when I peek in the rearview mirror his eyes are squinted shut. "Now that," he says, "is a heavy fuckin song."

"I'm glad you like it."

"Thanks, Chief. Now get the fuck out of here."

I rise slowly out of the cab like a mime. Slightly giddy, I back away and step between the parked cars, taking cover behind a Ford Pinto. In the quiet of the empty street, my mind is shouting orders: Crouch down, keep moving, get away. The thief, already in the driver's seat, revs the engine and jams on the gas. The cab shrieks up the street and I run after, sprinting as fast as I can, but when I reach the corner of East End it's gone, as I knew it would be, and as the night sky lightens toward the dawn, I stand there panting, massaging the spot on the side of my head where the squat leaden barrel of the handgun pressed against my scalp.

FORT GREENE

Not until I am riding in the front seat of the taxi I've flagged down and we are headed to the local police precinct do I begin to shiver. I don't realize it at first because of the condition of the side street, recently milled in preparation for being paved; the cab vibrates uncomfortably over the ridged, uneven roadbed. But on the smoother going of Second Avenue, I'm still shaking like I've got the flu. To calm myself I rub my knees and sway back and forth, as if at prayer. The burly driver, a black fellow named Mason with large, sympathetic eyes, tells me to breathe.

"Just breathe and relax, man. Breathe and relax. You'll be all right." When he repeats himself for emphasis, I find it wonderfully comforting. He assures me I did the right thing by not resisting. "It's a dangerous job," he says. "Yes, sir, a dangerous job, and we don't get paid enough for this shit. No, sir, not near enough."

The more I tell him about the robbery, the more incensed he becomes. "People think this gig be easy, man, but they don't know shit. You riskin your life every motherfuckin day out here and who be lookin out for you? The cops? Like the decoys they got ridin around in them yellows? Shit, man, don't make me laugh."

"I didn't even think I was in trouble," I say.

"You done the right thing, man. Someone be stickin a gun to your head, you got to play it cool. You ain't got no backup like Starsky and Hutch. I say give 'em the damn money and let 'em take the motherfuckin cab and don't be frettin none if you out of pocket. Because old Mase is here to tell you, man, you most definitely did okay if you sittin here with all your shit in one piece. Yes, sir, you got your mojo workin, son, you know what I'm sayin?"

I not only know what he's saying, I'm grateful for it. So when Mason drops me on Sixty-seventh Street before a soot-blackened, gray stone building where a half dozen police cars are parked aslant to the curb, I bound up the steps to the station house, because there's nothing like a brush with death to make you feel like you just won the lottery.

The lobby is dominated by a high wooden counter over which the desk sergeant leans, questioning an impeccably coifed middle-aged woman turned out in a turquoise beaded jacket over a floor-length black satin gown. She seems to be perturbed by the way she is being treated.

"You don't believe I was victimized, do you, Sergeant?"

"Answer my question, ma'am. Did you give him the keys or not?"

"Yes, but he never returned them."

"And when did he cease staying at the premises?"

"A week ago."

"So he made an unlawful entry into the apartment using the keys he should have returned to you."

"Precisely."

"And what did he steal?"

"Well that's the thing," she says. "He didn't actually steal anything. He took the clothes he had left in the guest room."

"You're saying he took his own clothes?"

"Yes."

I'm starting to get antsy. Another officer drifts in from a connecting office, but before I can catch his eye, he disappears back into it. I wish this woman would get a life and leave, but she persists, and the sergeant, who is lazily scratching the back of his head, the top of which is sheared as flat as the deck of an aircraft carrier, has all the patience of a saint.

"Ma'am," he says, "I'm sorry, but that's not stealing."

"I know that, Sergeant, but he entered my residence without authority."

"To recover his personal effects."

"Yes, but—"

"Does he still have the keys?"

"No. He left them on the escritoire."

"Whatever that is."

"The writing desk."

"I see. And he didn't take nothing else. Nothing that wasn't his."

"Come to think of it, Sergeant, he took a couple of apples from the crisper."

"And what would you estimate the value of those apples to be?"

"Negligible, I'm sure, but it's the principle of the thing."

"So let me get this straight," he says. "You're filing a complaint against this friend of yours for unlawful entry and the theft of two apples?"

"He's not my friend anymore, but, yes, I think I should. Don't you?"

"No, I don't," he says. "It's a lot of paperwork and nothing's gonna come of it. I think, Mrs. Vandeventer—"

"Miss. So you're not going to do anything because of the paperwork?"

He looks her over before he continues. "Let me ask you something, Miss Vandeventer. How long have you known this guy?"

"My heavens! I don't know, twenty years? But I don't see what difference that makes."

"If I was you, ma'am. I would go home, take a nice hot bath and forget about it."

"But he left the front door unlocked. Anyone might have wandered in. Any vandal or ruffian in the neighborhood."

"But they didn't, did they?" She answers him by looking away. "Please, Miss Vandeventer, go home." Dismissed, she pauses, unwilling to leave. Her hands clutch a small black evening bag, and her eyes dart about, birdlike, at the floor, at the sergeant, at me and then up to the ceiling, where the sea-green paint flakes away in patches, revealing the rough plaster. I'm not sure what the woman's problem is, but I figure she's wasted enough of my time and I take her silence as my cue.

"I'd like to report a robbery," I say, stepping up to the counter.

"One second," says the sergeant. He calls down the hall. "Pavetti," he yells, "get over here." A police officer, about my age and somewhat disheveled, shambles down the hallway, tucking in his shirt tail. "If I'm not disturbing you, Pavetti, would you be good enough to drive Miss Vandeventer home?"

"Love to, Sarge."

"And look around. Make sure everything's okay." Pavetti nods, sleepily.

"That's very kind of you, Sergeant Kopecky, but you may still hear from my lawyer about this matter."

"Yes, ma'am. Good morning, ma'am."

Miss Vandeventer takes the arm of the yawning patrolman like a debutante on her way to the ball. Kopecky watches them walk out, the hint of a smile softening the no-nonsense expression on his craggy face.

"Jesus," I say, shaking my head, "what was all that about?" Kopecky folds his arms and studies me accusingly. I can feel him sizing me up, noting the mass of curly hair, frizzy and unkempt from the humid summer night, the metal peace sign pinned to my jeans jacket, the Nixon T-shirt that inquires, "Would you buy a used car from this man?" Clearly we're on different sides of the political fence, and I wonder if he is going to take my story any more seriously than he did Miss Vandeventer's.

"You said you was robbed?"

"That's right. At gunpoint. A fare held me up and stole my cab."

"Where did this happen?" When I tell him, he says, "That's another one. The second this week."

"Could it be the same guy?"

"If it is, you're lucky. The other driver didn't live to tell about it." He lets me mull that over for a moment and I start to shiver again. "You the owner?"

"I lease."

"Better call your boss. And you have to fill out a complaint form." He looks around behind the counter, moving trays and opening drawers. "Where are those damn things? Maloney," he yells to the policeman in the connecting office, "you seen any 61s?"

Maloney yells back, "Right in front of you, Sarge."

"How do you like that?" he says, and hands me a form from the pile on the counter directly between us.

I call Lipschitz from the pay phone in the entryway and he answers on the first ring in an annoyingly adenoidal voice. "You're late, *shmendrick*. You were supposed to ring the bell ten minutes ago."

"I've got some bad news."

"You had an accident?" Without waiting for my reply he plunges ahead. "I knew it. You wrecked the cab."

"I got robbed."

"So you didn't wreck the cab?"

"Screw the cab, Alvin. A guy held a gun to my head. I'm a bit shaken up."

"Goddamn *shvartzes*," he says. "How many times did I tell you not to pick up those cocksuckers? I guess you won't be a liberal much longer."

"It was a white guy, Alvin." Lipschitz is quiet for a few seconds while this sinks in. I ask him to meet me at the precinct and hang up before he can whine about all the money he's losing and his goddamn rotten luck.

To fill out the complaint form, I'm directed to the waiting area, a trio of dilapidated folding chairs by the front windows. An ancient air conditioner, its cover removed to expose a soiled filter, wheezes loudly as if struggling to breathe out cooler air. Several plants occupy the broad windowsill in a half-hearted attempt at interior decoration. A plastic watering can loiters between a coleus and a spider plant, bearing the warning: "Do Not Remove— 19th Precinct Lobby." I complete the form, reread my statement, sign it, date it, hand it in. Still no Lipschitz, so to kill time, I check out the bulletin board, which is papered with children's drawings—thank-yous for a recent field trip. The best of the bunch depict a patrolman directing traffic, a police officer standing next to his cruiser and, my favorite, a cop slapping the handcuffs on a perp. As I study the image, it hits me they'll never catch the guy and that the detailed complaint form I have meticulously filled out is not only a pointless formality but a complete waste of time.

Lipschitz, who drinks six cups of coffee in the morning and likes to snack on NoDoz, shows up even more wired than usual. "Those bastards," he whines, "they won't let us live."

"I'm sorry, Alvin. I didn't see it coming."

"What can I say, kiddo? Chalk it up to experience. I just hope they catch the dickhead and cut off his balls." He nods repeatedly like a speed freak bebopping to a benzedrine rush. "By the way," he asks, "where did you park the cab?"

"They took it, Alvin. I told you on the phone." He stops moving, head cocked as if he were eavesdropping on the desk sergeant's breakfast order to the corner diner. It strikes me that I've never seen him so still.

"I thought I was picking up the cab."

"He used it to get away."

"You didn't tell me that."

"I could have sworn I mentioned it."

"Mention it? No, you didn't *mention* it. You said you had some bad news, and you were robbed." He stalks around the small waiting area, smacking his arms against his thighs like a pissed-off penguin. "Fuckin dickhead," he yells. "Cocksuckin, motherfuckin dickhead." He kicks at one of the folding chairs, and it slams to the floor as if shot.

"You," says the sergeant. "What the hell are you doing?"

"They stole my fuckin cab," he says, throwing his arms up and heaving them forward with an anguished bray of disgust.

"Do us a favor and calm down," says Kopecky. "And pick up the chair." Lipschitz does as ordered, righting the folding chair then slumping onto the flimsy slatted seat.

"I don't fuckin believe this." He looks like he's about to cry and I pat him gently on the shoulder.

"I'm really sorry, Alvin."

"I got to make the alimony payment."

"They want you to fill out a report."

"Shit," he says, "my ex isn't going to buy this."

"Sure she will. It's the truth."

"I used it already. In April." Lipschitz often bragged of the perfectly plausible excuses he fed Bettina, his ex-wife, to put her off. It killed him to have to pay her anything, and he took perverse joy in hearing her beg for whatever installment was past due. In December he said the Chanukah bush caught fire, causing smoke damage. In March he said he bit into a hamburger and cracked his tooth, which required a crown. In May he told her that he owed his bookie, who'd have his arms broken if he didn't pay; a cab driver with two broken arms, he argued, wasn't any good to either of them. She must have known he was full of it—the board-

ers in the hall were always sniggering in the background—but
what could she do? She had moved out to Phoenix for her aller-
gies and wasn't about to fly east every month to see for herself. So
she commiserated and played along, and sooner or later he threw
a check in the mail.

"You'll come up with something brilliant. You always do."

"At least give me the lease fee," he says. "That'll help."

"He took everything, Alvin. I don't have enough for the bus."

"That's okay," he says, "you can pay me later."

"I really don't think I should have to pay you."

"Look," he says, "you worked the shift so you owe me."

"Come on, man, that's not right."

"Well that's the way I see it."

"Let me ask you something. If I was shot in the head, would
you try to recover the money from my estate?"

"A, you're not dead. B, you owe me the money. And C, if you
don't pay, you don't drive."

"So I quit. What the hell do I care? I'm leaving for Europe in
a week anyway."

"Nice of you to give notice," he says. "When were you planning
to tell me? The day your flight leaves?" I had intended to inform
him this morning when I brought in the cab, but I didn't say that.
Smart ass that I am, I have to come up with something clever.

"Actually, I was going to drop you a postcard from Amsterdam." He tells me to pack up all my stuff and move out. Today. He
wants me out of the Penthouse by the time he gets back from
filling out the report. Even though I don't have the slightest idea
where I'm going, I tell him that's fine with me. Because of the
holiday, I have yet to pay July's rent, but I can see what he's think-

ing, the transparent worm, and his parting shot doesn't surprise me a bit.

"Say goodbye to your security deposit."

"You're an asshole, Alvin. I hope your cab is already in the chop shop."

"Where you going, dickhead? I'm not finished yet." He showers me with curses, raging like a betrayed adolescent. As I walk away, I hear Sergeant Kopecky shouting at him for chrissake to shut the hell up.

The first person I think to call is Gene, but then I remember the cramped décor of his one-room pad. The place has barely room enough for a bed. The last time I dropped by, I couldn't get over the fact that he didn't have a table to eat at. I sat on the edge of his bed while he occupied the only chair and we shared a joint under the glare of the overhead bulb. He didn't even have a lamp.

I decide to try Randi, who is never at her best first thing in the morning. "What the fuck do you want?" she growls. "I'm like really late for work." But when I tell her about the robbery, her attitude changes completely. "Jesus, Eddie, you could have been killed."

"And that's not the worst of it."

"Hold on a second." She strikes a match, puffs on her cigarette and exhales. "Poor baby," she coos, her voice deliciously low and sexy. "You must be totally freaked out."

"I've been better," I reply. I explain my housing quandary and ask to crash with her until my plane leaves.

She would like to say yes, but she really isn't sure it's a good idea. Her place is too small, she complains. Where would I store my stuff? She doesn't want to be a drag, but she can get very touchy about her space.

"Forget it," I say, wondering who to call next. "You can't hack the idea. I can dig it."

"Oh, shit," she says, "come on over. I get off work at one."

"Great, Randi, I really appreciate it."

"Yeah, well, okay, but if you're going to stay here, I think we should cool it for a while just in case."

"Somebody just put a gun to my head. Believe me, Randi, sex is the furthest thing from my mind."

By the time I show up in Brooklyn with all my earthly possessions crammed into a cab, I'm wondering if this isn't a big mistake. For one thing, Randi doesn't seem to know how to act. She barely says hello and won't help me haul my things up to her apartment. To smooth things over, I offer to buy her lunch after a quick shower. The warm water beating down feels incredibly relaxing after so many grimy hours and I close my eyes and float off dreamily to the white sands of Mykonos, where bronzed Scandinavian playmates frolic in the gentle surf, their pendulous breasts glistening with seawater. I'm so startled when Randi appears naked on the other side of the clear plastic curtain that the cake of Ivory dives out of my hand and dents itself with a thud against the floor of the tub.

"I'll get that," says Randi, stepping quickly in next to me, scooping up the soap and working it vigorously between her hands. "My, my," she says, "what do we have down here?"

"I thought we were going to cool it for a while."

"I thought so too," she says, "but then you got here, and I couldn't wait to fuck you." My reluctance vanishes with the playful teasing of her fingers and the purring of our shameful pleasure. She strokes my hard-on into a lather, and when she beckons me into her, the shower pelting us with lust, it is impossible for me to stop, especially when I imagine the cops bursting in, ripping down the curtain, and struggling in vain to pry us apart until we're sated.

We spend the rest of the weekend making love, which is not to say we huddle under the bedclothes for three days. Randi wants to turn me on to the charms of her adopted borough. Her actual words are: "I'm going to show you myself around Brooklyn." And, boy, does she mean it.

Over hotdogs at Nathan's, I mention the importance of being discreet, a concept that Randi, her lips pouty with mustard, completely agrees with. In practice, however, she has one small, insurmountable problem—her impulses. The risk of being discovered, especially in public, really turns her on. It isn't my style to initiate such escapades, but I can be persuaded without much effort to participate. Especially when she purses her lips, flashes a coy smile and entices me into yet another unlikely scene: under the boardwalk at Coney Island; crammed into a restroom stall at the Brooklyn Museum; behind the boathouse in Prospect Park. She seems to have a knack for choosing the perfect semipublic spots to drop her bell-bottoms.

Randi throws herself with abandon into each encounter, and while I am excited, I can't totally suspend my fear of being caught. At the Botanical Gardens, for instance, she surprises me by revealing the pantiless topography beneath her skintight hip-huggers. I lose myself in the impetuous licking of her pussy until a squalling child on the other side of the hedge turns me into a suspicious, unmoving sentinel. On the brink of orgasm, Randi pleads at me in hoarse, guttural urgings to press on, but I'm so nervous we'll be discovered, I can't help watching myself go through the not very enjoyable motions.

Sunday night we stroll through Fort Greene Park, share a joint, and amble uphill to the monument, a graceful marble column that occupies a quiet, grass-covered knoll. Concrete spheres like giant cannonballs mark the perimeter. "This must be the site of Fort Greene," I say.

"No, young man," says a woman's voice, startling us from the tree-covered shadows, "there was never a Fort Greene." We discern two seated forms, only a few feet away, which on closer inspection belong to an elderly black couple on a nearby bench. "It was called Fort Putnam," says the woman. "In 1776 this is where they fought the Battle of Long Island. Dig around here and you can unearth musket balls, flints, all kinds of things."

"Ooh, musket balls," whispers Randi, "just what I need."

"Go ahead, Didi, tell 'em about the retreat," says the old gentleman. In the dim light, his clip-on bow tie seems to match exactly the pattern of his plaid sport jacket.

"Oh, I wouldn't want to bore them, Isaac. It's ancient history."

"I'd like to hear about it," I say, ignoring the face Randi is making.

After Sullivan's troops were routed at Jamaica, Didi explains, the fort was in danger of falling to the British. The loss of the garrison would have dealt a severe blow to the Continental Army. "Luckily," she says, "the weather intervened, and they were able to ferry over to Manhattan under cover of fog. Had to use every skiff, barge and rowboat they could find."

"That is so fascinating," says Randi, trying to pull me away.

"You seem to have a lot of local knowledge."

The man chuckles and jerks his thumb at his companion. "Ought to," he says. "She taught high school for thirty years."

"So why do they call it Fort Greene?" I wonder.

She explains that the park was named after General Greene, who oversaw construction of the ill-fated Fort Putnam. Fort Greene, it turns out, is a misnomer. As she speaks, he watches her intently, nodding along with each point she makes.

"You mean *Nathanael* Greene?"

"That's right. Very good, young man."

"Yeah, history is my favorite subject."

Because of the Captain's wartime service, I became a military history buff—an interest I fed with a diet of books on the Civil War and the Revolution. Nathanael Greene, I knew, was Washington's most trusted subordinate—the general he had designated to assume command if something happened to him. In 1780 Greene replaced General Gates, whose army had just been crushed at Camden, South Carolina. Resistance in the Southern colonies was practically nil, but Greene displayed his tactical genius in devising a brilliant strategy of limited engagement. He never won an outright victory, but he inflicted such heavy casualties that in twenty months Greene succeeded in splitting the British Army in half and bottling them up in Charleston and Wilmington. His recipe for success he summed up in the following words: "We fight, get beat, rise, and fight again." It was a strategy that made an art of coming in second. When the Captain would do his Coach Lombardi riff and declare that finishing first was the only thing that mattered, I used to bring up General Greene and drive him crazy.

"Who's the monument for?"

"Tell 'em about the memorial, Didi," says the man. "The memorial is very interesting."

"I'm bored," whispers Randi, rubbing my ass. "Can we get out of here?"

"Be patient, will you." I brush her hand away.

Didi is telling us that the British kept their prisoners of war on ships anchored in New York Harbor, but the conditions were so deplorable, they died by the thousands. From disease, neglect, malnutrition—

"Bummer," says Randi.

"More than eleven thousand," says Didi. I let out a whistle of surprise. During the Revolutionary War, that number of men would have been sufficient to field two good-sized armies. "The monument," she continues, "commemorates the ship martyrs." As if on cue, we look up at the Doric column to where it merges seamlessly into the charcoal sky.

"Fact is," says Isaac, "Didi's relative died on one of those ships. Ain't that right, Didi?"

"My great uncle, I'm afraid."

"Is that true?" I ask her. I can feel the back of my neck tingling.

"Yes, my great great great great *great* uncle." Randi has drifted over to a bench, where she sits, legs crossed, tapping her foot. "Oh, my," says Didi, "look how late it is. You're very kind to humor an old lady. Now if you will take me home, Isaac, we shall leave these young people to their nocturnal pursuits."

"You folks take care now," says Isaac.

With the couple's departure the night reasserts itself and nature seems to turn up the volume of the crickets.

"God," says Randi, "I thought they would never leave."

"Come on, Randi. That was really interesting."

"For you maybe. I have other interests. Like these." Randi pulls me down onto the bench and burrows her tongue into my mouth in a long, tobacco-scented kiss.

"What does 'nocturnal' mean?" she asks.

"Pertaining to the night. Gazing at that star, for instance, is a nocturnal pastime."

"Guess what?" she says. "I just thought of another nocturnal pastime." She leads me into a grove of gingko trees, backs me against one of the slender trunks, unzips my jeans, slides to her knees, coaxes my stiffening cock into the night air, and as my Minuteman stands at attention she begins to lavish upon it a wild and wonderful Prison Ship Martyrs' Memorial blow job. Fan-shaped leaves flutter like tattered flags in the faint breeze as my hips move to the rhythm of her mouth. My fingers fumble at the buttons of her work shirt, fondle her pliant breasts and seize in triumph her swollen nipples, a foray that serves to further inflame her passions. Under her persistent assault, my defenses weaken, my knees buckle, and I feel myself surrendering to her charms. I close my eyes to concentrate on the forces gathering in my own Southern colonies and come close to counterattacking with a well-timed thrust of the main body of my desire when I hear a voice calling from the vicinity of the monument.

"Oh, young man. Young man! I remembered something else I wanted to tell you."

I freeze, as if startled by the glare of onrushing headlights. Randi, eyes spitting venom, expels my wilting penis from the soft recesses of her palate.

"Son of a fucking bitch," she whispers.

"Let's get out of here," I say, frantically zipping up my pants.

"Oh, young man!"

"Oh, shut the fuck up," hisses Randi, misfastening the buttons of her shirt so that it hangs askew.

"Jesus," I whisper, "she's coming this way."

"Didi, honey, those folks must have walked on."

We huddle on the ground among the fallen gingko leaves until their voices fade. Randi massages the denim at my crotch, but I take her hand and hold it. We lie like that, deflated by frustration, then get up and, taking a tip from the Continental Army, beat a hasty retreat out of the park.

I try to broach the topic of discretion, to no avail. "Eat me," says Randi. "You weren't complaining a minute ago when I was sucking your dick." Pissed off, she walks ahead of me up Willoughby, and though I want desperately to duck into the corner bar for a shot and a beer, I follow her to the apartment, where we avoid each other. The tension only increases as we brush teeth and get ready for bed. Randi makes me sleep for the first time on the floor.

In the morning Randi gets up early for work and stomps around until she slams the door on the way out. I climb onto the sofabed and doze until the phone rings. I lift the receiver to shut the thing up.

"Hello?" I mumble.

"Randi? You sound awful. You have to stop smoking." It's my Aunt Cele, Randi's mom, Gene's ex, and not anyone I want to be dealing with when I'm half asleep. The Gorgon Medusa, a mythical beast whose merest glance could turn a man to stone, has nothing on my Aunt Cele. Instead of a head coiled with snakes, a helmet of laquered hair encases the Halloween mask of her face. Excessive lipstick, a faint mustache and a prominent mole on her cheek conspire to shape a countenance that frightens babies to tears. As obese as Gene is thin, she also has a penchant for polluting the air with her perfume. There's a joke in our family that she spells *perfume* without the p-e-r. But her scariest physical quality is her voice, which too often imitates the painful screech of a subway grinding to a halt.

"I'm afraid I have bad news," she shouts. "Your father has been arrested at the Canadian border. Something to do with the coin business. I really don't understand it too well."

"Jesus," I say, "will you lower the volume?"

"What did you say?" Her voice scrapes like steel wool.

"I said lower the freakin volume."

"Who is this? Where's Randi?"

"She's at work," I whisper, endeavoring to disguise my voice.

"And who would you be?"

"Nobody. A friend."

"Nobody, huh? You have a name, nobody?"

I've done it now, I think. How do I worm my way out of this one? It doesn't occur to me to tell the truth—that I got robbed and I'm crashing here for a few days—so I give her the name of a college pal, Art Silverman.

"Listen, Silverman. Just be sure you tell her to call her mother."

Now that my Aunt Cele, like Macbeth, has murdered sleep, I throw on some clothes and go over to Durkin's, the greasy spoon on DeKalb where Randi has a job waiting tables. Through the front window I watch her negotiate a tray full of breakfast food along the narrow aisle of the crowded restaurant. She's wearing one of those white restaurant shifts that buttons down the front, and it hugs her body in all the right places. Under the stretchy material, the faint outline of her nipples is visible. In fact most of the guys in there seem to be checking her out.

"Nice uniform," I say as I walk up to her.

"What the hell are you doing here?"

"I have to talk to you, Randi."

"I can't right now. It's busy."

I sit at the counter and order breakfast. I can't believe how depressing the place is. The décor, as my mother would say, is strictly from hunger: orange Formica tables, harsh fluorescent lighting and a linoleum floor that looks like it hasn't been mopped in a week. When I visit the closet-sized restroom, a no-vacancy fly strip dangles obtrusively from the low ceiling. I hope at least that the food is okay, but the coffee is bitter, the eggs are overcooked and the home fries have a secret ingredient: lurking beneath the upper crust of sliced potatoes I discover to my chagrin an inch-long cigarette butt.

I catch Randi's eye and call her over with a slight jerk of my head.

"Look at this," I say, impaling the soggy butt on the tines of my fork.

"Sorry," she says. "The cook doesn't know his ash from his elbow."

"That's funny, Randi, but what I have to tell you isn't." I report her mother's phone call and the news of Gene's arrest.

"Shit," she says. "What a jerk he is." I want to calm her down and tell her that we don't know the whole story, but a wino weaves up to the counter and asks loudly who someone has to fuck around here to get service.

"What do you need?" asks Randi.

"You got any muff pie, sweetheart?" Although it's a warm summer morning he wears a heavy brown overcoat, stained and crusted with bits of dried matter. A pint of Night Train protrudes from the coat pocket.

"We have doughnuts," says Randi, patiently. "Doughnuts, danish and muffins. What can I get you?"

"All right," he says, pounding his fist on the orange counter, "Give me a cup of coffee, four sugars. And a nice, fat slice of muff pie." Customers close to the counter grow quiet as they become aware of the disturbance.

"We have apple pie, blueberry pie, Boston cream and lemon meringue. That's all the pies we have."

"Are you deaf?" he shouts. "I want muff pie. I know you got some." By now, most of the people in Durkin's have stopped eating and are watching the drama unfold.

"Listen," says Randi, "we don't have any muff pie, but we do have something almost as good." She pulls a takeout bag from under the counter, crumples the opening around her finger to form a tube, lifts it to her mouth, inflates it and hands it to him. "Here's a blowjob to go," she says. "Now get the fuck out of here."

The joint erupts with cheers and whistles as people yell and clap their approval. Flattered, Randi executes a quick curtsy. A few tables even give her a standing ovation. Smiling sheepishly, the befuddled wino retreats to the door, holding the paper sack aloft like a prize.

HICKSVILLE

My family loves to play games. Word games, card games, board games, all kinds of games. Crossword puzzles and Scrabble, Pinochle and Cribbage, Monopoly and Mah Jongg. But our favorite pastime by far is jumping to conclusions. We can't help ourselves. Answer the phone after the second ring, regardless of the time of day, and my mother says, "I woke you, didn't I?" Say hello to my uncle and he replies, "How you doing today, good?" Fail to agree immediately with my father and he screams, "What are you, an idiot?"

It's an embarrassing family trait, this tendency, almost like a curse, handed down congenitally from one generation to the next. Perhaps we can't deal with uncertainty or we're overwhelmed too easily by the complexities of experience or we just have a need to stereotype, but for whatever reason, we Sackses love to analyze behavior through the unreliable filter of our cockamamie assumptions.

Misplace your wallet: "Some son-of-a-bitch stole it." Flunk German literature: "That professor is an anti-Semite." Wake up with a stiff neck: "You better see a doctor. That's the first sign Aunt Gertie had of her tumor."

So when I learn that Gene has been arrested at Customs, I assume it's all his fault, and he must have done something incredibly stupid to screw up so royally. Though I have admonished Randi to wait for all the facts, I know my uncle too well to apply the rules of due process to his current predicament. In the court of family opinion, he is guilty until proven innocent.

Knowing as I do the sub-rosa nature of Gene's activity, I figure he hasn't sacrificed his only phone call to his ex. I dial the store number and Tiny answers.

"Your father's looking for you."

"How's it going there?"

"Things are crazy, Ed. Absolutely nuts. Leo is apoplectic."

I can hear the Captain's agitated voice in the background: "What are you talkin?" he says. "Is that my son?"

"I'm warning you," says Tiny, "he's on the warpath. Hold for Crazy Horse."

"Very funny," says the Captain. "Gimme the damn phone."

"Hi, Dad—"

"Jesus, Eddie, where the hell have you been? I'm trying to reach you since yesterday."

"I've been around."

"Don't give me that crap. Lipschitz said you moved."

"Oh, yeah? What else did he say?"

"That you quit without giving notice."

"He did, huh? Did he tell you about the robbery?" I wanted to keep it to myself, but I'm so pissed at Lipschitz that I blurt out the whole story—the robbery, the argument at the precinct, getting fired and kicked out of the apartment, all of it, except for the de-nouement where I move in with my first cousin. For once my father listens without interrupting.

"You get hurt?"

"Just shook up. Don't tell Mom."

"What do think I am, an idiot?"

"No, Dad, I just—"

"You think I want to give her a heart attack?"

"I'm just sayin—"

"You don't have to tell me. Jesus." During the pause that follows, I wonder if I should say something for bruising his feelings. Should I apologize or keep my mouth shut? If I apologize he'll tell me to forget it, but if I don't say anything, he'll be pissed off. While I'm deliberating, he lets me off the hook by changing the topic. "So where are you staying?"

"With friends in Brooklyn." In the background I hear Tiny shout out someone's name.

"One second," he says. "Who is it, Tiny? Who? No, tell him I'll call him back. So you heard the news about Gene?"

I figure I better play dumb. "You got me. Did he win at the track?"

"That putz? He's a loser. An also-ran."

"What happened?"

"Stupid cocksucker."

"Don't tell me he screwed up again."

"No good deed goes unpunished, Eddie."

"What the hell does that mean?"

"It means every time I do your uncle a favor, it winds up costing me a bundle."

"For godsake, Dad, you going to tell me or do I have to read about it in the papers?"

He finally lays it out. Gene was busted at the Thousand Islands Bridge with undeclared bags of Canadian coins. He's being held at some county lockup in upstate New York.

"Something must have gone wrong," he says. "All I know is, I got to go to hicksville."

"Hicksville? You mean on Long Island?"

"No, not that Hicksville. I mean hicksville, like the middle of fuckin nowhere. Some dinky town named Canton up by the Canadian border."

"Canton? That's like a seven-hour drive."

"Oh, yeah? How would you know?"

"Because we used to play St. Lawrence in hockey and I went up there once to watch a game."

"Good," he says, "you can come along and keep me company. It'll be like old times."

I wonder to what "old times" he is referring. The last time we traveled together I was a high school senior and we drove to Boston for my Harvard interview. I had applied reluctantly, at the Captain's insistence, tormented with the awareness that I wasn't Harvard material, especially when I compared myself to Eric Glantz, my Harvard-bound classmate who was widely acknowledged to be a genius. I felt like a fraud, but there was no way out of it. So I went through the motions and by the time the assistant dean of admissions called me in for "our little chat," I had pretty much psyched myself out. I was so intimidated that I clammed up, unable to elaborate on any of my terse, unimaginative replies. At some point, I made reference to a severe upset stomach; then, exhausted by this tenuous effort to save face, I sank back as far as I could into the high-backed leather chair, gripped the armrests for courage and rode out the remainder of the interview. Mercifully, it was brief. I told the Captain it had gone great, better than expected, though my behavior suggested otherwise. On the return trip, I was sullen and withdrawn, resentful of my father for engineering this humiliation and livid with myself for not opposing him and refusing under any circumstances to apply.

Later that morning I rendezvous with the Captain at Radio City, where his forest-green Caddy is idling in a No Standing zone. Behind the wheel, the Captain studies a roadmap and puffs on a Sultan. "Here," he says, dispensing with the more common forms of greeting, "fold this." I gather in the map, a crumpled, crinkled mass, which I straighten and refold while the Captain jogs crosstown toward the elevated West Side Highway. I'm using the folded map to wave away the curling ribbons of cigar smoke when a delivery van cuts us off, gasoline sloshing from its uncapped fuel tank.

"You see that, Eddie? You see what that son of a bitch did?"

"Relax, Dad, it's not the end of the world."

"Fuckin vans think they own the road," says my father. "You want to play, shithead?" He jams on the accelerator, pulls alongside the passenger door, deploys his middle finger, then tattoos the horn until he gets the driver's attention. We race neck and neck across Fifty-fifth Street, the Captain laughing with maniacal glee at every bump and pothole as jets of gas erupt from the fuel tank like geysers. There's something to be said for cheap thrills, I guess, especially when they put my father in a good mood. Half an hour later, as we're sailing up the Palisades Parkway, he's still laughing about it.

I may be twenty-two, but I'm not supposed to touch the radio in my dad's car. He tunes in "The Make-Believe Ballroom" until I pester him to play something that I'd like to listen to, a demand I regret after sitting through a couple of god-awful selections that represent his warped idea of rock and roll: "Tie a Yellow Ribbon 'Round the Old Oak Tree" and "Killing Me Softly." Long before Roberta Flack can wrap up her nauseating ballad, I flick off the radio in disgust.

"What the hell are you doing, Eddie?"

"I can't listen anymore. The song sucks. I wish he would go ahead and kill her already."

"Don't touch the radio," he says, but at least he doesn't turn it back on.

The sound of the road serenades us, and I feel as if we're going on vacation, even if it's just an overnight.

"Hey, Dad, maybe we can do some fishing if we have time."

"This isn't a pleasure trip, Eddie. We're gonna take care of business and get the hell out of there."

"I know. I'm just saying it would be fun to go fishing together."

"You want to go fishing? I'll take you when we're down in Miami over New Year's. And I don't mean lake fishing. We'll do some real fishing, sport-fishing. You try reeling in a hundred-pound swordfish, you'll never forget it. Believe me."

"Sounds great, Dad. I can't wait."

I ask about Gene's situation and he fills me in, grudgingly, salting the details with expletives that colorfully assail my uncle's

character: "He got caught with sixteen bags, the fuckin putz."
"He'll be arraigned tomorrow in Watertown, the cocksucking cretin." "We'll have to arrange for a lawyer and a bailbondsman, unless of course he happens to drop dead, the stupid no-good rotten son of a fucking bitch."

I need to tell him about the trip to Europe, but this hardly seems like the time. As the Captain stews, I lapse into silence and mull on my own predicament—how to extricate myself as quickly as possible from the awkwardness of this fling with Randi. I know once I leave for Europe, things will naturally cool down, but I'm not sure I can make it another week. God, what a jerk I was to move in with her. I could kick myself. I mean, what the hell was I thinking? I'm sorry, Randi, but that's it. As soon as I get back to the city, I'm moving out. That's definite. But where? My parents' house in Valley Stream? Jesus. I gaze absently at the reflectors whizzing by on the graveled shoulder of the highway, finding some small comfort in the fact that each green mile marker takes me farther away from the impetuous and demanding arms of my pathologically indiscreet cousin.

At Utica we abandon the Thruway and head north on a two-lane route that skirts the piney foothills of the Adirondacks. As the state road arcs north by northwest, the forest recedes, the land clears, and we speed through rolling farmland past weathered barns with picturesque silos amid fields of unripe corn.

It's almost six o'clock when we pull into the sleepy, tree-lined town of Canton, but of course the Captain refuses to ask for directions, so we drive around aimlessly looking for the St. Lawrence County Jail. It's supposed to be at the county complex, an area of courthouses and office buildings, which eludes us as we cruise Main Street and then stumble onto the campus of St. Lawrence University. An old joke pops into my head: Why does it take fifty million sperm to fertilize one egg? Because none of the sperm will stop to ask directions. I tell it to the Captain, who is not amused, though he allows me to question a pedestrian out walking his dog. The man, whose eyes are as sad and heavy-lidded as his dachshund's, speaks in such a halting, exasperating cadence that it takes him five minutes to explain how to get to Judson Street, which is only two minutes away.

Twice we drive past the jail, a handsome three-story structure of gray stone block, which appears to be a turn-of-the-century historical landmark rather than a correctional facility. The deputy at the door informs us that visiting hours have just ended and points us toward the office with instructions to ask for Sheriff Lephart. Into the hall steps a lanky, middle-aged man whose face, badly scarred from acne, is strangely attractive, lean and angular with thoughtful, deep-set eyes. The sheriff says there's nothing to be done about it, that rules are rules so why don't we return tomorrow.

"I was wondering, Sheriff, maybe you can give us some advice."

"I'll try."

"Let me ask you something . . ." The Captain takes him by the arm and walks him down the institutional gray hallway out of earshot.

A hairnetted lady in a blood-stained butcher's apron and white crepe-soled shoes emerges from the stairwell, beams at me and says, "It's so nice and quiet around here at mealtimes."

"That explains it," I say. "I expected it to be, I don't know, busier. More activity."

"It's the meatloaf," she says. "Everybody loves the meatloaf. I'll tell you a secret," she confides. "Lipton's Onion Soup. That's what gives the chopped meat its special flavor."

"I'll have to try that sometime."

"You won't be disappointed." She enters the office, the heavy wooden door closing behind her with a report that echoes in the quiet corridor.

The sheriff and my father walk toward me deep in conversation. The taller man says something to the Captain, who stops, throws his head back and laughs, *hee hee hee*, a high-pitched, staccato bleating that never fails to remind me of our distant simian relatives.

"Unbelievable," says the Captain.

"One of a kind," says the sheriff.

"Remember what he said when we were surrounded?"

"I'll never forget it," says Lephart.

They start reciting in unison: "'Well, boys, we've been looking for the enemy and now we know where they are.'"

"He was something else," says the Captain.

"Yeah," says Lephart, "they broke the mold."

"You said it, Dan. They'll never be another like him."

"That's for sure."

"So about this other thing. What do you say?"

"Tell you what," says Lephart. "Seeing as you outrank me, Leo, I'll give you ten minutes. That's about the best I can do."

"Beautiful, Dan. I really appreciate it."

"No problem, Leo. I'll just be a minute." Lephart ducks into the office and we wait by a bulletin board papered with news and notices: the menu for the week; a memo with the new date for a rained-out softball game; a flyer for the annual pancake breakfast at the local firehouse.

"Damn, I'm good," crows the Captain.

"How did you manage that?"

"Tell you later."

Lephart steps out of the office and leads us down the hall to a small gray room with three visiting booths. The booths are side by side and separated by a sheetrock partition. Prisoners are seg-regated from visitors by a secure wall interrupted by a trio of two-foot-square plexiglass panels, one per booth, which permit conversation, as does a teller's window, through a ring of perfor-ated holes.

After several minutes, Gene appears behind the plexiglass looking haggard and unshaved. He acknowledges the Captain, then takes me in, cracks a smile and nods. He looks so out of place in his jailhouse garb, a dark green work shirt and pants, that he might as well be playing the role of an inmate in one of those made-for-television prison dramas.

"I wish you got here earlier," he says. "They're in the middle of serving dinner."

"How's the chow?" I ask.

"Great," he says. "You wouldn't believe it. The sheriff's wife runs the kitchen and, man, can she cook. Last night we had chicken with some kind of honey-mustard glaze that was deli-cious. And they say the meatloaf tonight—"

"I'm so glad you like the food," says the Captain.

"Hey, man, not only is the food good, but I haven't been this regular since I don't know when. This morning I took a dump that was unbelievable. Looked like a pound of sausage. And I'm not talking those thin little breakfast links. I mean the thick Italian kind like you get at the—"

"Hey, genius, I'm happy for you your bowels are in working order, but since we only have a few minutes, would you mind telling me, if it's not too much trouble, what the fuck happened at the border?"

"What can I say, Leo? I had a little problem."

"I don't get it," says the Captain. "We never got stopped before."

Gene starts to say something but stops. He looks down, shifts his position, folds his arms, looks at the ceiling and shakes his head. "I fucked up," he says. Then, leaning right up to the window, he adds, "I guess I got a little greedy."

"What does that mean?"

"*Oy,*" Gene sighs.

"Will you spit it out already? I feel like I'm pulling teeth."

"Thirty bags, okay? Listen, Leo—"

"Thirty? Are you nuts? You were supposed to handle sixteen."

"I know, I know. I fucked up. I wanted to make a little extra, so I could pay you off faster."

"So where did the other fourteen thousand dollars come from?"

"I scraped together everything I could. I didn't think there would be a problem."

The Captain mimics him like a little kid: "I didn't think there would be a problem."

"I didn't."

"Thirty bags—that adds fifteen hundred pounds to the weight of the vehicle."

"I know that, Leo, but with the heavy-duty shocks, I thought the Camaro would handle it. But when I get to the border, they say the car is riding low and pull me over."

"You mean to tell me you used your own car?"

"Yeah, why, is there a problem?"

"What are you, an idiot? You're supposed to use a rental."

Gene looks away and says nothing. He doesn't have to. My father stares at him, his mouth agape, as if he were about to say something, but he doesn't know where to begin.

"They're not going to keep my car, are they?"

"I don't know," says the Captain. "It might depend on what they charge you with."

"They haven't charged me with anything yet."

"I'm aware of that, genius. Why do you think I'm here?"

"Okay, Leo. I get it. So now what?"

"Tomorrow you'll be arraigned in Watertown. You'll get formally charged with something, either smuggling or, if we get lucky, failure to declare. I'll have a lawyer there and we'll get you out on bail. What else? I called Lenny and told him you were in an automobile accident. I said you got some whiplash but you're okay and you need to take a couple of sick days. He said no problem, he'll see you Wednesday."

"What can I say, Leo? That's beautiful. Thank you."

"What can you say? Nothing. Don't say anything to anyone. That's what you can say."

"What do you think I am, stupid?"

The Captain looks at him. "Why would I think that?" he says.

"All right, already. I made a mistake. I'll make it up you."

"Yeah, I know. You're always making it up to me." The Captain takes a breath and exhales, trying not to lose his temper. "Answer me this, Gene. Who have you talked to so far?"

"Nobody. Not a soul. I swear."

"You weren't interrogated?"

"Well, yeah, the special agents from Customs questioned me. They asked me where I got the coins. I said I purchased them legally but that's all I said. I didn't mention any names. They said something about 'bolos,' that they would talk to me again after they check for 'bolos,' whatever they are." He looks at me and shrugs.

"Let me edify you," says the Captain. "'Bolo' means 'be on the lookout for.' It's a bulletin issued by a law enforcement agency."

"Really?" I say. "I didn't know that."

"They had to check to see if a bank was knocked over or if a robbery of silver coins was reported."

"Yeah, that makes sense because they left for a while and when they came back they didn't try to pressure me. They just asked if I wanted to sign a release. Tell them my side of the story. You know, get things off my chest. Where was I taking the coins? What was I going to do with them? Who was I working for? Stuff like that."

"And what did you say?"

"I said thanks but no thanks. Name, rank and serial number, like you told me. So they read me my rights and brought me here."

On Gene's side of the wall, a deputy comes over to tell us we have two minutes, then returns to his post by the door.

"You did the right thing for once," says the Captain. "You didn't talk and you didn't sign any waiver. Now listen to me and listen good." My father leans forward and drops his voice to almost a whisper. "You can get a lot of people in trouble. I don't think I have to mention any names. But if you give me your word you'll continue to keep your mouth shut, then we'll pay for the lawyer, we'll pay for the bail, and we'll get this situation straightened out."

"You got it, Leo. You can count on me."

"I hope so," says the Captain. "Because if you fuck me this time, Gene, we're through. You understand? You can rot for all I care."

Duly chastened, my uncle stares at his hands, which are folded on his lap. "I promise," he says. "I won't let you down."

The Captain pushes himself out of his chair and the three of us stand. "Get some sleep," he orders. We got a big day tomorrow."

"Thanks, Leo. I'm lucky to have a brother like you."

"Don't forget it," he says. "See you in the morning."

My father walks out, but I tarry to have a few words with Gene.

"How you doin?" he says. "Good?"

"I'm okay," I say. "What about you?" The corrections officer comes to within a few feet of Gene and waits. "Hey, man, it's just a little speed bump on the highway of life. I'll be cruising again before you know it." He mimes a race car driver shifting into second and third. "Vroom. Vroom."

"That's the spirit," I say. "We'll go to the track when you get home. Just the two of us. Have a few laughs."

"Root home some longshots, eh, kid?"

"Hit the daily double," I say. "A few exactas."

"Now you're talking," he says. "Hey, thanks for coming. It

means a lot to me." We nod to each other. As he's led away, he calls out, "Don't let your meat loaf."

In the hallway the Captain is chatting with Sheriff Lephart.

"Be sure to give my regards to Chesty," he says.

"Will do," says the Captain. "*Semper fi.*"

As soon as we emerge into the summer twilight, I feel lighter, as if some oppressive feeling has lifted. The Captain unlocks the Caddy and we backtrack to Main Street to pick up Route 11.

"So what did you say to him?"

"Lephart? I told him he looked familiar. He asked me if I was in Korea, I said yes and we got to talking. Somehow he got the idea that we were in the same outfit."

"You mean you lied to him?"

"How else am I going to get preferential treatment?"

"I guess it worked."

"You're damn tootin it worked."

The funny thing was, the Captain never talked about his wartime experience. Whenever I'd ask him about it, he would change the subject. After a while I caught on that it was a forbidden topic, which wasn't unusual. A lot of vets didn't talk about their experiences. But then my mother told me something interesting a couple of years ago. According to her, my father didn't want to go to Korea since he had already served in the Second World War. His big mistake was signing on with the reserves for extra pay. He didn't expect to get called up since yours truly had just been born, but the Army had a little surprise for him: It needed experienced officers. I was six months old when he left. My mother, who had to raise me by herself for a year and a half, was fit to be tied. And who could blame her?

"So who is this Chesty person? She sounds like a hot one."

He laughs. "That's not a broad," he says. "We were talking about an officer. A division commander."

"Chesty?"

"Yeah, Chesty Puller. A legend in the Marines. Everybody knew about him. He was the hero of Chosin Reservoir."

"Never heard of it."

"Of course you never heard of it. Kids today don't know about Korea. But listen carefully and I'll give you a little history lesson." He flips down the visor to shield his eyes from the setting sun, which is strafing the windshield with blinding glare. "By November 1950," he begins, "our forces were almost to the Yalu River—the border between China and North Korea—when China entered the war. A quarter of a million Chinese troops waited in ambush on the heights above the Chosin Reservoir. They counterattacked and pinned us down."

"Wait a minute," I say, "I thought you didn't get there until the following year."

He looks at me a moment before answering. "I'm talking about our soldiers. Not me personally."

"Okay, so what happened?"

"So it's winter up there in the snow-covered mountains and it's freezing. They don't have proper winter gear and they're getting shot up left and right. When they run out of water, they start eating snow. The situation was desperate but Chesty orchestrated a textbook retreat in which he commanded the rearguard. He saved a lot of lives."

"I see now why Lephart was so impressed that you and Chesty were pals."

"It worked, didn't it?"

"Like a charm, Dad. *Semper fi.*"

"Maybe I led him on a bit. So sue me."

"Well I learned something. I had no idea you were in the Marines. All this time I thought you were in the Army."

"You see," he says, "you don't know everything about me."

"Apparently not."

"Yeah," he says, "I joined up briefly. Just long enough to visit your fuckin uncle."

WATERTOWN

My father hates motels. He calls them "rinky-dink" operations with little service and less class. Better to stay in a hotel, he says, and preferably the best there is, which is why we'll be stopping at the Woodford in Watertown. The Captain once stayed there for a coin convention sponsored by the North Country Numismatic Association. This was back when he had the store in Lynbrook and to make a few bucks he hustled to regional events a couple of weekends a month. So he's familiar with the Woodford, but it's also convenient.

Gene is to be arraigned in the morning before the honorable Alonso Larson, U.S. Commissioner for the Northern District of New York, whose law offices occupy a third-floor suite in the same hotel.

Spanning much of the long block fronting Watertown's Public Square, the five-story, red brick hotel, built in 1851, is by far the most imposing edifice in the heart of downtown. A shoe store, a travel agency and a candy shop rent space on the ground floor, but the windows of JJ Newberry's—a cut-rate department store—are empty. The vast lobby is still impressive, though the classical marble columns, the lazily revolving ceiling fans, and the decorously placed palm trees shading candy-apple-red couches seem far less appropriate to an industrial town half an hour from Canada than to some boiling equatorial capital. Several guests brandish after-dinner cigars, which serve to reinforce the pervasive odor of stale smoke. The Captain inhales deeply and looks around to reacquaint himself. Sure it's faded now, he concedes, but it must have been quite a scene in the 1890s, especially the grand lobby where Boswell P. Flower, Watertown's native son and the newly elected governor of New York, held court. He gestures across the black-and-white tiled lobby to where the polished mahogany balustrades of a marble stairway rise toward the mezzanine. If he's not mistaken, the bourse for the coin convention was located in the ballroom at the top of those stairs. I follow him to the front desk, with its antique wrought-iron grill, behind which a descendant of Ichabod Crane cannot seem to locate our reservation cards.

"Look again," says the Captain, leaving a five-dollar bill on the counter.

"Nothing to worry about, sir," says the gangly clerk, who suddenly whirls about and halfway through his pirouette plucks a key from a cabinet of pigeonholes. "Five twenty-one," he says, tapping a silver bell on the counter. "If you wait a moment, Harry will show you up."

"The dining room serves until what time?" asks my father.

The clerk grimaces. Dining services, it seems, shut down a month ago, but there's always the Italian place down the block. He smiles perfunctorily and hopes we will enjoy our stay.

"I'd enjoy it a lot more," my father says, "if it wasn't so damn hot." He uses the sleeve of his sport jacket to wipe the sweat from his eyes.

"All the rooms are air conditioned, sir. I'm sure you'll be comfortable."

"If I'm not, you'll hear about it." The bellhop, a grizzled cuss who looks to be pushing seventy, picks up our bags and plods across the lobby toward the bank of vintage elevators between the candy concession and the shoeshine stand.

"You look tired, Dad."

"I'll be fine as soon as I freshen up."

The Black River Restaurant is empty, save for the lone customer finishing his coffee. The waiter shows us to a table, deals out menus, insists that everything is good and urges us to order quickly as the kitchen is closing. The place is incredibly dark— above the walnut-stained booths, chocolate walls run up to a black, pressed-tin ceiling. A few frosted glass lamps fight the losing battle of illumination.

After we order, the Captain surprises me by asking about the robbery. I give him a full account and he listens carefully.

"It's a dangerous job," he says. "Thank God you're all right."

"Well, I'm through with it, Dad."

"That's good because there's no future in cab driving."

"I see that now."

"You need to concentrate on making something of yourself. You knuckle down now, Eddie, you can take it easy later."

"Okay, Dad."

"You know how many years it took me to make good? You're lucky. With the opportunities you have, you can do it in half the time. I just don't want you to waste them."

"I know, Dad." The Captain usually reserves his impromptu pep talks for the beginning of a semester. I assume he's referring to summer school, which has only been in session for two weeks.

"I know you think I'm hard on you, Eddie, but you don't know what life was like growing up in Rockaway. It was rough before my father got his patronage job. I remember one time when I was nine, my friends and I went down the block to the beach. My mother packed me a bologna sandwich and when she asked me later about lunch, I told her I wasn't that hungry so I threw half of it away. 'In this house,' she yelled, 'we don't throw out food,' and she cracked me across the face. Then she marched me down to the boardwalk and we went through all the garbage cans looking for it."

"Jesus, Dad, that's humiliating."

"That ain't the half of it. When we found the sandwich, she made me eat the damn thing, sand and all. You think I want you to live like that? So if I'm tough on you, it's because I know what it takes to get ahead."

The lecture is cut short by the arrival of the entrées. I could eat a horse, but the processed veal is deep-fried and coated, as is the overcooked spaghetti, in a maroon-colored sauce with a faintly metallic flavor. In addition, the bread is stale and the salad is swimming in dressing. Even the ginger ale is flat. You know the food is awful when you start yearning for half a bologna sandwich covered in sand.

The waiter trudges over to clear the dishes and inquire about dessert. My father shakes his head no.

"Me neither," I say. "Couldn't eat another bite."

The Captain shoots me his *Let's get the hell out of here* look, peels a twenty off his roll and drops it on the tablecloth. "Tell you one thing," he says. "It ain't Nino's."

He's so disgusted, I feel obliged to cheer him up. "Too bad we couldn't eat at the jail, huh, Dad?"

"Who knew?" he says. "Remind me next time to get Lephart to invite us to dinner."

After the morose interior of the restaurant, the lobby of the Woodford is bright and welcoming. We repair to the leather comfort of one of the couches, where the Captain goes through the ritual of lighting a Sultan. On the sofa opposite, a bearded man in an ink-stained khaki shirt nods to us and raises a brandy snifter. His brown hair is bushy and unkempt and he smokes with the deliberate movements of a man who has been drinking for hours.

"What do you think, Dad? Is the hotel like you remember it?"

"It wasn't as quiet," he says, "but then again there was a convention going on."

"She's dying," announces the man with the beard.

"Excuse me?"

"The hotel. She'll probably close in a few months."

"It's a shame," says the Captain, looking around the lobby as if to fix in his memory the details of its doomed design.

"Another victim of urban renewal," says the man, attempting to light a fresh Pall Mall from the remains of a filterless butt. "They're hoping to bring in new businesses to revitalize downtown, but the only thing that's booming is the fast food strip that runs out to the interstate. Makes me sick," he says, beckoning to the waiter. "People flock to the malls while the center of town goes to hell."

"Sounds like Long Island," I say, thinking of the cluttered

commercial avenues that feed on the unchecked development of Nassau County.

"They'll kill this town, the bastards." He points to a copy of the *Watertown Daily Times* that sprawls on the coffee table between the couches. "The local paper is all for it. You watch. Pretty soon they'll take the wrecking ball to this place, and they'll demolish the city's soul. Then where will I drink? Howard Johnson's? The Marriott? God help me." The man orders another cognac and insists on buying us a round.

I glance at a headline that reads, "Inquiry Links the White House to Political Sabotage Scheme." I skim the article, which mentions GOP attempts to disrupt the campaigns of Democratic presidential candidates in 1972. A sentence catches my eye: "The secret operations at their height embraced a widely scattered and sometimes disorganized network of amateurs who engaged in political pranks as well as more serious, and even violent, activities."

The man is explaining the role of the hotel as a gathering place for the city's residents.

"Mind if I take the paper?"

He waves me off and keeps talking. "Old Norris must be turning over in his grave," he says. My father and I look at each other and the man laughs. "I take it you have yet to be introduced to Norris Woodford. Fellow who built it." He points to the portraits in the gilt frames on either side of the fireplace, where Mr. and Mrs. Woodford gaze stoically across the lobby with an air of resignation. "Good old Norris," he says. "They say that when the hotel first opened, it would get so cold in the rooms the guests would come down here and finish dressing in front of the fireplace. Isn't that right, Nick?"

"That's what they say, Mr. Dexter."

"But not in this heat," he says. "I doubt anyone will be dressing in the lobby tomorrow morning." The waiter is centering our drinks on cocktail napkins: Courvoisier for Mr. Dexter; Chivas neat for the Captain; Heineken for me. My father lifts the glass to savor the aroma of the whiskey. "Gentlemen," says Mr. Dexter, raising his snifter, "may you already be in heaven before the Devil knows you're dead." We drink and exchange introductions.

"What line of work are you in, Mr. Dexter?"

"I indite, sir."

"You work for the D.A.'s office?" asks my father.

"God, no," he says."

"So where do you practice?"

"I don't."

"He's not a lawyer, Dad, he's a writer." Mr. Dexter regards me for a moment, his eyes bright with interest or booze.

"That is correct, young man. 'To indite' as in 'to write' or 'to compose.' Your son, Mr. Sacks, is a clever young man."

"I wish he was clever enough to get a haircut."

"I can't help you there," he says, running his hand through a mass of wild hair. "Afraid I'm not much for neatness."

"What kind of writing do you do?"

"Well, Mr. Sacks, my work tends to occupy that ambiguous no-man's land between fiction and nonfiction. My publisher calls it 'fictional memoir.'"

"So you're published?"

"I am, sir. The book gods have smiled upon me."

"Sounds autobiographical," I say.

"What writing isn't?" he asks, though the question comes out more like a statement. "Let's just say I manage to salvage art from the shipwreck of my ill-adventured youth."

"What does that mean?" the Captain wants to know.

"It means I live a self-destructive life, sir, but people will pay good money to read about it."

"Must be tough on your liver," I say.

"Not to mention my other organs."

A gentleman in a three-piece suit who is passing by pauses to pat Mr. Dexter on the shoulder. "What are you up to, Dex?"

"Not much, Jack. Biding my time until football season." As he departs, Mr. Dexter raises his glass in the man's direction. "One of our prominent defense attorneys. He handles a lot of drug-related cases."

"I wonder what he thinks of the new law," I say. In September, when Governor Rockefeller's draconian drug law takes effect, jail sentences for sale and possession will be much stiffer.

"They had to do something," says the Captain.

"Have you looked at the penalties, Dad? Somebody who gets convicted of selling a joint can go to jail for seven years. It's ridiculous."

"You have to get the pushers off the streets somehow."

"The jails will be so full of nonviolent offenders, there won't be any room for the violent criminals."

"You don't know what you're talking about, Eddie. Stiffer penalties will act as a deterrent. It's as simple as that."

"That's right, Dad, a deterrent to plea bargaining. More defendants will opt to go to trial because with mandatory sentencing they'll have nothing to lose. In the end it will be far more expensive for the state, and the court system will be inundated."

"Inundated my ass," says the Captain. "They're going to hire a hundred new judges."

"Actually, Mr. Sacks, I believe your son has a point."

"Is that so?"

"Judges will have far less discretion in their sentencing guidelines. Imagine, Mr. Sacks, some harmless guy who likes to smoke a little pot. A college kid, not unlike your son. He gets caught with an ounce of grass—a small bag that takes up no more volume than one of your cigars—and now he's looking at fifteen years."

My father eyes me through the haze of cigar smoke. "Then he's an idiot to be fooling with marijuana."

"People do a lot of illegal things, Mr. Sacks, especially when they don't perceive them to be immoral."

"The way I see it, Mr. Dexter, the law is the law, whether we like it or not, and we owe a certain responsibility to our families to abide by it."

"Come on, Dad, you've never broken a law when you thought it was inane or archaic or out of touch with reality?" Although I'm not about to bring it up, smuggling silver in from Canada comes to mind. "How about speeding, Dad? How many times have you gotten a speeding ticket?"

"Speeding doesn't kill you. Drugs do." Mr. Dexter and I look at each other and I roll my eyes, an impulse that provokes his immediate and boisterous laughter.

The Captain stands abruptly. "I'm ready for bed."

"Wait a minute, Dad. I haven't finished my beer."

"Now, Eddie."

"Big day tomorrow?"

"I'm afraid so, Mr. Dexter."

"Well, don't let me keep you," he says, lighting with difficulty another Pall Mall.

"Thanks for the drink."

"Don't mention it, sir. Goodnight." He punctuates these pleasantries with a slight bow of his head. "Oh, and don't be alarmed if you hear any strange noises during the night. They're pretty common in an old building like this. The maids say it's the ghost of Mrs. Woodford making her rounds, but I wouldn't put any stock in it."

"Let's go!" the Captain says, and strides off toward the marble staircase, which he takes two steps at a time. I find him on the mezzanine, bent over and breathing hard.

"You okay, Dad?"

Refusing to look at me, he straightens up and hurries down the hall.

"What the heck is the matter with you?"

He stops abruptly and glares at me, arms folded, as I approach.

"You know, Eddie," he says, "it's one thing to make me the butt of a joke, but to enlist a stranger to do it, that I don't appreciate."

"I didn't realize you were so thin-skinned."

"There's nothing funny about your disrespect."

"Oh, for godsake."

"I'm waiting."

"All right, I apologize. Now will you lighten up."

"I got news for you," he says, "this *is* light for me."

Our room is roasting. The a.c. drones ineffectually as if it were set to fan. I suggest that we keep running it for the white noise, but my objection is overruled. The Captain wrestles open a window to the listless night, and we bake in our underwear while my father complains that his mattress reminds him of the Great Depression. I sympathize but I have my own problem, a lumpy pillow. I turn it repeatedly, searching in vain for a cool spot on the pillowcase. Finally I drift off to the faint creaking of floorboards, as though some overstimulated guest were trying to pace off his insomnia.

At five-fifteen I thrash awake, entangled in a sweat-soaked sheet, to find the Captain, already dressed, playing solitaire at the writing desk.

"You might as well wake up," he says, and lobs a small bottle of shampoo onto the bed. I groan and roll over. "Let's go, Eddie. Shit, shower and shine." I grope my way to the bathroom, hoping a quick shower will somehow compensate for a lack of sleep. When that fails, my brain yearns for caffeine. Across from the hotel, on the other side of the square, a neon sign in the window of a hash house proclaims the WORLD'S STRONGEST COFFEE. Either the waitress mismeasured or, more likely, the boast is the punch line to a local joke. We dawdle over breakfast and three cups of the insipid brew, then stroll back to the hotel where we still have hours to kill. My dad fires up a Sultan while I read the *Watertown Daily Times*, poring over John Mitchell's testimony before the Senate Watergate Committee. Mitchell claims he vetoed the Watergate break-in and believes that Nixon didn't participate in the cover-up. I don't buy a word of it, but I know better than to vent to my father the depths of my skepticism. I steal a glance at him as he puffs and fumes—a man with no capacity to wait.

The arraignment takes no more than ten minutes. When we enter the law offices with the local lawyer and the bailbondsman,

Gene is already there, standing next to a couple of guys in khaki slacks and plaid sport shirts. They are special agents from the Customs Service with whom he banters easily as his cuffs are removed. The commissioner, having ascertained that the necessary parties are present, explains the purpose of the appearance, which is simply to lay a formal charge that serves to jumpstart the legal proceedings and, if appropriate, to set an amount for the bond. Gene will not be asked to enter a plea because under federal rules a commissioner cannot accept one—only a district court judge can do that. The Customs agents, who represent the interests of the U.S. Attorney's office, inform the commissioner of the criminal violation: 18USC545 of the U.S. Code. In layman's terms, smuggling. The commissioner poses a series of questions to determine if Gene is a flight risk: Is he married? Does he own a house? Does he have a job? Luckily, Gene's status as a New York City employee qualifies him for a bond, set at four thousand dollars, of which the Captain puts up ten percent. As soon as the documents are signed, Gene is free to go. He's so happy, he shakes hands all around, even with the commissioner. The Customs agents clap him on the back and tell him to stay out of trouble.

"Don't worry," he says, "I won't even jaywalk." He bounces out the door and when we get to the elevators he executes an impromptu jig. "Man," he says, "I feel great."

"Tell us in the car," says the Captain. "It's a long drive back to the city." Gene wants to take a walk, get some fresh air, and savor his freedom. We agree to meet in the lobby in twenty minutes. The Captain insists I chaperone my uncle to make sure he doesn't get into trouble, then takes an elevator up to the room.

Gene throws an arm around my shoulders and wants to know if I'm holding.

"You really think that's a good idea, man?"

"Come on, will you. I'm dying for a hit." We jaywalk across to the Public Square, past an empty fountain in which an ornate stone pedestal supports the statue of a dancing woman, barefoot beneath a diaphanous gown. Without a pool of water to set her off, she seems incomplete, like a diamond without a setting. "Nice-looking babe," says Gene.

"I guess every man wants a woman he can look up to."

"I'll tell you something, kid, as soon as I get back to the city, I'm ready for some R & R. I know this place in Chinatown. For twenty bucks you get a massage and a hand job."

"Places like that actually exist?"

"Oh they exist all right. This one's on Bayard, right behind the court buildings. You go in, you put your stuff in a locker, you take a steam, then they give you an hour-long massage and— " He mimes an obscene gesture.

"Good hand job?" I ask, prying the flattened joint from my wallet.

"Not bad."

"Do you have to give the girl a tip or can you just stiff her?"

"Very funny," he says.

"How's the massage?"

"Pretty good. They walk on your back in their bare feet."

"Nice looking?"

He shrugs. "Asian women—thin, nice ass, no tits—but good personalities. Very accommodating."

"Who goes to this place?" I ask. I'm rolling the joint between my fingers, reshaping it into a cylinder. "I mean, besides you."

"Look, it's for guys who don't have wives or girlfriends and stay out till all hours. It gives them somewhere to go to round out the night. You shoot your wad and you go home and fall asleep."

"So what do they use to perform this particular service?"

"Baby oil."

"They use both hands?"

"Yeah, they use both hands. Sometimes they rub your balls at the same time, but the best thing is when they massage your sphincter."

"With a finger?"

"Sometimes the finger, sometimes the big toe."

"Get out of here."

"I'm telling you, these Oriental women are unbelievable. They know how to do this stuff."

"They push their big toe into your asshole?"

"Well they use lubrication, don't forget. What do you say? You want to check it out?"

"I'll think about it."

"While you're thinking, would you mind lighting up the joint?"

"Listen, Gene, you sure we should get stoned out in the open like this? What if a cop comes by?"

"Give me a break, man. Who the hell is going to see?" The driver of a red pickup looks us over as he whizzes by within spitting distance.

"Look around, will you. We're in the middle of everything here."

"I got an idea," he says. We hunker down in the dry bed of the fountain, cross-legged like little kids, so that the rim of the stone basin obscures our activities from the glances of passing motorists and the prying eyes of guests on the upper floors of the hotel. Gene has several tokes and hands me what's left of the joint. I take a huge hit and hold it, but only for a few seconds before exhaling in a spasm of coughing.

"You'll be all right," he says, and slaps me on the back. I double over, eyes tearing, gasping for air. To catch my breath I scramble to my feet and steady myself against the wrought-iron railing that rings the fountain. I could use a drink of water and consider a short walk to the WORLD'S STRONGEST COFFEE shop, but a pleasant inertia renders such exertion hypothetical. World's strongest coffee—what a laugh! And you want to hear another good one? How about "Public Square"? Look at it—it isn't a square at all but an elongated oval not twenty feet wide. Aside from the fountain, there's just a Soldiers' and Sailors' Monument at one end and some old stone benches at the other. I mean, what were they thinking, the city fathers, trying to squeeze in such a piss-poor excuse for a park? Beyond the meager shade of a half dozen trees, the withered turf is an uninviting patchwork of faded green and straw-colored tufts. Not that it matters. The narrow common is encircled by one-way thoroughfares, and traffic careens around it with such velocity that only a couple of desperate potheads like us will risk using it. No wonder the center of town is dying.

"What's wrong with you, Ed? You're giggling like a moron."

"Oh, man, I'm stoned."

"Get a hold of yourself. You see me acting like an idiot?"

We start back to the hotel and Gene darts into the street like a halfback cradling an imaginary pigskin, stiff-arming would-be tacklers and dodging oncoming cars. He celebrates a touchdown as Leo walks out of the hotel with our bags. Our frivolous behavior dissipates under the Captain's sobering gaze.

"Get in the car," he says. He flips me the keys to the Caddy. "You drive."

"That's okay, Dad. I really don't feel like it." I've driven stoned any number of times but never while the Captain was in the car.

"Don't argue with me, Eddie. I've been up most of the night and I'm exhausted."

"I'm kind of out of it myself." I cast about for any excuse that can free me from the task of driving, but I'm so high that words and phrases struggle vainly in the scrum of consciousness to cohere into organized thoughts.

"Go ahead. Take the wheel."

"Why don't I take the first shift?" says Gene.

"You?" says Leo. "I wouldn't let you drive my lawn mower."

"Jerk," mutters Gene. He climbs in next to me while my father stows the bags in the trunk. I buckle the seatbelt, adjust the mirrors and fiddle with the electronic controls to the front seat. Then I take a deep breath and let it out.

"Look at you," whispers Gene, "you're fuckin wrecked."

"Got any advice?"

"'Yeah," he says. "Keep your eyes on the road and your hands upon the wheel."

My father sprawls across the rear seat and tells me to put it in gear. I throw the transmission into drive and we lurch forward, the powerful engine straining against implacable resistance. "The car rides a lot smoother," he says, "when you disengage the emergency brake."

My uncle cracks up.

"Shut up, Gene." I release the brake and ease the enormous Caddy into traffic. My eyes are constantly roaming. I survey the road, consult my mirrors and monitor the instrument panel. Every stop is smooth, every acceleration gradual. By the time I merge onto the interstate, my father is snoring peacefully. Gene is describing the spanking new unmarked Ford the Customs agents drive—a snazzy, two-tone Galaxie with a black roof and an orange-brown body. Although agency regulations prohibited them from discussing the actual specs of the police interceptor engine, Gene estimates the maximum horsepower and the volume it displaces in cubic inches. The police package is decent, he admits, but his souped-up Camaro would "wipe its ass" in a quarter-mile heat. This is Gene's specialty—suppositions that can never be verified.

The hours pass. I drive, Leo sleeps, Gene talks. He relates the story of his arrest in agonizing detail, kicking himself for being so greedy, second-guessing the way he greeted the Customs inspector and pitying himself for his legal troubles. He claims he's learned some bitter lessons from his misadventure.

"Like what? Not to engage in illegal activities?"

"Fuck, no," he says. "Not to get caught."

We stop for dinner in the Catskills, after which the Captain takes the wheel and we ride the rest of the way back to the city in silence.

From the George Washington Bridge, the riverside down to the Seventy-ninth Street boat basin is laid out in the soft summer twilight like an old-time postcard. I wish I could enjoy it, but all my problems are rushing back like rowdy students from recess. Where am I sleeping tonight? When do I get my things? Where am I taking them? What do I say to Randi? When do I tell my parents about Europe?

I don't want to think about any of it.

The Captain has business in Midtown, so we drop Gene at the subway and pull into a parking lot.

"Where are we going?"

"A restaurant. Walk faster."

"I'm not that hungry. We just ate." The Captain gives me that look of exasperation my questions never fail to elicit.

"Why do you have to know everything?"

"Why do you have to keep me in the dark?"

"There's someone I want you to meet. Okay? You happy now?"

"Who?"

"When I want you to know I'll tell you."

He ushers me under a rust-colored awning into Gallagher's Steak House. After a tantalizing peek through the street window into its meat locker, the reception area offers a more expansive view of the cold room. Through large picture windows underscored by polished brass rails, shells of porterhouse bound in layers of fat sit on rows of slatted shelves like bookcases stacked with beef. I follow my father to the horseshoe-shaped bar, where the bartender greets him like a long-lost Irish cousin.

"A pleasure it is to see you, Mr. Sacks."

"How's everything, Pat?"

"Oh, grand," Pat says, "everything is just grand," and raps his knuckles smartly on the bar.

"Have you seen my friend around?"

He nods to the alcove, a small dining area just beyond the bar. "Corner table," he says, "under Man O' War."

The room has the generic look of a lot of steak houses: red-checked tablecloths, oak-paneled walls, unpolished plank floors. A gallery of champion thoroughbreds decorates the far wall—Citation, of course, War Admiral, Assault. Displayed above their portraits are colorful caricatures of well-known jockeys.

An elderly gentleman is bent over his plate, his well-tanned scalp showing off his thinning white hair. He's dressed immaculately in blue blazer and white shirt—no tie—with cufflinks fashioned from ten-dollar gold pieces that catch the light as he saws away at his meal, a slab of calf's liver smothered in onions.

"Look who's here," he says, without looking up. "I hope you'll forgive me for not waiting."

"Sorry we're late. It was a long drive."

"I'm sure it was. Sit, sit," he gestures. "What can I get you?"

"We're fine," says my dad. "We ate a couple of hours ago."

"This must be your son," he says, fixing me with his milky blue eyes. "He could use a haircut, of course, but he's good-looking, Leo. Reminds me of myself when I was his age."

"Eddie, meet Foxy Rosenthal." My benefactor carefully sets down his utensils and picks up a napkin before offering a bony liver-spotted hand.

"So you're the great underachiever. What do you have to say for yourself?" Right away he starts giving me the business, the old bird.

"Right now I'm just an old lump of coal, sir, but I hope to be a diamond some day."

He pounds his fist on the table and laughs until he starts to cough. "That's a good one," he says. When he coughs, wattles of loose skin tremble at his neck.

"And with your help, Foxy, we can polish him up."

"We'll see what we can do, Leo. He's got a sense of humor."

"Yes, he does," says the Captain, "but humor and charm only get you so far."

Foxy waves over the waiter. "Would you be good enough to take this away, Kevin, and bring us some coffee?" He's left half his portion untouched.

"Shall I wrap it up for you, Mr. Rosenthal?"

"Are you kidding? That's tomorrow's breakfast." The waiter laughs with forced enthusiasm and I wonder how many times Foxy has used the same line. "Best liver and onions in New York. Right, Kevin?"

"Right, Mr. Rosenthal."

"And we'll have cheesecake all around." Foxy takes a pill from a small enamel box and chases it with water. "It's no good to get old, my friends." He gazes wistfully at the photos of old ballplayers on the wall. "I'll tell you something," he says. "You know when I first came in here? 1927, the year it opened."

"That's going back," says my father.

"You know who opened it, don't you?"

"Let me take a wild guess," I say. "Gallagher?"

"*Helen* Gallagher," says Foxy, "and a hell of a gal at that."

"Wasn't she a Ziegfeld girl?" asks the Captain.

"That's right. A real beauty, and the wife of Ed Gallagher who was half of Gallagher and Shean, the great vaudeville act. Well after Gallagher died, Helen married Jack Solomon, who was a gambler and a restaurateur and kind of a Runyonesque character, and the two of them opened this place. Not as a steak house, mind you, but as a speakeasy. And everybody came."

"How do you like that?" says the Captain. "I had no idea."

"It wasn't till after Prohibition that the place became a steak house. But it was really the first one to have that flavor of a country inn with the red tablecloths and the wooden walls and the oak beams in the ceiling."

"So if I'm hearing you right, Mr. Rosenthal, you're saying this is the original steak house and everybody copied it."

"Very good. But that's what happens in this country when you have a good idea. Imitation is the highest form of compliment." The waiter sets out cups of coffee and places before each of us a hefty wedge of cheesecake. Foxy samples the coffee and dabs his lips with a napkin. "Take Morningside Chapels," he continues. "We were the first to conduct simultaneous funerals so that the guests at each ceremony perceive theirs is the only event happening in the building. That concept, which we call 'intimate grief,' the industry learned that from us. And you know how we did that?" He waits for a reply like it's a pop quiz.

"I don't know," I say, "staggered starting times? So all the services don't start at once?"

Foxy stares at me. "How did you know that?"

"Lucky guess."

"Get a load of this kid, Leo. It took me years to figure that out. Tell you what, Eddie, your law career doesn't pan out, you can come work for me in the funeral business."

What should I say, I wonder? That I'm dying to work for him? "Thank you, sir. I'll keep that in mind."

"You do that. So what's the news, Leo? Good or bad?"

"It's all taken care of." My father attacks his dessert.

"You sure? Because at my age, I can't afford this nonsense."

"He's playing ball. I promise you."

"I hope so. You know I just got word Columbia wants to name a building after me."

"That's a great honor, Foxy. Mazel tov."

"But they don't name buildings after felons."

"Believe me, Foxy, you got nothing to worry about."

"Congratulations, Mr. Rosenthal. You must be very proud."

"Thanks, kid. Of course there is one catch. Before they get the money to start construction I have to die first." He tastes a tiny piece of cheesecake. "Mmmm," he says, "delicious."

In the panoramic photo above the table, Man O' War is winning the Dwyer at Aqueduct by two lengths. The date, oddly enough, is July 10th, 1920, fifty-three years ago to the day. I wonder if this is some kind of sign that I'm supposed to be here tonight shmoozing with the great Foxy Rosenthal—funeral home mogul, philanthropist and Columbia Law School booster—who, out of the goodness of his heart, is going to pave my way to a golden future. I sip my coffee as he enjoys another fastidious forkful.

"Don't forget to take care of your end," says the Captain.

"I'll put Kornblatt on it. Tell Gene to expect a call."

"Sounds good, Foxy."

"Then we can put this business behind us." He notices I'm not eating. "What's the matter, kid? You're not hungry?"

"I'm full," I say.

"You don't know what you're missing," he says.

"Take a taste," says the Captain. "Live a little."

"That's okay. I don't want any."

"Go ahead. Eat some cheesecake."

"No, thank you."

My father, having demolished his massive piece, eyes mine greedily. "You sure?"

"I'm sure. Would you like it?"

"Have a bite. It isn't going to kill you."

"For the last time, Dad, I'm not hungry."

To Foxy, he says, "Do you believe this kid?"

"It's his loss," says Foxy. "No one's going to force him."

The two of them look at me like I'm nuts as I push away the untouched plate of cheesecake. My father pulls it toward him and goes to town.

AMSTERDAM

We're zipping along the L.I.E., where the hills stretch away, landscaped in tombstones. The Captain is whistling "Sidewalks of New York," his pudgy fingers tapping out the rhythm on the steering wheel, when he smacks the dashboard and his high-pitched cackle bursts from the back of his throat like a machine gun.

"I gotta give it to you," he says. "You killed him. You charmed the fuckin pants off of him. Staggered starting times! And that line about the lump of coal..." He shakes his head like he can't get over it.

"You think I passed the audition?"

"Are you kidding? Foxy loved you."

"Why? What did he say?"

"Nothing. I could tell."

"You couldn't warn me?"

"For what? You would have been nervous."

"Well don't get too excited. Things can still go wrong."

"What are you worried about? You're as good as in." He waves away any doubts with a sweep of his hand. "I see great things for you, Eddie. Great things. Hey, what could be better than Columbia Law School? It's a dream come true." He resumes his whistling and I realize I haven't seen him this excited since he hit the big exacta at Belmont.

Unfortunately, one man's dream is another man's nightmare. While my father is convinced that the only route to my future lies on the well-traveled expressway to law school, I keep itching to exit onto some unexplored side street, where through luck and serendipity I might stumble on a passion and a calling. Coward that I am, I'm afraid to propose what I desperately desire because I know he'll blow up.

I roll down the window to get some air. The cemetery rests in peace in the summer night and why the hell shouldn't it? What do the dead have to kick about? Nothing. They've got no worries now, the lucky bastards. You think any of them are turning over in their graves? Don't bet on it. Maybe it's a failure of my paltry imagination, but the notion of restless spirits who haunt the places where they died or the homes in which they once resided is just too silly for words. As the Captain would say, it's a load of crap. What seems all too likely, I'm afraid, is that consciousness expires with the body and that in the democratic country of death the mortal coils of the *hoi polloi* decay as inexorably under their headstones as those of the rich and powerful inside their marble monuments.

A white-columned, neoclassical memorial occupies a private knoll above Maspeth and I wonder whose remains are entombed within. What was it Foxy said? There was only one catch to having a building named after him; he'd have to die first? Could that

be the sort of extravagant resting place where Foxy plans to molder
for eternity? Because that is one old buzzard who won't be buried
in a simple grave. He'll have one of those shiny caskets lined with
satin and a thousand mourners to see him off and Mayor Lindsay
himself as one of his pallbearers.

"What are you thinking about?" asks the Captain.

"Nothing."

"Well think about this. I want you to work for me again. You
don't have a job, and I need someone I can trust to run silver in
from the airport."

"Are you asking me or telling me?"

"Would I force you to do something you didn't want to?"

"Not you, Dad."

"You drove my car so well, I'm going to let you take the Caddy."
He lets this sink in for a moment before adding the inevitable
conditions. "Just remember one thing. You can listen to any of
that rock crap to your heart's content but leave the radio set to my
stations."

"Whatever you say."

"Good. You start tomorrow."

I ought to get it out in the open right now that I'm quitting
summer school and leaving for Europe, secrets that loom ahead
like the pair of brick-red gas tanks that dwarf the homes of Elm-
hurst. But I can't. My father is in too good a mood and I don't
have the heart to confront him. I'll do it tomorrow, I decide, when
I'm not so exhausted. Tomorrow will be soon enough for the
opening salvo of the next war.

If my mother is happy to see me, it's hard to tell from her
greeting: "Hello, stranger. What are you doing here?"

"It's nice to see you too," I say. "I thought I'd visit for a while."

"What's a while?" she demands, as I peck her dutifully on the cheek.

"I don't know, Ma. Until I find a place."

"What's wrong with this place?"

"Who said anything was wrong with it?" I trudge up the stairs and enter the time warp that is my bedroom. Same wallpaper of cowboys around a campfire; same volumes of the Hardy Boys on the bookshelf. A Battle of Gettysburg diorama, a poster for an anti-war rally, my college pennant tacked above the doorway, it's all here—the familiar roomful of eclectic items that constitutes the permanent collection of the museum of me.

I flop on the bed, my eyes drawn to a framed front page of the *Daily News* that memorialized Woodstock: HIPPIES MIRED IN SEA OF MUD. Except for vacations, I haven't lived at home for four years and thought I never would again. True, it's only for a week, but the words *I have to get out of here* cycle in my mind like a mantra. When my parents retire to their bedroom, I sneak downstairs to watch TV. *Invasion of the Body Snatchers* is on, but I fall asleep before the small-town doctor discovers what is turning his neighbors into aliens. Next thing I know, my mother is standing over me, tapping my shoulder, and the TV is broadcasting a test pattern, which is accompanied by an unpleasant whine. "Eddie," she shouts, her curlers secure under a plastic shower cap, "it's three o'clock in the morning. Wake up and go to bed."

I don't bring up Europe at breakfast, and I say nothing on the way to the station, where the Captain catches the 8:17 while I head over to the air cargo depot at JFK. There's no time to discuss it at the store after I drop off the day's shipment and before I leave for class. Neither can I see broaching the topic on the afternoon run to Wall Street, where we deposit thirty-eight thousand-dollar bags of silver coin in the theft-proof vaults of Irving Trust, nor on the hour-long commute home.

After dinner while Goldie tidies up the kitchen, the Captain and I adjourn to the den to watch the rebroadcast of John Mitchell's testimony before the Watergate Committee. Mitchell, the former attorney general, is admitting he withheld information from the President regarding the break-in and the cover-up. Had Nixon been informed, Mitchell explains, the President would have had no choice but to punish the culprits. The public repudiations of those involved would have tarnished Nixon's credibility and damaged his reelection bid, an outcome Mitchell intended to prevent by keeping the President in the dark.

To someone who despises Nixon and his cohort, Mitchell's defense presents an irresistible irony. During his tenure as the nation's chief law officer, he knowingly obstructed justice. Mitchell's story is that he concealed from the President not only the larcenous behavior of the "plumbers"—the men who broke into Democratic National Committee Headquarters—but also the criminal actions of the White House aides who paid off the burglars to maintain their silence. Mitchell describes three disturbing meetings with G. Gordon Liddy, who laid out in elaborate detail a variety of crackpot schemes. These included kidnapping protestors at the Republican National Convention, hiring prostitutes to compromise Democratic candidates, engaging in electronic surveillance, even deploying a "chase plane" to shadow the Democratic nominee's airliner and bug its radio communications. All of these stratagems Mitchell claims to have rejected out of hand.

Three times. The Watergate burglary, part of the scaled-down version of Liddy's secret operation, was somehow implemented, but Mitchell swears he never endorsed the plan. Yeah, right.

My mother brings in dessert, a tray of attractive parfaits—layers of raspberry Jello and Cool Whip, topped by a maraschino cherry.

"Something new," she says.

"Looks great, Mom."

"I think you'll like it. I got the recipe from—"

"Be quiet!" thunders the Captain, as he pounds the padded armrest of the Stratolounger. "I'm trying to listen."

"Jesus," she says in a forceful stage whisper, "what a killjoy."

Senator Weicker is questioning the witness from a seat on the elevated dais: "Now you have indicated that in hindsight you probably should have thrown him out of the office—"

Mitchell removes the pipe from his mouth and interjects, "Out of the window," delivering the line with perfect timing.

"Do you believe this guy?" I say. "It's like the emperor's new clothes. Everybody knows he's full of it, but they have to take him seriously. I wouldn't be surprised if he turned to the camera and gave us a big wink."

"What the hell is wrong with you?" says my father. "The man is incriminating himself. He may be looking at a prison sentence and you think he's playing some kind of game."

"According to you he's going to some minimum-security country club."

"Don't be so high and mighty."

"Honestly, Dad, you don't think he knew what Liddy was up to? Even if he didn't, which I doubt, he had to have briefed Nixon."

"I believe him."

"Give me a break. The guy's a stone-faced liar. Look at him: So witty and arrogant and full of himself. None of the senators are buying this."

"Buying what?" asks my mother. "What's going on?"

"Mitchell says he didn't tell Nixon about the break-in or the cover-up. He's taking the fall so Nixon won't be implicated."

"You don't know what you're talking about," says the Captain. "His testimony is completely plausible."

"Oh, come on, Dad."

"I have news for you, wiseguy, not every Republican is a liar."

"No, Dad, not every Republican. Just the politicians."

"Don't talk to me, will you please?"

"What did I say?" I ask my mother.

"You know what your problem is?" he snaps. "You got no respect for authority."

"You had to get him started," says Goldie.

"It doesn't take much."

"Shut up!" he says, collapsing the footrest and rising out of the recliner. "Do me a favor and shut the hell up."

"Why should I?" I shout, squaring off with my outraged father, armed with a slender parfait glass in one hand and a long-handled dessert spoon in the other.

"Will you two grow up? You're behaving like children."

Silenced by my mother's rebuke, we stare at each other warily.

"Honestly, do you have to fight about every little thing?"

"Nobody's fighting," my father says, taking his seat. "We're having a heated discussion is all."

"Oh, is that what you call it? I know five-year-olds who act more mature." We stare morosely at the TV screen as my mother berates us. "At least have the decency to fight over something important."

"This is important, Mom. The President could be impeached."

"Impeached, my ass," says the Captain. "There's no way that'll happen."

"Explain something to me," my mother says, nibbling a cherry. "It's Mitchell's word against Dean's, right? So how will they ever be able to prove what Nixon knew? It's a big waste of time, if you ask me. But don't let that stop you. Go ahead and kill each other."

Goldie has a point. Without evidence to verify the truth, the whole Senate inquiry is little more than a charade to satisfy the public.

The telephone rings.

"Hi, honey. When are you coming to dinner?" Goldie laughs. "That's cute, Randi, but I don't think one meal will jeopardize your standing as a starving artist. Hold on." She hands me the receiver. "It's your cousin."

"What a surprise!" I say, much too blithely.

"When the fuck did you get back?" Randi's husky voice is playful and taunting.

"Great. Oh, yeah, terrific. How are you?"

"How the fuck should I be?"

"No kidding? That's fantastic."

My father tells me to take the call elsewhere so I run up to my bedroom and grab the upstairs extension.

"Ooh," Randi says, "heavy breathing. I like that."

"I've been meaning to call you," I say, disregarding her remark.

"But you lost my number. Is that it?"

"I've been really busy, Randi. I started working for my father again and I'm attending classes and—"

"You know what I'm doing right now?"

"I have no idea."

"I'll give you a hint. It's erotic." She whispers into the phone how she is fingering herself and pinching her nipples. "Fuck, that feels good." She moans and I imagine a languorous hand plucking indolently at those enticing thimbles of flesh while a trembling fingertip explores the moist, exquisite folds of her cunt.

"Come on, Randi, what the heck are you doing?"

"You know what I'm doing, so why don't you come over here and fuck me?" Visions of Randi submitting to my masterful will increase the burgeoning pressure of my erection. I want to go over there and fuck her, all right, fuck her for hours until her legs turn to jelly. But then the grip of my sexual fantasies abates and I remember my resolve to end it, grasping with trenchant clarity the stupidity of overriding my intuition.

I tell her it's impossible tonight. I can't.

Of all her spur-of-the-moment invitations since we started seeing each other in March, this is the first one I've rejected, and I don't know which of us is more surprised. I should add something definite—that I don't feel good about what we're doing, that it's time for us to move on—but I know such endgames are best played out in person and surely I've dropped, for the time being, an unmistakable hint.

"When can I see you?" she wants to know.

"Soon."

"What the fuck does that mean?"

"Saturday." I resolve to end it when I see her.

"Okay. Not too early. I have to work."

"Not too early" probably means one, so on Saturday I borrow the Caddy and pull up to her building about ten. After mulling it over for three days I've decided to get my stuff, dash off a note and split. Sure it's a cop-out, but I know myself too well. If Randi shows up, I'll probably take one look at her and jump into bed.

Inside her place I feel like an intruder. I gather my possessions as quickly as possible. I never think I own very much until I have to move. I'm surprised at how many trips it takes to lug my clothes, furnishings, books, record albums and stereo components down to the car. When it's all stowed snugly in the trunk and the back seat, I run upstairs to take one last look. I'm taping a note to the refrigerator when Randi walks in.

She looks incredible. Her white uniform, transparent with perspiration, adheres to her skin in dark, alluring patches like damp caresses. Brushing her hair from her eyes, she smiles and is about to say something but stops when I look at the floor instead of smiling back.

"I didn't think I was going to see you," I say, gesturing to the note on the fridge.

"What the fuck is this?" she says. "You're not staying?"

"My father needs the car."

"You weren't going to see me?"

I shrug. "I was going to write from Amsterdam."

"You mean you were just going to disappear? 'Thanks a lot, babe, but I gotta ramble on'?"

"Come on, Randi, I can't hack this. I'm constantly worried that we're going to get caught."

She shakes her head, lights a Marlboro, exhales and looks at me.

"You're a real shit, you know that?"

"You're right. I could've handled it better." Even as I'm ending it, part of me is hoping I'll come to my senses, rip off her uniform and have her right here on the floor. *Are you nuts, Eddie? You'll never have sex as naughty and exciting as this. Apologize before it's too late!*

"Where's my ashtray? I hope you didn't take my fuckin ashtray."

"Just a bath towel and the complimentary shampoo."

"Asshole."

"The only thing I took is that drawing of you. The self-portrait."

"The nude?"

"Well, you gave it to me, didn't you?"

"Have fun jackin off to it."

"Come on, Randi—"

"Fuckin bastard."

"I'm sorry. Okay?"

"Leave me the fuck alone."

My father always says, "Get out while the getting is good." So I go quickly, without a last lingering look or a final hurtful remark, fleeing down the creaky flight of stairs to the merciful refuge of the Caddy.

At home I find a postcard protruding from the brass mail slot of the front door. Van Gogh, ear bandaged, smokes a pipe, accusing me with his eyes. (It seems to be my day for self-portraits.)

Except for the address, which has been outlined in black marker and walled off into an eye-catching rectangle, the capital letters of my friend's neat, precise hand occupy all available space on the back of the card:

SACKS, AMSTERDAM IS OVERRUN WITH UGLY AMERICANS AND I REGRET TO INFORM YOU THAT SHAPIRO IS ONE OF THEM. HE HATES MUSEUMS AND REFUSES TO "PIPE DOWN." I MENTION I LOVE VERMEER; HE SAYS HE PREFERS HEINEKEN. HE HAS A WAY, I ADMIT, WITH THE COMELY DUTCH GIRLS, WHO FOR REASONS I FAIL TO FATHOM FIND HIS BLATANT INSINCERITY AMUSING. DID YOU KNOW HE SNORES? SPEAKING OF WHICH, OUR LODGING IS QUITE EXOTIC—A HOUSEBOAT ON ONE OF THE CANALS. I MIGHT EVEN FIND IT ENCHANTING WERE I NOT SUFFERING THROUGH A SEASON IN HELL. I ANXIOUSLY AWAIT YOUR ARRIVAL AS I AM DEPENDING ON YOU TO RELEASE ME FROM THIS TORMENT AND SAVE ME FROM A FATE WORSE THAN VAN GOGH'S. DISCONSOLATELY YOURS, CASTELLI

In no time at all, the tensions of travel have strained the hell out of their tenuous friendship. Without me, they have little incentive to make amends. It seems to be incumbent on me to get my ass over there before they come to blows or split in different directions to God knows where.

"What you got there?" says the Captain, looking over my shoulder.

"Just a postcard."

"Let's see it," he says, reaching for the incriminating piece of mail.

"You mind? It's addressed to me." I bound up the stairs to the safety of my room.

"Get your crap out of my car," he yells. "I'm late for the track."

I run down to unload while the Captain sits in the driver's seat, poring over the *Racing Form*. "Move your ass," he says. "I don't want to get shut out of the daily double."

I look at my watch. "You'll be fine, Dad. I'll be finished in a few minutes." I pile my belongings on the otherwise useless strip of lawn between the sidewalk and the curb.

"You coming?"

I walk up to the passenger window and lean in on my elbows.

"I don't know, Dad. What's the feature?"

"A good one. The Dwyer Handicap. Stop the Music's a stick-out."

"I'd like to, but I think I better hang around and sort out my stuff." I have to pack for my trip, and with the Captain out of the house I can do it without fear of being caught.

"You're sure?" Next to him on the front seat is the weathered leather case with the heavy old pair of beat-up binoculars.

"Maybe next time."

"All right. Suit yourself." He turns over the engine and floors it, the big car accelerating around the corner and out of sight.

I carry everything up to my room, then go to the kitchen for a glass of water. "You should let the faucet run till it's cold," says Goldie, addressing me through the cut-out counter that separates the kitchen from the dining room. She is bent over an ironing board, working on the last of a stack of my father's handkerchiefs. "That's that," she announces. "Oh, God, look at the time." She picks up the keys to the Riviera and pauses at the back door. "If anyone wants to know, I'm at the hairdresser's, and then there's a rummage sale in Woodmere. And don't forget, your father's taking us to Nino's."

Two minutes after Goldie leaves, the doorbell rings and Gene is standing at the screen door.

"Where's the Captain?" he says.

"You missed him. He just left for the Big A."

"Son of a bitch," he says.

"What's the matter?"

"Nothing. I need to talk to him." Parked at the curb in the spot vacated by the Caddy is a battered Dodge Dart. The rear door is bashed in, the vacant window protected by a plastic garbage bag secured with duct tape. An intricate web of twine restrains the door from swinging open.

"Nice wheels."

"Piece of shit," he says, "but I gotta drive something."

He follows me down the hall to the kitchen.

"Got any tea?" he asks.

"Lipton okay?"

"I don't want to drink it, you moron, I want to smoke it. Roll me a stick of that green kind you got around here somewhere."

"Well how am I supposed to know? Come on upstairs." We have to sidestep the packing boxes and the stereo equipment, which are stacked like free-form sculptures on the floor.

"Jesus," Gene says, "what hit this place?"

"I'm flying to Europe on Tuesday." I retrieve my stash from its secret hiding place in the base of a statue of Seabiscuit that occupies a corner of my desk.

"You got a ticket and everything?"

"Of course I have a ticket. What do you think?"

"How come I didn't know about this?"

"Didn't I tell you?"

"No, you didn't tell me. I can't believe you're going to Europe." He sounds like he's either angry or jealous.

"Yeah, for six weeks. I can't wait." I hand him a small baggy that contains the last of my pot. "Roll a number from this, but do me a favor and blow the smoke out the window."

"Now you're telling me how to smoke?"

"Look, I'm trying not to antagonize them, so can you please just do as I ask?"

"Stop whining. You sound like an old lady." He takes a packet of rolling papers from his shirt pocket, removes a sheet, creases it and sprinkles in some grass. He rolls it, seals it and anchors the joint between his lips. "Aren't you in summer school?"

"I'm quitting."

"Oh yeah? What did the Captain say?"

"He doesn't know yet."

"Are you nuts?" he says. "You like to live dangerously, don't you."

"I haven't been able to find the right moment."

"You don't think that's going to antagonize them?"

"I know, I know. I keep putting it off 'cause I'm positive he'll freak."

"He'll do more than that, pal. He'll hit the fuckin ceiling."

"What the hell am I going to do?"

"I'll tell you what you don't do," says Gene, lighting up. He puffs on the joint and holds it before exhaling a huge cloud into the room.

"Oh for godsake, I asked you to blow it out the window." I get a can of Right Guard from the bathroom and spray till the air has the sickly aroma of deodorant.

"Enough, already. It stinks in here."

I sniff the air several times. "Maybe I should light some matches."

"Here, have a hit. You won't smell anything at all." He hands me the joint.

"Oh what the hell."

"Listen," he says, laughing, "whatever you do, don't leave a goodbye note on the kitchen table like you did for that rock concert."

"I don't know what's funny about it."

"You know what your trouble is?" says Gene. "You're only worried about yourself. You think you got problems? Don't make me laugh. You don't know what problems are."

"What's eating you?"

"What's eating me? You want to know what's eating me? This fuckin court case. I'm eating my *kishkas* out."

"You got a lawyer, don't you?"

"Yeah, I got a lawyer. This big shot named Kornblatt who works for Foxy. He's got these fancy offices in Rockefeller Center."

"Yeah, I heard about him. What did he say?"

"He said I had nothing to worry about. He'll cop a plea down to failure to declare. I'll pay a fine and that'll be it."

"That's great. What's the problem?"

"The problem is I can't stand the guy. He keeps me waiting an hour and when I finally see him, he's one of these real arrogant types. Okay, I know I'm not picking up the tab, but this bastard doesn't even shake my hand. 'Get in here. Sit down. Listen to me.' The kind of schmuck who likes to give orders. But with a really bad toupee and, get a load of this, he's wearing a blue shirt with white cuffs and a white collar. You know what I'm talking about, right? He thinks he's a real snazzy dresser. Anyway, he gives me all of five fuckin minutes of his precious time and boom, it's over. Here's your hat, what's your hurry. He's got an important meeting so he's giving me the bum's rush. You see what I'm saying? It doesn't sit right."

"Calm down, Gene. You're overreacting. Don't forget you're getting five thousand dollars of free legal help."

"A lot of good it'll do me."

I hand him the roach. "Would the condemned man like a last hit?"

"I tell you, that fuckin Kornblatt is a boil on my ass. I know you want to go on this trip and all but who else can I depend on? You're smart, you know about the law and you're the only one I can count on to give me a straight answer. I don't trust that bastard."

"What do I know, Gene? I'm not a lawyer. I'm not even in law school."

"All right, but you know the terms and you have some background and you can explain stuff to me. And what's more important, you're the only one I can trust."

"Let me get this straight. You don't want me to go to Europe because you need someone to hold your hand?"

"Just think about it. That's all I'm asking. Look, I have to go."

"Fine. I'll mull it over." But I'm kind of pissed off that my uncle is running a guilt trip on me.

"Do me a favor, kid. I'm down to seeds and stems so lay a little something on me."

"Sure. Take what you want." He opens the baggy, sniffs it, and helps himself to half my meager stash. I'm so surprised I don't say anything. All I can think of is Louie Ragusa from down the block, who when you offered him a taste of your ice cream bar ate half of it in one huge bite. I can't say I'm unhappy to see Gene leave.

I've decided to confront the Captain when he returns from the track, but the minute he steps in the door, there's a rush to leave for the restaurant. I tell myself he'll be far more amenable after a good dinner, which indeed it is. In fact the food at Nino's is so good, the Captain becomes quite expansive, even recounting some stories from his service in North Africa I've never heard before.

"So, Dad, when did you enlist?"

"September 1942. I was twenty years old. And I'll tell you something, my folks were none too happy. They wanted me to finish college."

"You mean you disobeyed your parents?"

"They came around after a while. Don't forget, everybody was joining up and it seemed like the right thing to do."

This is as good an opening as I'm going to get. My father never graduated because there were other things he deemed more important. Okay, he quit to serve his country, back when there was a war worth fighting. But my transgression is small compared to his. I'm not going to abandon my degree, just delay completing it by a few months.

"Look, I want to talk to you about going to Europe. I know I'm in summer school and everything—"

"For Chrissake, Eddie, you're not going to bring that up again."

"But Dad—"

"Your father's right," my mother chimes in. "You're making good progress now. We don't want you to interrupt your studies."

"But Mom—"

"This is no time to go gallivanting around with your friends."

"You're mother's right."

"He doesn't fool me," says my mother. "I know why he wants to go to Europe. He wants to get all potted up and sleep with girls."

"Well, of course," says the Captain. "But, remember, Eddie, when the penis gets hard, the brains turn to mud."

"Can I just say something?"

"Look," says the Captain, "you want to go to Europe, you can go to Europe."

"I can?"

"Yeah! You wait till next summer after you've finished up and you've been accepted to law school, and you can go to Europe. In fact we'll all go. I'll pay for it."

"*Ooh la la,*" says Goldie. "I've been dying to go back to Paris."

"Paris it is," says the Captain.

"And don't forget Geneva, dear, so you can buy me that new watch you promised."

"Geneva too. Why not?"

"That's very generous of you, Dad, but—"

"I insist. It'll be our graduation gift."

"But I want to go this summer."

"Out of the question."

"Can't we talk about this?"

"No."

"Did you buy a plane ticket?" asks my mother. "Ask him if he bought a plane ticket."

"Why?" says my father. "I don't care if he bought the whole damn plane, he's not going." I stare at the remains of my tortoni, or more precisely at the pleated paper cup in which it came, all too conscious of the lump in my throat that won't subside no matter how much I swallow.

"Dad—"

"We're not having this conversation. It's over. And you better not disobey me if you know what's good for you."

My father disobeyed his father and it worked out for him. But I can't stand up to the Captain. So I sit and refuse to meet his gaze. It's easier to watch the busboy ply a loaded tray into the kitchen through the double-hinged doors or to imagine my plane ticket as so much confetti wafting down like flakes in a snow globe, settling gently on the sauce-stained tablecloth, on the shoulders of my father's fuchsia sportcoat, and on my mother's perfectly lacquered hair.

OUT OF TOWN

Weekend nights in high school we'd get stoned—Shapiro, Castelli and I—and drive out to JFK to watch the planes take off. Our favorite terminal was TWA—the one that looks like the wingspan of a giant bird sculpted in concrete. We'd kick around the concourses and laugh ourselves silly, making fun of the straights and the geeks and the squares, even as we wondered where the jets revving up the flood-lit runways were headed. It was hilarious until the high wore off and the passengers who had been the butts of our ridicule were all winging their way to new and exciting tomorrows. Stuck on the ground, we hungered for change but always wound up at Nathan's or Jahn's where, hunched over hotdogs or sundaes, we nodded to our friends or kids we knew from other schools, all of us huddled in our comfortable college-bound lives, biding our time till gradu-ation, a bunch of budding Prufrocks without a Kerouac among us.

First thing Tuesday morning, I shoot out to TWA with the intention of converting my plane ticket to an open-ended depar-ture good for a year. As soon as I enter the sweeping space of the terminal, that old familiar melancholy rushes over me like the cold blast from the air conditioning. I'm summoned to the counter by a perky young woman with a bob of blonde hair, a pert nose, a southern accent and a permanent smile. I smile back and break the ice with a little of the Eddie Sacks charm.

"I'm very well, ma'am, and how are you this fine morning?"

You ever say something so ridiculous you regret it as soon as it pops out of your mouth? I doubt I've ever said *ma'am* before in my life, which is probably why she's squinting at me like I'm Woody Allen trying to play Rhett Butler.

"You're not from the South, are you?"

"Are you kidding? Born and bred on the South Shore."

"You're pulling my leg." I could think of other parts of her anatomy to pull, but her leg was not one of them.

"Swear to God."

"The South Shore? Where is that, Florida?"

"Actually it's Long Island."

"Wait a second. You're not from the South."

"You got me. I'm a Yankee, but I hope you'll help me just the same. I was supposed to fly out this morning, but something personal came up, and I have to postpone my trip." I appeal to her with my best sad puppy dog eyes. It would be her pleasure to assist me, she beams, if I just explain the circumstances that forced me to change my plans.

"As I said, it's personal and I really can't discuss it."

"I understand, sir, but the airline requires a reason on the change of ticket form." With her perfect teeth and her singsong voice, she is unbearably chipper at this early hour.

"I don't care. Put down anything."

"I'm afraid I can't do that, Mr. Sacks. I need a reason."

I take a deep breath and think for a moment. "You might say the passenger is indisposed."

"I'm sorry to hear you're not feeling well." At least she reduces the wattage of her smile, which still radiates plenty of light but no warmth.

"Thanks. Just put down that I'm sick. Better yet, you can write that I'm sick and tired."

"And you have a note, of course?" I look at her blankly. "In cases of illness, sir, we do need to see a note from your doctor."

"I don't have a note. I'm not ill. I'm just trying to give you an excuse." I don't believe this woman.

"Perhaps if you told me the truth, I would know what to put down on the form."

"You want to know what to put down? It's very simple, lady. Put down, 'It's none of your damn business.'"

In a huff she calls over her boss, whom she addresses with exasperation as if she were a school teacher reporting to the principal the behavior of an incorrigible student. The supervisor, a Mrs. Merquit, listens politely then dispatches the agent to deal with another passenger. I breathe easier as I detect that Mrs. Merquit has a New York accent, doesn't smile and isn't from some Hallmark-inspired corner of the South where every trace of irony has been assiduously rooted out. Still I am embarrassed to have to explain that I had a fight with my parents, who will practically disown me if I leave the country. I can't ask our doctor for a note because he might mention it to them. And though my mother may have divined in her uncanny fashion that I bought a ticket, she'll really give me hell if she finds out for sure.

"There's been a slight misunderstanding," she says. "You only need a note if you want us to waive the twenty-five-dollar penalty fee."

I glance at my nemesis, who is still smiling at me furiously. Mrs. Merquit at least is professional and efficient. She promptly writes me a new ticket, which I flaunt at Miss Grits-and-Collard-Greens on my way out.

Back in the Caddy, I tune in the FM band, which is set to an all-Sinatra station. I push a button, Barbra Streisand: "*People . . .*" I push another, the classical Muzak of Montevani. Next station: "That was Perry Como and here's the great Robert Goulet—" Last button, Burl Ives. He swallowed a fly; perhaps he'll die. He will if there's any justice in the world.

"Jesus, Dad, how do you listen to this slop?" I cry out loud. I cut the engine and lean back, feeling the heat of the midsummer sun bearing down on the windshield. A jet roars overhead, its contrails defacing the blue sky. Some vacation this is. I should be soaring over the ocean on my outbound flight, but I'm tethered to the ground with that same empty, left-behind feeling I used to have in high school. Europe. What a joke. At this rate the closest I'll ever get to Amsterdam is the Holland Tunnel.

With an hour to kill before I'm due at air cargo, I decide to go somewhere and relax. I remember a nature preserve near the airport where Mrs. Breslow, my old high school English teacher, once brought us on a field trip to do "nature writing." I jump on the Belt Parkway and cruise by the vacant Aqueduct grandstand to Cross Bay Boulevard. Beyond the clam houses of Howard Beach, the causeway to Rockaway crosses Broad Channel, the largest island in Jamaica Bay. Most people heading to the beaches of Riis Park or out to Breezy Point speed right by the entrance to the refuge, an unobtrusive habitat encompassing thousands of acres of salt marsh, mudflats, woodlands, ponds and trails.

I pull into the small parking area and leave the Caddy next to the only other vehicle, a Volkswagen Bug. Skirting the wall of the small visitor center, still closed at this hour, I set out on the circular trail that loops around a pond, enclosing it from Jamaica Bay, which shimmers beyond the mudflats where seagulls perch on the gunnels of a partially submerged rowboat. A dark, heronlike bird glides in from the bayside, its landing spot obscured by vegetation. I feel like I'm down the coast somewhere, far away from New York, until I recognize a city landmark. Spanning Rockaway Inlet is the Erector Set structure of the Marine Parkway Bridge, its familiar towers rising like steel parentheses.

I don't normally smoke on the job—too much responsibility— but today I say screw it, fire up a roach, and take a couple of good, lung-filling drags. As the high comes on, sounds become strangely amplified: I have the odd sensation that my jeans are rubbing at the thighs then realize it's only the crunch of my shoes on the packed gravel berm.

On the path ahead a woman peers through a telescope that is affixed to the top of a tall tripod. So preoccupied is she, she doesn't move as I scrunch on by to a wooden bench overlooking the pond. There's not much to see except a pair of swans gliding idly past some ducks, which seem to be bathing themselves—they take turns dunking head first, their fuzzy rumps shimmying comically. They are undeterred when the breeze stiffens, furrowing the surface and billowing the feathery plumes of the reeds that crowd the waterline. It's so tranquil here, as if the morning has swallowed a

Quaalude. It seems implausible that only a few miles away people are rushing anxiously to work.

The woman is paused a few feet from me, the tripod slung over her shoulder like a rifle. She looks like a grandmother on safari. Her khaki bush hat matches her shirt and shorts, and in her thick-soled hiking boots she looks ready to strike out across the savannah.

"Excuse me, would you mind if I set up over here?"

"Be my guest."

With astonishing quickness, the elderly woman steadies and adjusts the tripod to observe some large black birds that perch with wings spread on what look to be broomsticks, jutting through the surface.

"What are they?" I ask.

"Those are what you call Double-crested Cormorants."

"Double-crested, huh? They must be rare."

"The cormorants? No, not really. They're here all the time."

"Are they courting, the way they display themselves like that?"

"No. They do have courtship rituals," she says, "but the breeding season has passed. They're just drying their wings."

"You mean they're hanging out? Catching some rays?"

"I suppose, but it's not recreation for them. They have to." She explains that cormorants do a lot of sunbathing because their wings aren't water-repellent. But their reduced buoyancy allows them to stay underwater longer when they dive for fish.

"That's pretty neat."

"Would you care to have a look?"

The cormorants are eighty yards away, but when I peek through the scope one of them materializes, outsized, in front of me. It poses with dramatic nonchalance, its dark gray wings dominating the field of vision. I take in the long, black neck; the smooth, rounded head; the orange face tapering to a hook-tipped bill; but it is the lustrous bright green eye, sparkling like a precious stone, that ultimately compels me.

"This is something else," I say.

"Can you see the crests on top of the head?"

I don't know if it's because I'm stoned, but I laugh when I notice the tiny little tufts that give the bird its name. I feel like I'm grinning crazily as I step away from the eyepiece to thank her.

"Look over there," she says, pointing to a solitary black bird standing by the edge of the water. Head down, it seems to be probing the mud with its bill.

"Hey, that's the heron I saw as I was walking in."

"No, that's not a heron. Herons have straight bills," she says, adjusting the angle of the scope. "It's probably an ibis; the bill is longer and downcurved. Let's see," she says, fine-tuning the focus. "Yes, it's a Glossy Ibis. Take a look."

Magnification does indeed reveal an elegant curve to the bill, but the big surprise is the bird's coloring, which isn't black at all, but a beautiful rich chestnut with iridescent patches of purple, green and pink.

"I can see every feather."

"It helps to have a spotting scope. Or at the very least, a good pair of binoculars."

"I can see why."

"Is this your first time at Jamaica Bay?"

"Not exactly. I was here four or five years ago. And you? You come here a lot?"

"Every day. I'm studying certain bird populations for the Museum of Natural History."

"Do you have a degree in ornithology or something?"

She laughs. "I have a doctorate in biology, but I was a math major in college. I taught high school for a while, but I didn't like it very much." She leans over as if she were telling me a secret. "The kids seemed to be more interested in grades than in learning. It took me a long time to figure out what I wanted to do."

"How *did* you figure it out?"

"I don't know. One thing led to another. After I got divorced, I took a trip to the Galapagos, which got me interested in biology. That's when I went for my advanced degree. I ended up studying distraction displays, if you know what they are."

I shake my head. "Not a clue."

"It only means that birds that have nests close to the ground will often feign injury, such as a broken wing, to lead predators away from their young. I wrote a boring book about it."

"I doubt it," I say.

"And now I'm studying another hot topic, site tenacity, which is the tendency for birds to return each season to the same nesting site."

"Sounds pretty cool,"

"Well, it's not what you want to do, I always say. It's what you want to do next."

"I'll keep that in mind," I tell her.

I wish I could play hooky, hang out and look at birds, but I have to make a pick-up, then tackle the rush-hour traffic to Manhattan. I thank her for letting me use her scope and start to retrace my path to the car.

"Come again," she says. "And bring binoculars."

"Don't worry. I'll be back."

I can't get over how I feel. Twenty minutes ago I was depressed as hell. Now I'm laid back and relaxed, but also excited. Can you be relaxed and excited at the same time? I'll have to think about that.

On my way to the city, I tune in to get a traffic report. The big news story is the Watergate testimony of a former White House aide, who inadvertently mentioned the existence of an automatic taping system. Outside of a small coterie, nobody knew Nixon had been secretly recording all official phone calls and conversations until this guy Butterfield spilled the beans. The implications for the scandal are obvious. By listening to the relevant tapes, investigators will be able to pin down when Nixon knew about the burglary and if in fact he participated in the cover-up. It's really too funny. All this time Nixon has been surreptitiously bugging people and now like Claudius he may be hoist by his own petard.

As the calendar crawls through July, the headlines are dominated by the high-stakes chess game to win the tapes' release: The White House verifies the existence of recording devices; the Watergate Committee requests the tapes; Nixon rebuffs it, citing executive privilege. Special Prosecutor Cox also subpoenas the tapes, and again Nixon refuses, claiming that they contain sensitive information bearing on national security. To placate the public, the President releases the reassuring statement that he has listened to the tapes and they are, quote, "entirely consistent with what I have stated to be the truth." Unquote. The case seems destined for the Supreme Court—even Nixon admits as much—but when it will be heard, and how the impasse will be resolved, is anyone's guess.

"Don't you love all this executive privilege shit?" asks Gene. "I wish I could use a defense like that." We're escorting my uncle upstate to his plea hearing, and he hasn't been in the car five minutes before he brings up the one subject I was hoping to avoid.

"It wouldn't help you, genius. They caught you red-handed."

"I don't know, Leo, I think your boy is trying to pull a fast one."

"You don't know what you're talking about," says the Captain.

"Please," I say, "do we have to discuss politics before breakfast?"

"For your information, genius, presidents have been using executive privilege for a hell of a long time."

"Is that so?"

"It goes all the way back, big shot. You couldn't run the country without it." The Captain reels off several kinds of secrets—from troop deployments to the names of CIA agents—that the government has a need to protect.

"I don't know," says Gene, "it sounds like something they just cooked up."

"Dad's right," I say, giving in to a yawn. "George Washington came up with it to deny documents to Congress."

"You see," says the Captain, "Eddie knows all about it."

In the interest of domestic tranquility, I hold my tongue and suggest we listen to music.

"Nixon, Mitchell, Haldeman—what's the difference?" says Gene. "They're all crooks, the whole fuckin lot of 'em."

My father slams on the brakes so hard, I think we've blown a tire. The Caddy fishtails to a halt in the middle of First Avenue as cars honk and swerve around us. Speaking into the rearview mirror, he addresses Gene in measured tones.

"Listen, you stupid dingdong, I'm wasting my whole goddamn day doing this, so if you want me to be nice to you, I suggest you think before you open that big fat trap of yours. Because so help me the next time you piss me off, I'll dump you on the side of the road, I don't care where the hell we are, and you can find your own fuckin way there."

"Give him a break, Dad. He's a little nervous today."

"Mind your own business," my father says. "I'm not talking to you."

After a while it's uncomfortably obvious that the Captain isn't talking to anyone. He spends the next twenty miles cleaning his ears with his house key. Furthermore his disapproving presence makes it clear to Gene and me that we better refrain from even the slightest communication if we know what's good for us. The enforced self-absorption is especially hard on my uncle, who sits forward in the middle of the back seat drumming endless rhythms on his knees. When we stop for a bite, he refuses to eat, sticking to black coffee even if it isn't doing his *kishkas* any good. Finally, after five boring hours of fitful naps and furious silences, we arrive at the small Finger Lakes city of Auburn, where the rotating Northern District of New York is winding up its summer session.

The court is located on an upper floor of the old post office, an arrangement that is not in itself unusual, although the excesses of its Romanesque Revival style defy expectation. A fortress-like, steep-roofed building of limestone and brick replete with towers and gables and turrets, it seems an unlikely structure for a federal courthouse. I forget who said architecture is frozen music, but I can practically hear a fanfare as we mount the front steps and pass through a rounded archway.

Our lawyer, it turns out, is AWOL. Kornblatt was supposed to fly in to Syracuse and rent a car, but something has delayed him. We bide our time watching Judge Meehan conduct business, a performance I alone among us find entertaining. For one thing, he looks more like a stevedore than a judge. A man of about sixty, Judge Meehan has the crooked nose of a prizefighter and the bushy eyebrows of a silent screen villain, which in interviewing the unfortunate defendants or their lawyers he arches to humorous effect.

I can see why Gene isn't chuckling. Judge Meehan has no compunction about humiliating people.

"Where did you go to law school?" he asks one unprepared attorney. "You should get your money back."

In another case he sticks it to a dumb, insolent kid who won't shut up. "On behalf of the defendant," he says, gesturing at the scruffy figure before him, "I must apologize to the courtroom that his parents did not utilize appropriate birth control." When this remark incites the foul-mouthed hothead to further outbursts, Judge Meehan waits him out to have the last word. "I was going to sentence you to time served," he says, "but obviously you need another year to think things over."

"Whatever you do," I say to Gene, "don't talk back."

After several hours the clerk announces "Docket number 6580, *The United States versus Eugene Aaron Sacks*, and all appearances for the record." The three of us approach the judge, though Gene lags behind, looking as eager as a condemned man. Luckily, Kornblatt rushes in at this moment, striding down the aisle to join us at the bench. His hair perfectly coiffed, his chalk-striped suit immaculately tailored, he is a sight to instill confidence. He shakes the Captain's hand, introduces himself to the judge and apologizes perfunctorily for his lateness.

Compared to Kornblatt, the prosecutor—a balding, pasty-faced public servant—seems unimposing. "Your honor, Anthony Francis Carbone, assistant U.S. attorney on behalf of the government. Marvin J. Kornblatt on behalf of Eugene Aaron Sacks." Mr. Carbone recites his lines in the thin, tired voice of someone who has been through the same song and dance a thousand times. "Judge, we're ready to proceed."

"Let's get on with it, Mr. Carbone."

"Your honor, Mr. Kornblatt is not admitted to practice in the Northern District of New York. However, we know him to be an attorney in good standing and respectfully move for his admission *pro hac vice.*"

"What are they're talking about?" asks Gene.

"It's Latin," I whisper. "It means 'for this instance' he'll be allowed to defend you."

"Have you consulted with your client, Mr. Kornblatt?"

"I have, your honor," intones Kornblatt, adjusting the gold cuff-links in his French cuffs. I can't help noticing that the cuffs and the collar on his light blue dress shirt are white.

"Mr. Carbone?"

"We're here today, your honor, pursuant to a plea agreement

for defendant's plea of guilty to the charge of smuggling. The background of this case is as follows: Approximately three weeks ago he was arrested at the Canadian border by the Thousand Islands in possession of thirty thousand dollars of Canadian silver coins, which he had not declared."

"All right," says Judge Meehan. "Will the guilty man please step forward." I glance at my uncle, who appears to be smiling in pain. Kornblatt motions for Gene to join him, which he does reluctantly. Dwarfed by his taller attorney, Gene clasps his hands before him as if they were handcuffed. "I have to advise you, Mr. Sacks, to go through the advice of rights regarding the plea and the panoply of rights you will be giving up by admitting to this crime. Mr. Carbone, will you please set forth for the record the essence of the plea agreement and tell us what the maximum penalties are."

The assistant U.S. attorney reads the particulars of the plea agreement as if he were bored to death, a delivery that makes the possibility of a ten-thousand-dollar fine and five years in prison especially jarring. Gene, however, isn't listening. He is whispering furiously at Kornblatt, who responds with a shrug of his shoulders.

"Is there a problem?" asks Judge Meehan, raising both formidable eyebrows at Kornblatt.

"If I could have a moment with my client, Your Honor."

"What the hell is going on?" says Gene. "I thought the charge was failure to declare."

"Lower your voice," says Kornblatt.

"You stabbed me in the back, you son of a bitch?"

"There was nothing I could do," says Kornblatt. "The best they would offer is smuggling with a suspended sentence. At least you won't have to do jail time."

"Did you know about this, Leo?"

My father has moved a discreet distance away. *I can't hear you*, he mimes.

"I don't understand," says the judge, throwing up his hands. "I thought this was all arranged." He looks at Mr. Carbone and shakes his head. "Did you not tell me, Mr. Kornblatt, you had already conferred with the defendant?"

"I'm sorry, Your Honor. If I may beg the court's indulgence for another moment."

"Listen, Mr. Kornblatt, I don't know what kind of game you're playing, but I can assure you, sir, in my courtroom I don't appreciate these surprises at the last minute."

"Just a slight misunderstanding, Your Honor." Kornblatt pulls Gene aside and lays down the law, unleashing a torrent of whispers that has a deflating effect on my uncle. His eyes lose their anger and turn inward, surrendering to despair.

"I hate to interrupt," says the judge, "but what's it going to be, Mr. Sacks? Is the plea voluntary?"

Kornblatt leans over and whispers angrily at Gene, who meekly relays his assent.

"Now we're getting somewhere," says the judge. "I find the plea to be voluntary, knowing and with full understanding of the consequences. I will accept the plea, I will accept the agreement, and I will incorporate the provisions of the plea agreement in conviction at the appropriate time. I will fix sentencing in this case for two months from now." Judge Meehan taps his gavel and we're dismissed.

My uncle stares daggers all the way home. I try to get out of him why he's so incensed, but he ignores me. I don't get it. He won't have to do time and it's not as if he'll have to pay the fine or the legal fees. So what's he so upset about?

A month later my uncle is fired from his city job as an elevator inspector for having been convicted of a felony.

BELMONT

Since losing his job, Gene takes it out on everybody. His favorite targets are Kornblatt, the Department of Buildings, and the ineffectual leadership of Local 237 of the International Union of Operating Engineers. When he's tired of them, he complains about the Captain or the Customs inspectors or Assistant U.S. Attorney Carbone or Judge Meehan. And it doesn't take much for him to rip into his ex-wife or his daughter, who are always bugging him for money. He holds everyone accountable but himself.

Leo urges him to look for work in elevator repair, but Gene is damned if he's going back to maintenance. Somebody puts him on to the Policemen's Retirement Benevolent Association, an organization run by ex-cops who solicit contributions over the phone. They make it sound like they support former policemen in their old age, but the only policemen they support are themselves. They'll take any donation, of course, but a hundred bucks will buy you a bronze plaque with a seal of the PRBA to affix to the chrome bumper of your car: "Cops take one look at that plaque and they treat you like a state assemblyman or a judge. That's right, pal, you'll never get another summons. It's like a Get Out Of Jail Free card for beating speed traps." That's the spiel, though Gene doubts the plaque has any influence at all. Not like his elevator inspector's badge, which resembles a detective shield. By flashing it, he has avoided a slew of traffic violations and a dozen speeding tickets. It's a crying shame it didn't work at the Canadian border. "So what do you say? Can you help the boys out this week with a little something?"

While Gene goes to work cold-calling prospective pigeons, I return to school. For my last semester at City College I move out of my parents' house into an apartment share with some actors in Morningside Heights. Shapiro and Castelli are also in Manhattan—Shapiro at NYU law and Castelli in the architecture program at Columbia—but they won't have anything to do with each other, or with me for that matter. When I phone Shapiro, the schmuck hangs up on me. At least Castelli invites me over. He describes the escalating war of insults that culminated in a drunken fight on the deck of the houseboat, which ended with Shapiro pitching Castelli's bicycle, and then Castelli, ignominiously into the canal. I nearly bust a gut laughing, but the more I laugh, the more uptight he becomes. "People outgrow each other," he says, and maybe he's right. "Such are the vicissitudes of friendship, Edward." Then he asks me to leave.

All I can say is, thank God for the track. A Saturday at Belmont is still a welcome diversion, especially when Secretariat is running. In the recent Marlboro Cup, a race created expressly for the Triple Crown winner, the horse shattered the world record for a mile and an eighth. He's facing older horses again in today's

Woodward, but over a surface rendered sloppy by a light but steady rain.

"What do you think, Dad? Will Secretariat handle the wet track?"

"It won't make any difference," says the Captain. "Great horses win no matter what the conditions."

"So let me ask you," says Gene, "what happened in the Whitney?" In August Secretariat had lost at Saratoga to a non-stakes winner named Onion, an upset that reduced more than a few chalk players to tears.

My father waves Gene away as if he were a mosquito. "He wasn't right that day."

"Maybe he's not right today," says Gene.

"Secretariat will toy with this field. Mark my words."

"You and your chalk," says Gene. "We've watched six races and a favorite hasn't won yet."

"Bet against him, genius. See if I care."

"I'm not only going to bet against him. Twenty bucks says I find a way to beat him."

"You're covered," says the Captain. It's a ridiculous wager, betting against Secretariat without getting odds, but my uncle is in a jovial mood. For once he's not complaining; he's crowing. He won't let us forget that his Mets, who only a month ago were in last place, are on the verge of clinching a playoff spot, while the Yankees with an almost identical record are sixteen games out in their division. On top of that, he's the only one of us who has cashed. He had a sawbuck on a 15-1 shot in the second, then nailed a $200 exacta in the fourth. Feeling flush, Gene offers to spring for a beer and a hotdog. "You go ahead," says the Captain,

"I'll sit and handicap." Being around Gene when he's winning gives my father indigestion.

I accompany Gene to the concession stand.

"Two with kraut," he says, gesturing to the hotdogs that are rolling hypnotically on the spinning steel cylinders of the grill. "So how is college going, good?"

"Great, so far. If I keep it up, I'll make dean's list. What about you? How's the Policemen's Retirement Benevolent Association?"

"I quit that crap a few weeks ago," he says. "Aside from the draw they paid me, I couldn't make dipshit."

"It sounded like a tough sell."

"Don't get me started," he says. Our order comes and he crams the frank into his mouth, talking away as he chews. "I was just keeping my head below water." By way of explanation he places a level hand over his bald spot. "Look," he says, "I didn't exactly quit. I got fired. But I got a better gig now—office supplies." Central Office Supply, he tells me, is run by a bunch of Hungarians, real *gonifs*, who resort to an elaborate but highly effective ruse. "Listen to this," he says, and lays out the rap they use to gull their unsuspecting leads:

Mr. Sussman? I got your name from Meyer Isaacs in Miami.

Oh, sure, I know Meyer. How can I assist you?

Well, Mr. Sussman, my father-in-law, who recently passed away from a heart attack, rest his soul, was Meyer's best friend. They used to do everything together: golf, go to the beach, jai alai. It turns out my father-in-law had some boxes of office supplies in the garage—pens, pencils, paperclips, stuff like that—and I'm trying to give my mother-in-law a hand. Meyer took most of it, and he thought you might be willing to help.

I'd love to. How much stuff do you have?

Let's see, it probably comes to about fifteen hundred, give or take a few bucks, and now of course that she's a widow ... Hello? Mr. Sussman? Are you still there?

Yes, I'm here.

What do you say? Can you do something for her?

Well, I'd like to think it over.

Sure. I understand. And I'll certainly give Meyer your regards.

You say that Meyer took most of it?

Oh, he took four or five times that. What a mensch he is.

Well, if Meyer took that much ... Sure, count me in.

"And you actually hook people with this line?"

"I'm telling you," he says, "it's beautiful. That's because we sell them something they can use."

"Like what? Pens and pencils?"

"Don't forget the paperclips."

"Of course you do mark it up a ton."

"What do I give a shit? People are idiots. All I care about is that twenty-percent commission." He blows his nose into a paper napkin. The rims of his nostrils are red.

"Have you closed anyone?"

"I got a few deals ready to drop."

"I see."

"Okay, I haven't hit anything yet, but there's money in this phone room. I can smell it."

"How can you smell anything with that cold?"

"Very funny."

"So how's your head these days?"

"How should it be? The sentencing is Monday."

"What are you worried about? The Captain will pay your fine and it'll be over."

"I just want this nightmare to end." He takes a slug of beer.

"Look on the bright side, Gene. Something good has to happen. It's the law of averages."

"I'm winning ain't I?"

"Must be your lucky *Playboy* shirt."

"It's about time I hit a few."

"You see. Every cloud has a silver lining."

"Yeah, and every casket has a satin one."

"Boy, are you in good shape."

"Hell of a fortieth birthday present. Fifteen years and they fuck me out of my pension."

"Hey, I forgot it's your birthday. Let me buy you a shot."

"Now you're talkin," he says. "I could use a little hair of the dog."

I go to the bar and bring back a couple of shooters.

"Happy birthday, you old fart." We tap our plastic cups and sip our Canadian Club.

"Listen, kid, what do you say we celebrate Tuesday?"

"Sure. Why not?"

"Meet me at that Irish pub in Midtown next to Orange Julius."

"Whatever you want, Uncle."

"Good. I could use a few laughs."

"By the way, Gene, what happened to your mezuzah?" As long as I've known him, he's always worn a mezuzah shaped like a silver ingot attached to a chain around his neck. In its place hangs a miniature spoon, such as you might find on a girl's charm bracelet.

Before he can answer, the customary trumpet flourish calls the horses to the post and the announcer intones, "The horses are on the track for the twentieth running of the Woodward Stakes."

"I got to make a bet," he says.

"Who do you like?"

"I don't know. I'll figure it out at the windows." He knocks back the rest of his rye.

"I think I'll save my money."

"You're probably right," he says. "Stay and finish your drink." He pats me on the shoulder and as he walks away I page through my *Racing Form* to the feature. A scan of the past performances and a quick check of the toteboard—Secretariat is the odds-on favorite at 3-10—reinforces my inclination to skip the race.

I hurry back to the seats a few minutes before post time. The skies are clear, but the stands are far from crowded, which is understandable given the sloppy condition of the track.

"Seems familiar, huh, Dad? Belmont Park, a mile and a half, Secretariat in a field of five. You think he'll win by thirty-one lengths?"

"Against older horses in the slop? Not likely, but who knows? With this horse anything is possible." A Sultan is clenched between his teeth as he pats himself down looking for his pills. He finds the vial, digs out a nitroglycerin tablet, removes the cigar and secures the small white pill under his tongue.

"If you're not feeling well, Dad, maybe you shouldn't be smoking."

He shoots me a look that shouts, *Mind your own business*, so I ignore him and study the horses. The colts and their stable ponies are strung out before the grandstand, each pair ambling toward the starting gate, which is positioned below us at the finish line.

Gene joins us at the seats looking much less sure of himself. By the way he is worrying his nails and darting his head about like a nervous squirrel, I assume he's put a bundle on a longshot.

As soon as Secretariat steps in, the last to load, the announcer informs us, "It is now post time." A moment later the gates spring open and the horses charge through the slop. The 5 horse, Prove Out, comes away with the lead. Secretariat on the outside is easy to follow, or at least his jockey is. Meadow Stable's blue-and-white blocks are instantly recognizable. The favorite sprints easily into second, just off the flanks of the 5 horse, whose rider's silks are a blur of bright orange. Around the clubhouse turn, Prove Out establishes a short lead, but only five lengths separate the entire field. As they move onto the backstretch, the leader maintains a slim half-length advantage. Secretariat seems content to lay off the pace, but at the mile pole, his jockey makes a move. After pulling even with Prove Out, Secretariat quickly draws off by a length and a half. The move is so effortless, the Captain lets loose a triumphant cackle. "Forget it," he says, "the 5 is cooked." He has good reason to be confident: Passed horses almost always fade.

"Shit," says Gene, whacking his folded *Racing Form* in disgust. Secretariat is coasting around the far turn and will surely fire once he hits the straightaway. But against all odds, Prove Out somehow finds a second wind, ranges up along the rail, collars Secretariat at the top of the lane and vies for the lead.

"Come on, Red," calls the Captain. "You can do it, baby." Even through binoculars I can't tell who's winning when the horses are so far up the track, but Secretariat appears to be coming on again.

"Come on, 5!" screams my uncle. "Go get him, 5! Let's go, 5! You can do it, 5!" As if he can hear Gene rooting him on, the 5 horse surges ahead, putting daylight between himself and Secretariat. Velasquez whips Prove Out down the stretch and the horse responds gamely, splattering through the slop and streaking past the lighted toteboard to finish more than four lengths ahead of his celebrated rival.

"How do you like them apples?" shouts Gene. "Sixteen to fucking one. The longest shot in the race." He waves a black-edged fifty-dollar win ticket at the Captain and says, "Is that beautiful or what?"

"Even a blind squirrel sometimes finds an acorn," says the Captain, forking over a crisp twenty.

"You sure you don't want to wait till it's official."

"That won't be necessary."

"Way to go, Genie." I pat my uncle on the back. "How did you figure it?"

"I went with Jerkens, man. The guy's on a roll. After what he did at the Spa, I figured why the hell not." It was a pretty smart move when you think about it. Allen Jerkens, who trains Prove Out, also engineered Onion's improbable upset in the Whitney.

"So tell me," says the Captain, "does this mean you can finally pay back some of what you owe me?"

"Your old man is hilarious," says Gene, nudging me with his elbow. "A regular laugh riot." He sidesteps toward the aisle and hurries toward the betting windows.

"Where's he rushing?" says the Captain. "Does he think they're going to run out of money?"

"Give him a break, Dad."

"Why should I?"

"Why do you have to rain on his parade?"

"Because he's an ungrateful bum. He thinks he's so fuckin smart. Well this time he got what he deserved."

"What are you talking about? He won."

"I'm talking about he never listens to me. No, he's got to do everything his way, the big fuckin genius, and look where it gets him."

"Relax, Dad, don't have a conniption." But I know my father and it's no use trying to placate him when he starts flying off the handle.

"Like I always say: 'You can coat shit with honey but underneath it's still shit.'"

"What does that mean?"

"It means I'm sick of his bullshit. He won't vary his route, he gets clipped. He gets greedy in Canada, they bust him at the border. One fuck-up after another and I always have to pay for it. Well it's too bad about him, but I'll be damned if I'll shell out another sixty Gs to save his miserable ass. He should've thought of that earlier."

"I think you lost me, Dad."

"The plea bargain, Eddie. What do you think I'm talking about?"

"What about it?" I have a queasy feeling in my stomach that I fear has little to do with the hotdog I wolfed down.

"Let me clue you in. Gene wanted to plead to 'failure to declare' because it ain't a felony. What your uncle don't know is, Carbone said he was willing to go for it, but then we found out the fine would run us twice the amount confiscated: Sixty Gs! And that's on top of the sixteen they got at the border and the eight thousand in legal fees and all the rest." The Captain pauses to let the grand total hit home. "We talked it over with Kornblatt, Foxy and me, and he convinced us not to take it."

"Kornblatt convinced you?"

"Kornblatt said Gene needed to learn a lesson and I had to agree with him. Think of it as a wake-up call. Gene won't have to go to jail, but the suspended sentence will give him plenty to think about."

"Look at him, Dad. He's lost without that job."

"You're not listening to me, Eddie. It's too bad about the job and the pension, but it serves him right. If you think your uncle is worth sixty thousand bucks, you been smoking too much pot. I know you got a soft spot for him, but I've known him his whole life, Eddie, and believe me, he'll never amount to anything."

"He's still your brother, isn't he?"

"He's an embarrassment."

"So you turn your back on him? That's not right. What if it was me?"

"You're not like him. He's a loser. He'll never change, your uncle."

"He's your family, Dad."

"He's got nobody to blame but himself."

"Okay, he made mistakes, but he didn't kill anyone. For god-sake, have some compassion. A little *rachmunis*. Isn't that what you always tell me?"

"He's not *my* family. I don't want to deal with him anymore."

"If this is what it means to be a winner, you can have it. This is not how you treat a brother."

"How long am I supposed to carry him? Kornblatt says I should cut my losses already. He says I'm a pushover and he's right."

"Kornblatt? What does he know?"

"A lot, for your information. He's one sharp cookie."

"He's a pompous ass."

"That pompous ass makes two hundred grand a year."

"There's more to life than making a truckload of money."

"Says who? Some schmuck who doesn't have a pot to piss in?"

"I don't get it, Dad. You're always telling me, *Go to law school. Go to Columbia.* What the hell for? So I can turn out like Kornblatt?"

"You could do a lot worse than Kornblatt, believe me."

"Open your eyes, Dad. He's a scumbag in a silk suit."

"What did you say?" He leers at me menacingly, the edge in his voice a warning that I've gone too far.

"Nothing."

"You got a big mouth on you, Eddie, just like your uncle."

"You want to know what I said? I said, 'Screw him,' Okay? Screw Kornblatt and screw Columbia and screw you." The words fly out of my mouth before I can stop myself, but I don't give a damn because for once I've told him to his face exactly how I feel.

"Where you going?" he yells, his blood pressure rising. "Come back here, mister. That's an order." I've seen this act before, the Captain bellowing and blowing his top, but with that absurdly large cigar protruding from his twisted mouth his antics seems less threatening than buffoonish. People are shushing him and telling him to calm down, but he ignores them. "Don't walk away when I'm talking to you. You hear me, Eddie?" I hear him all right, but I can't stop. I jog up the steps and keep right on going out of the clubhouse, down the long, litter-strewn grandstand and out the concrete walkway to the platform of the Long Island Rail Road, where I board the Belmont Special to Manhattan.

I make my way haltingly through the densely packed train until I happen on a window seat in the last car. People are chatting, laughing, yawning. A loudmouth is excoriating Secretariat for a lack of heart. As the train clacks along I lean my forehead against the tinted glass, hoping to lose myself in the neglected backyards of Queens, but I can't stop reliving the scene with my father, relishing the euphoria of having told him off and dreading the certainty that the next time I see him there'll be hell to pay. The argument replays itself obsessively, triggering short-lived sensations of anger, excitement and apprehension, and though I would dearly love to lose myself in sleep, I'm much too anxious and overwrought to nap.

ON THE TOWN

New York has no shortage of cozy, well-appointed pubs to which revelers might repair to raise a celebratory glass, but the dive I meet Gene in is not one of them. A narrow saloon with six stools up front and as many beer-stained tables cluttering the dingy linoleum in the rear, McAnn's offers no distractions to serious drinking: No steam table, no pool table, no TV, no pay phone, no jukebox, no dartboard, and no decorations to speak of, save for the neon beer ads in the window and the KISS ME, I'M IRISH sign taped to the smoky mirror behind the bar. Gene has the place to himself and the yawning bartender is pouring him a cheap whisky from the speed rack. Judging from the glint in my uncle's eyes, I can see it's not his first.

"What are you doing, Gene? You can't drink that rotgut on your birthday."

"Why not?" he says. "It does the job." And to prove it, he tosses back the caramel-colored liquor in one shot.

"Let me at least buy you something off the top shelf."

"Well if it isn't my long-lost pal, Mr. Rockefeller. Sit down,

Mr. Rockefeller. Say hello to Frankie. Frankie, meet Mr. Rocke-feller." Frankie nods at me. "Frankie's a great bartender. You know how I know? He works in a place called McAnn's and he ain't even Irish. Now how do you figure that?"

"Must be karma," I say, but if Frankie has to work in this crummy joint, his karma can't be too good.

"It's a wonder they hired him, ain't that right, Frankie?"

"Like I told you before, the wife is Irish. I guess that was good enough for them."

"There you go. His wife is Irish. And that's good enough for me, Frankie. Is that good enough for you, Mr. Rockefeller?"

"'Tis, indeed, it is," I reply in the pathetic accent I acquired from an Irish Spring soap commercial.

"I'll have a Black Label, Frankie, since he's buying." Gene pats me on the back. "So how you doing today, good?"

"I will be after a few beers." I order a Heineken and ask him how the sentencing went.

"We got a lot to celebrate," he says and slugs down the scotch.

"Why don't you pace yourself, Uncle?"

"You pace yourself. I'm going wire to wire."

I sip my beer, glancing furtively at his reflection in the mirror. He hasn't shaved, his thin mustache is untrimmed and the tips of his nostrils are still irritated.

"It's your birthday."

"That's right. It's my fuckin birthday."

"And since you're so pleasant and all, I got you something."

"You're kidding me." His belligerence instantly disappears. "I don't believe it," he says. "A present?" He holds it up to show the bartender. "Look at this, Frankie? Is that beautiful or what?" He might as well be a kid holding a moon rock, he's so delighted.

"Go ahead, open it."

"What is it?" he asks, ripping off a strip of the gold gift wrap and then the rest of it. Studying the picture on the box, he says, "Is this what I think it is?"

"Compact binoculars, like I got the Captain."

"Fantastic."

"But don't do what he did and bounce them off the floor."

"Don't worry," he says. He fumbles with the packing tape, the booze having compromised his fine motor skills. "Fuck! They really seal the shit out of these things." After several clumsy attempts, he gives me the box to deal with.

"Another round, boys?"

"Don't you think we should eat something, Gene?"

"Yeah, we'll eat. Let me have a look at those." I hand him the field glasses by the strap, which he drapes with some difficulty around his neck.

"I can't see a damn thing," he says.

"Try removing the protective caps."

"Oh. Oh, yeah, I got it." He focuses on the small sign next to the men's room and reads, FACILITIES FOR CUSTOMERS ONLY. Then he swivels on his stool, almost losing his balance, and trains the glasses through the front window. Man, these are boss, Ed. They're so light."

"Glad you like 'em."

"Listen," he says, focusing on something across the street, "I invited some more people to dinner. You don't mind, do you?"

"Why should I?"

"Hey, I can read the parking sign over there."

"Anybody I know?"

"Just the immediate family: Leo and Goldie, Randi and Cele."

I stare at him, open-mouthed.

"You're kidding, right?"

"The six of us. Like old times. Make it a real celebration." The walls of the bar seem to be verging closer, like in one of those B-movies where the hero is about to be crushed to death. I start to giggle, and then I'm slapping the bar and laughing like a lunatic until my eyes tear.

"I knew you'd get a kick out of it," he says.

"Hey, yeah, this is, uh . . ."

"It's a good one, right?"

"I think I'll have a shot now."

"Great," says Gene. "I'll join you."

"And Frankie," I say, "you better make it a double."

A misty rain is falling as we slide out of McAnn's, arm in arm, warbling with intoxicated gusto, "When Irish Eyes Are Smiling..." Our voices are as erratic as our gait, but who gives a damn? If you're going to your own funeral, you might as well show up singing.

Beneath the bright-red awning of the Carnegie Deli, the immediate family is waiting. We greet them with exaggerated bonhomie, ignoring the scowls and the heads shaking with disappointment and the conspicuous rolling of eyes. I kiss my aunt on the cheek (the one without the mole), embrace my mom and smile weakly at my cousin. My father and I exchange a curt nod.

"This must be the place," says Gene. "Look at that thing." A three-foot-long plastic pickle hangs in the window, surrounded by a curtain of slender salamis. "What are we waiting for? Come on. Let's eat."

Gene leads everyone into the restaurant, but Randi lags behind, gesturing me aside. I haven't seen her in months, but she looks hot in her black plastic slicker, her dark hair glistening with pearls of rain.

"How's it going?" I say. "You look great."

"Why the fuck should you care?"

"Come on, don't be that way."

"How should I be?"

"Guess what? I'm taking a photography class and I really dig it."

"You're confusing me with someone who gives a shit."

"Do you want to talk, Randi, or just insult me?"

"I don't *want* to talk. I have to."

"Great. What did I do now?"

"Plenty," she says, taking a drag of her cigarette.

"Wait a second," I say, "I bet my parents put you up to this. Let me guess. You're going to give me a pep talk about my responsibilities, ask me to apologize to the Captain and urge me to get serious about my future. Am I right?"

"You are such a jerk," she says. "Not everything is about you."

"My father didn't ask you to talk to me?"

"I don't know what the fuck you're talking about."

"Oh. So what did you want to tell me?"

"Never mind. What's the point of talking to you? I'll figure it out on my own."

"Figure what out?"

"Forget it. I don't need your fuckin help. Just leave me alone."
She yanks open the door to the restaurant and stands there holding it for two couples who are leaving.

"Come on," I say, tugging her away from the entrance. "Talk
to me."

"You don't make it easy."

"I'm sorry."

Refusing to make eye contact, she smokes and watches a taxi
speed by, its tires spitting rain.

"I didn't want to ask you," she says, finally, "but I need a loan
for something. An emergency."

"And what's the big crisis this time?"

"I have a problem I have to take care of."

"Such as?"

"Let me put it this way: *We* have a problem."

"We have a problem? You and I?"

She nods. "I'm afraid so."

"I don't have the slightest idea what you're talking about."

"Don't be so dense," she says.

I step back to take her in, studying her face and then the shiny
plastic of her raincoat. "Jesus, you're not . . ."

"Jesus had nothing to do with it, Eddie. But you did." She taps
off the ash for punctuation.

"God, this is terrible."

"It's not good."

"And you're sure it's mine?"

"Yeah," she says, almost inaudibly.

"You're absolutely certain?"

"Yes, asshole. I haven't slept with anyone else."

"Okay, let's just calm down and think about this. First of all, when did it happen?"

"It had to be that weekend after the Fourth of July."

"That was three months ago. Why would you wait so long?"

"I don't know. I was angry. I didn't want to deal with it. What difference does it make?" She smokes and we eye each other warily.

"I thought you were on the Pill."

"I was."

"Well you did something wrong."

"Yeah, I slept with you."

I want to blame her for her stupidity, but how can I blame her without blaming myself? I can recall a couple of times she forgot to take her daily cocktail of estrogen and progesterone, and it may even have troubled me momentarily before I blithely disdained the consequences.

"God, Randi, I'm sorry." I put my arm around her and she leans against me. "How are you feeling?"

"Awful," she says, holding back tears. "I'm like nauseous all the time and now I'm starting to show."

"Does anyone else know?"

"No."

"You didn't tell your parents?"

"No, I'm not *that* crazy."

"Well, that's a relief."

"Fuck you."

"Why didn't you tell me sooner?"

"I've been busy hating you."

"I can see that. But meanwhile you've been going through the whole thing by yourself."

"I haven't exactly been alone," she says, patting her tummy.

"So now what?"

"I made an appointment for Saturday. A clinic in Queens. You don't have to come, but I'll need to bring three hundred dollars."

"Don't worry. I'll be there. Someone has to look after you."

"What about the money?"

"I'll take care of it." The conversation is sobering, and whatever swagger I donned with the whiskey has disappeared. "We should go," I say, patting her shoulder. "They're waiting for us." She flicks away the cigarette, sparks peppering the wet pavement.

Inside the Carnegie I follow her past a deli counter stocked with jars of marinated peppers, platters of pickled tomatoes, stacks of knishes, and trays of coleslaw and potato salad. Herb, who does the seating, is perennially harried and bustles around like a large, flightless bird. We follow him into a small, windowless dining room, which is papered practically to the ceiling with the auto-graphed head shots of actors, entertainers, celebrities and news-men. Our parents are already noshing on pickles, trying to decide what to order.

"I see the joint is jumping, Herb," says my dad.

"Pre-theater rush, Mr. Sacks. All I know is, my feet are killing me." He looks miserable, but he always does, his sad eyes like small black olives garnishing a pale, bloated face. I glance at the orthopedic shoes that are delinquent in relieving his foot pain—bulbous black oxfords with thick soles, molded arch supports and a high toe box.

"Anybody here tonight?"

"Henny Youngman was here earlier," he says, coming closer to deliver privileged information, "and Debbie Reynolds will be in after her show."

"You're kidding!" cries Cele, putting a hand to her mouth, though not close enough to muffle the outburst. Herb tells us to enjoy and waddles out to seat another party or perhaps to escape my aunt's ear-splitting enthusiasm. "Oh, my God. Debbie Reynolds. Did you see her in *Irene*? She was fabulous."

"Lower your voice, Mom. We're not deaf."

"I feel for you, Randi. It's very hard bringing up parents nowadays."

"Every time I see that guy," says my father, "he looks like he's put on another fifty pounds."

"What a shlub," adds Gene. "If he's not careful, one of these days he's going to keel over from a heart attack."

"They sure give you a lot of choices," says my mom.

"Did you see those desserts?" says Cele. "I'm starting my diet tomorrow."

The waitress wants to know if we have questions.

"How's the beef flanken?" asks Cele.

"A little bland for my money. Better to go with the goulash."

"I can't decide between the tongue and the pastrami," says Gene.

"Have 'em both," says the Captain. "What's a couple of sandwiches to a *fresser* like you?"

"Leo," warns my mom.

Gene orders a tongue sandwich. "I want it sliced from the tip," he says, "and a beer. But only if it's ice cold. Feel it with your hand to make sure."

Randi looks at me and rolls her eyes.

"Don't you think you've had enough?" says Leo.

"Who asked you?"

The waitress jots down the rest of our orders and collects the menus.

"So Gene," says Cele, "what is that you have around your neck, opera glasses?"

"Do I go to the opera?"

"How should I know? Maybe you acquired some culture since the divorce."

"Very funny. For your information these are special for the track. I'll show you how they work." He pans the binoculars as if he were watching a race: "And down the stretch they come. It's Secretariat in the lead, but here comes Prove Out. They're neck and neck, but Prove Out is digging in. Prove Out is edging away. At the finish, it's Prove Out in front. Prove Out at 16-1, a stunning upset."

I glance at my father, who does not look happy.

"When they help you win a lot of money," says Cele, "maybe you can find the time to pay your daughter's overdue tuition bill."

"I'm working on it," says Gene. "Don't hock me."

"Maybe you could work on it a little faster."

The waitress brings our drinks—five cans of Dr. Brown's and a bottle of Beck's. Gene picks up the beer and says, "No good. Not cold enough. Bring me another." The waitress stalks off, but he immediately calls her back. "Leave it," he says. "I'll drink it." He picks up his water glass, gulps down the contents and pours the

Beck's over the half-melted ice. The head threatens to overflow the glass, which he raises quickly to his lips to down the foaming suds.

"Ah!" he exclaims, lowering the tumbler onto the table with a sharp *thwack*. "Now that's a cold beer."

Great, I think, this just gets better and better. To escape the unpleasantness at the table, I take an exaggerated interest in the head shots that are higher up on the wall: John Wayne, in cowboy duds, looks ornery; Phyllis Diller laughs herself silly; Jerry Vale croons an incongruous duet with his neighbor, Brian Wilson. The prize, though, for the most esoteric 8 x 10 would have to go to a grinning Alfred E. Neuman from *MAD* magazine. I only wish I could share his light-hearted attitude: "What, me worry?"

"So Eddie," says my aunt, "I understand you're finally going to graduate."

"It looks that way."

"If you wait long enough," says my mother, "you see all kinds of miracles."

"And you're going to Columbia, right? For law school?"

The waitress is distributing entrées and sandwiches.

"Eddie seems to be having second thoughts," says my dad, filling a glass with Cel-Ray Tonic. "We're hoping he comes to his senses."

I hate it when he refers to me in the third person. I'm tempted to shout, *Eddie is never coming to his senses. And get it through your thick head, will you, he's not going to law school.*

"Children can be very demanding," says Cele, glancing at Randi. "Believe me, Leo, I know how hard it can be."

"Kids are like pancakes," says the Captain, slathering mustard on his pastrami. "Sometimes you have to throw the first one out."

Inwardly I cringe, but I refuse to show it. "Like my father always says," I counter, "'You can coat shit with honey, but underneath it's still shit.' Right, Dad?"

"Lovely table manners," says my mother, sawing away at her stuffed derma.

My vulgar remark hasn't affected anyone's appetite. Gene and Leo attack their sandwiches; Aunt Cele tucks into her goulash. Everybody is eating with relish except Randi and me. I glance at my plate, the effort of digesting my father's verbal slap having obliterated my interest in the thick mound of sliced brisket. Randi extends her hand under the table and I take it, comforted by its passive weight.

"What's with you two?" says my aunt. "You're not eating."

"I don't feel well," says Randi.

"She looks pale," says my mother.

"What do you expect?" says Cele. "She doesn't take care of herself."

"Please don't start, Ma."

"Who's starting? All I'm saying is—"

"I'm going out for a cigarette," says Randi, standing abruptly.

"My daughter," says Cele, consoling herself with a forkful of stew.

"She looks sick to her stomach," says my mom.

"I should take her to the doctor," says Cele. "Her digestion has been lousy for weeks."

Gene belches loudly. "It wouldn't hurt her to miss a few meals," he says.

"Don't you make any cracks to her about her weight," says Cele. "Besides, they all gain in college with the pressure."

"I hope she isn't pregnant," says Goldie.

My stomach flips and everybody looks in my direction as if on cue. My aunt asks the question everyone seems to be thinking.

"When you were outside with her, did she say anything?"

"No," I lie. "She hasn't said a word."

"If I find out she's pregnant—" says Gene.

"I'll make an appointment tomorrow," says Cele.

"She's not," I say, laughing it off. "She had to pull an all-nighter to finish a project. She's exhausted."

"Well why didn't you say so?"

"Stop jumping to conclusions," I say. "She just needs some rest."

My aunt looks doubtful and seems certain to renew her interrogation. "I don't know what to think," she says. "I'll have to—"

"Hey, have you heard this one?" I ask, launching into a joke I heard at the racetrack: "Riva Ridge comes into the barn and Secretariat is just hanging up the phone. 'Who was that?' he says. 'That was Nixon,' says Secretariat. 'He wants me to be the next vice president.' His stablemate says, 'You got to be a shoo-in for that job. You're even a bigger horse's ass than Agnew.'"

"It's a load of crap," says my father. "The Democrats are trying to discredit Nixon any way they can. They're just—"

"Let me guess," I say. "Nattering nabobs of negativism?"

"Don't be such a wiseguy."

"Agnew's going down, Dad. You know why? Because he's the best vice president money can buy."

"Again with the wisecracks."

"It's a prediction, not a wisecrack. He'll be lucky if he doesn't go to prison."

"Ah, you don't know what you're talking about."

Our waitress comes over to ask us how we're doing. "Anybody save room for chocolate layer cake?"

The mere mention of dessert, like a fleeting glimpse of Barbra Streisand in the dining room, is enough to make my family forget what we were discussing. The topic of Agnew's troubles is lost amid the relative merits of rugelach, cheesecake, babka and strudel.

The waitress takes orders, then starts to clear the dishes.

"Not the beer," says Gene. He drains another glass in one long swallow and looks around with a stupefied air. "You want to hear a good one?" he says. "You know what they hit me with at the sentencing? A five-thousand-dollar fine and—"

"I'll pay it," says the Captain.

"I'll pay it myself."

"I said I'd take care of it."

"Who's asking you?"

"Consider it a birthday gift."

"Some birthday this turned out to be."

"What are you bitching about," says my dad. "You got off easy."

"Oh, I got off easy, all right. Except for the five years in jail."

"Oh my God!" shouts Cele.

"He's making a joke," says Leo.

"It's no joke," says Gene.

"Kornblatt assured me—"

"Kornblatt said a lot of crap and none of it was true."

"What are you talking about?" says Leo.

"Kornblatt said first offenders don't do time. Kornblatt said I'd get a suspended sentence. Kornblatt said the sentencing was a formality. Kornblatt said this, Kornblatt said that." Gene's voice is rising now above the din of the neighboring diners. "Kornblatt said it was a done deal. A piece of cake. Well Kornblatt is a lying sack of shit. You know what Kornblatt can do? He can drop dead and kiss my fuckin ass."

I stare at my father, who won't look me in the eye.

"Nice job, Dad."

"Shut your mouth," he says.

Efforts to pacify Gene are fruitless until dessert arrives. The waitress bestows on each of us the best palliative known to New Yorkers—obscenely large wedges of cake and pie. Gene's cherry cheesecake is topped by a thin flickering candle, which he grudgingly blows out after what seems like an endless pause. If I know my uncle, he probably wished for Kornblatt to contract testicular cancer. Between soothing mouthfuls of the dense, creamy dessert, Gene is coaxed into filling us in on the details. It turns out he exaggerated a bit. Under federal law, he'll have to serve a third of the sentence—twenty months—before he can be paroled. He has to turn himself in Friday at the Manhattan Federal Detention Center on West Street.

I steal a glance at my uncle, whose eyes are distant with worry. He doesn't seem strong enough to handle prison. I think about *Angels with Dirty Faces*, and Jimmy Cagney acting yellow on the way to the electric chair.

"Shit," says Gene, "this isn't a birthday party. It's a farewell party."

"It's only a year and a half," says the Captain. "It's not the end of the world."

"It's not the end of your world," says Gene.

"All right, already. Calm down."

"That's easy for you to say. You and your charmed fuckin life."

"He's having a rough day," Leo says to the waitress, who is handing him the check. She rolls her eyes, sympathizing with what my father must have to put up with.

"I'll take that," says Gene, ripping the check from Leo's grasp.

"Stop playing games," says the Captain. "Give it back."

"You've paid enough."

"What do you think you're doing?"

"I'm taking care of this."

"No you're not," says my father.

"That's what you think."

"Cut the crap. Let me have it."

"Not this time."

"Ridiculous," says Goldie, "two grown men acting like babies."

"Forget it," says my dad, throwing up his arm in disgust. "Pay for it yourself. See if I care."

I don't believe what I'm seeing. Nobody picks up a check on the Captain. Especially not my uncle. It's unheard of. Gene studies the tab as if the prices are written in a foreign currency. He makes a show of sorting through his cash and counting out the amount four or five times before he's satisfied. My father, red-faced and breathing heavily, searches his pockets for pills.

Randi sweeps back in, her hair wet from the rain.

"Where the hell have *you* been?" Cele wants to know.

"I took a walk," says Randi. "What's all the commotion?"

"You better sit down," says Cele. "Your father's going to prison."

"I thought Uncle Leo got him off," says Randi.

"Five years they gave him! How are we going to live?"

"A year and a half," I correct her.

"I don't understand," she shrieks. "How could they do that?"

"Will you lower the freakin volume?" I say. "Everyone's staring."

My aunt looks at me strangely, as though she were squinting at the bottom line of an eye chart. "Lower the freakin volume," she repeats softly. "That's just what your boyfriend said."

"What are you talking about, Ma?"

"Silverman!" she shouts. "When I woke him up. Art Silverman."

"I don't know any Art Silverman."

"Wait a second," says Cele, staring at me. "He's the boyfriend."

"What are you talking about?" I say. "I only crashed there a few nights after I got robbed."

"So what's the big fuckin deal?" says Randi.

"You were robbed?" says my mother. "When did this happen?"

"But why should he lie to me?" says Cele. "Unless he was . . . Oh my God!"

"I don't get it," says Gene.

"He's the boyfriend," explains Cele. "The one I told you about."

"You?" Gene's eyes bore into me with confusion and hurt.

"I think we should all just take a deep breath," I say.

"You son of a bitch," he says, leaping up. "I'll murder you." But he gets no farther than the back of his chair, with which he steadies himself before he vomits over it.

"What a fuckin mess," says Randi. "We better clean him up." With Cele's assistance, they steer Gene toward the restroom. My mother goes to look for our waitress.

The Captain and I face each other from across the table, like gunfighters waiting for someone to make the first move. He wipes his forehead with a napkin and drops it on to the floor. He seems to be breathing with difficulty.

"You *shtupped* your cousin?" says my father. "You're disgusting."

"You're going to lecture me on morality?"

"Look at you. How can you live with yourself?"

"Me? What about you? The big *macher*. You said you'd take care of him if he kept his mouth shut, and you hung him out to dry."

"You don't know what you're talking about," he says. He pats himself down, in search of his medication.

"Everyone thinks you're Mr. Magnanimous. What a laugh."

"I'm warning you, Eddie. You better watch yourself."

"You're nothing but a phony."

"I don't have to listen to this," he says, getting up and storming past me.

"You don't get off that easy," I say, following him to the deli counter. "Look what you did to him. He's ruined."

"He brought it on himself," he says, stopping to catch his breath. "He's a loser. He's not like us."

"You think I'm like you? I got news for you, Dad, I wouldn't do what you did in a million years."

"The judge screwed us. He wasn't supposed to go to jail."

"No, Dad, you screwed him. You got all the money in the world, but it's more important to you to save a few bucks."

"You'll understand better when you're older. When you get out of law school, Eddie—" But that's as far as he gets. As if recoiling from an invisible blow, he slumps against the angled glass of the deli case, massaging his chest.

I try to get Herb's attention, but it's useless. He's too busy freaking out. Diners are fleeing toward the door. Arriving parties are waiting impatiently to be seated. Sinatra is on his way over with an entourage. "Get a mop," he yells, "and something to spray the air." A busboy runs up to him with an aerosol can. "Not disinfectant, you *shmendrick*! Air freshener! For the odor! The odor!" he cries, a mock-heroic Kurtz amid the corned beef and the kosher pickles.

ALL AROUND
THE TOWN

The ambulance rushes my father to Roosevelt, where Goldie and I camp out in the waiting room. The doctor who briefs us is encouraging. The Captain has suffered a heart attack, but he seems to be doing well.

We sit for hours leafing through outdated magazines. Every now and then Goldie looks at me and shakes her head. She can't quite bring herself to say *How could you?* but I gather that's what she's thinking.

I wish she would accuse me so I could defend myself, but she's too well versed, my mother, in the art of guilt. Her disapproving silence is impossible to ignore and my thoughts soon riot with worry and recrimination: How could I have slept with my first cousin? What an idiot I was to get her pregnant. You don't have to be a genius to realize that a few months of sexual ecstasy are not worth a lifetime of disgrace. But did that stop me? Did I weigh the consequences? Did I take time to think things out? Did I once remember my father's favorite expression? Not me. I had to learn the hard way that "when the penis gets hard, the brains turn to mud."

When my mother finally talks to me, it's to suggest I take a nap. Though I'm beyond exhaustion, I cannot relax enough to nod out until my mind hugs like a pillow the reassuring thought, *Thank God for Roe v. Wade.*

I'm playing tiddlywinks with the Captain's nitroglycerin tablets when Goldie shakes me awake. "I'm afraid I have bad news, Eddie." Her voice is flat and faraway. "He didn't make it," she says, absently handing me the death certificate, which reads, "Massive myocardial infarction."

We drive back to Valley Stream in the wee hours, and it's only when I enter the den and see the empty Stratolounger that I know he's gone. My mother goes straight to sleep, but I'm still geared up from the drive. It feels like trespassing to sit in the recliner so I opt for the couch instead. The tube offers little of interest except for an old flick in which Bill Holden plays a talented violinist who defies his father, Lee J. Cobb, to become a prizefighter. Cobb reminds me of the Captain, physically prepossessing in a way that made him seem larger than he was. He was often cast as the heavy—a character with an iron will who, depending on the role, could be either an upright citizen or an outright villain. By coincidence, Cobb, like my father, had suffered a heart attack in his thirties, while doing *Death of a Salesman* on Broadway.

It's after four when I click off the TV, douse the lights, check that the doors are locked, and lie down on the sofa fully clothed. A dog up the block is barking, my mother is snoring, the porcelain clock is ticking, the fridge in the kitchen seems to be chanting, *Om.* Every so often the house groans. It can't get settled either.

Goldie has always complained that the walls are too thin. "A person sneezes in the attic," she's fond of saying, "and someone in the basement says 'Gesundheit.'" But tonight the place seems even flimsier than usual. I play an old game, trying to identify each discernible noise: the faucet's languid drip, the barking dog again, the oil burner as it drones and stops. And then a new sound joins the symphony, an intermittent squeaking of loose boards, like someone stealing up the cellar stairs.

I go to the kitchen and open the fridge. A can of Reddi-wip tempts me from the top shelf. Uncapping it, I throw my head back and cock the nozzle. A jet of cold whipped topping snorts into my mouth and I wash it down with a swig from a carton of milk. No longer drowsy, I imagine I am the only person awake on Robin Road, if not the entire avian subdivision. No doubt it's too early even for the early birds of Sparrow Lane, Warbler Way, Oriole Drive and Phoebe Court. I part the living room curtains and survey the street. A suburban still life lies before me with the clarity of a Magritte: All is tenebrous and deserted down the prosperous row of split-level homes; not a single night light shines; the goose-necked street lamps burn weakly; above the darkened houses a luminous half-moon hovers among pale apparitions of clouds.

Now that the sky has cleared, I ought to go for a walk, or at least throw open the windows behind the couch, but they're frozen fast with excess paint. Without ventilation, the air is stale in the small living room, which seems further diminished by all the pictures and keepsakes and *tchotchkes* that crowd the end tables, the glass étagère, the piano console, the top of the liquor cabinet. For the first time in years I examine the iconic images of old family photos. On the piano is a likeness of myself to which I've always been partial: an eager-eyed sixteen-year-old, calmly surveying the Hudson Valley from an escarpment in the Catskills. He projects such assurance, such focus and ability. Yet at this instant I feel no kinship with that clean-cut, ingenuous kid full of initiative and promise. He was going to be a lawyer, but you might say I sabotaged his future. Derailed his plans. Rebelled against his fate. He probably hates my guts for what I did to him. In an adjacent frame, my father as a handsome young lieutenant stands at ease. The resemblance between father and son is striking not just in the similarity of facial features, but in the correspondent qualities of character their portraits manage to convey: An air of confidence and determination that one can read easily in the bearing of the head and the identical cast of the eyes. I wonder if I'll ever again feel so sure of myself, and I'm seized by the sudden impulse to apologize.

"Sorry, Dad," I say out loud.

"Sorry for what?"

"Mom, is that you?" But how can it be her when the fickle silence is punctuated by my mother's snoring?

"What are you sorry for?"

Am I hearing things or is that the sound of the Captain's brusque, authoritative voice emanating from the darkened dining room? Peering intently into the dim, unlighted space, I am unable to apprehend a form but sense a kind of presence, animate and near.

"I'm sorry for disappointing you."

"Remember, Eddie, the clubhouse is littered with losing tickets. You want to be a loser or a winner?"

"Dad? Dad, is that you? Are you in there, Dad?"

"The trouble with you, Eddie, is you think you know it all. You never listen."

"I'm listening now, Dad. What did you want to say?"

I sound very strange to myself, vague and disembodied, as if someone else were using my voice. My father does not reply. Staring into the shadows, eyes bright as dimes in the pin-drop-silent middle of the night, I will my father's being to materialize. I want more than anything for him to speak to me, but there is only the suggestive scraping of a maple branch against the brick, and the blustery wind sweeping away the spent leaves.

"I'm waiting, Dad. I'm ready to listen. Are you there?"

Nothing.

My eyes burn as I fight the urge to blink; my ears strain to hear his voice; my pulse throbs; my foot falls asleep. Ignoring the discomfort, I exhort myself to pay attention. Never have I felt more alert. I seem to be coursing with a definite electrical charge—hair, neck, skin, fingertips all conducting a faint but palpable current. Intent on listening, I persevere, studying, sifting, probing the ambiguous darkness. The room grows blacker, then seems to lighten before darkening again. A car with a noisy muffler passes, and its headlights irradiate the dining room like time-lapse photography of the sun rising and setting. Try as I may, I cannot conjure my father's voice, and after a quarter of an hour of sustained concentration, I concede, collapsing with a sigh onto the stiff prophylactic slipcovers of the sofa.

We spend the day drifting through the house like clouds. When not making phone calls or funeral arrangements, my mother and I speak in whispers, as if it is a quiet Sunday and the Captain is taking a snooze.

Around noon I retreat to the picnic table with a cup of coffee. It's the first chance I have to reflect on my pre-dawn experience and I hardly know what to make of it. Drained and confused, with a pounding headache and eyes like sandpaper from lack of sleep, I wonder if I achieved some form of paranormal communication or if my febrile imagination just hallucinated the whole thing. Had my father addressed me or had I addressed myself? I'd like to think that I have some unusual powers, but the more I dwell on it, the more I'm convinced I slipped into a suggestive state that fueled a harmless delusion. All I know is, I haven't felt so strange since I was tripping.

Weird as it sounds, I need to remind myself that I'm in mourning, because I really don't feel like it. I'm not weepy. In fact I haven't cried at all. I guess I'm sad, but I'm not dragging my ass around. Just the opposite. I feel strangely buoyant. While Goldie trudges around in her housedress, I float through the day like an astronaut in a state of weightlessness.

No, my mother is not doing well. She breaks down while dusting the Captain's portrait or carrying his shoes into the bedroom or moving aside a can of Fresca in the fridge. And when she learns that Rabbi Tuchman is unavailable and we'll have to use another rabbi to conduct the service, one we've never met, she starts sobbing inconsolably. She does better with other people around and is more composed in the afternoon when neighbors drop by to pay their respects or when we go over to Green Acres to buy a suit I can wear to the funeral.

Goldie worries that the threat of torrential rain will keep people away, but as it turns out, the main sanctuary at the Morningside Funeral Chapel in Forest Hills, which Foxy has been kind enough to reserve, cannot accommodate the crowd. Mourners pack the aisles and spill into the hallway. People come from all corners of my father's life—friends and relatives, colleagues from the coin business, neighbors from Robin Road, people he grew up with, even old army buddies.

I keep an eye on Goldie, who so far seems to be holding up. She's greeting the Sukenicks, our elderly neighbors from down the block, as Cele and Randi stand on either side of her, ready to lend assistance. Foxy is also over there, leaning on a cane, waiting to express his sympathy. Frail and shrunken, he looks exhausted with the effort to remain upright, and I can't help thinking that he's next. It occurs to me that Kornblatt isn't with him and I hope to hell he doesn't show up.

Gene pushes his way over and stares at me menacingly.

"I ought to beat the crap out of you right now," he says.

"You want me to step outside?"

"Never mind. You get a reprieve because of the funeral, and because you're going to drive me to the city later."

"When do you have to turn yourself in?"

"I was supposed to report this morning, but Kornblatt got the time changed to seven. The one thing the bastard was able to do for me." He looks around. "You want to get stoned?"

"Before or after you kill me?"

"I hate to smoke alone."

"You go ahead. I think I better be straight for this."

"Suit yourself," he says. "You need a blast?" He opens his suit jacket to reveal half a pint of Canadian Club stashed in his inside pocket.

"Go easy on the schnapps, why don't you?"

"Relax," he says, "I'm not going to puke on the corpse, if that's what you're worried about." He turns and snakes his way through the crowd.

Fortunately the coffin is closed, in keeping with Jewish custom.

My father's partner comes up and hugs me, burrowing his face in my chest. "What can I say, Ed?" says Tiny in his high, boyish voice, his supplicating palms more eloquent than any words of condolence. "Your father was a giant. There was no one . . ." His hand covers his quivering lips.

"Thanks, Tiny," I say, patting his shoulder.

"What are we going to do without him?"

"I don't know," I say, but of course I do know. I know I'm not going to law school.

"I feel like it's my fault," he confesses.

"Don't be ridiculous, Tiny."

"I begged him to take care of himself, but he wouldn't hear of it."

"Since when did he listen?"

"You don't know the half of it," he says. "Last couple of months he's been popping those heart pills like candy. 'See a doctor,' I told him. You know what he says to me? 'Go fuck yourself.'"

"Nobody could tell him anything."

"Stubborn cocksucker. That was your father to a T."

Someone is tapping the microphone and asking people to take their seats. A few minutes later Rabbi Melnick, a recent seminary graduate whose wire-rimmed glasses and well-trimmed beard cannot conceal his youth, ascends to the podium. He places a small packet of index cards on the lectern, which must contain what little information he gleaned from his fifteen-minute interview with Goldie and me. What could he possibly have to say, I wonder as I take my mother's hand. But he seems confident enough as he waits for the syncopated coughing to abate.

"We are assembled to say farewell to Leo Jacob Sacks," he begins, "who has been called too soon to his eternal rest. It is difficult to speak of a man who until a few days ago carried on his daily routine, and then all of a sudden, poof"—he snaps his fingers—"his routine has been terminated, for he has been charged with the task of completing his sojourn here on earth."

Cele leans across my mother and whispers much too loudly, "I don't think it's right for the rabbi to snap his fingers."

"I don't know," shrugs my mother. I don't think it's right for my aunt to wear so much perfume, but do I tell her that?

Rabbi Melnick plods on in the deliberate singsong that is the rhetorical hallmark of his trade: "Leo's death comes as a painful shock to his wife, Goldie, his son, Edward, and his brother, Gene, for he was such a dynamic person. Yet in the midst of tragedy we endeavor to confer meaning on this sad event. How do we do that? We do that by recalling from the Bible the story of Jacob, which is altogether fitting and proper as it is Leo Sacks's middle name. In the Book of Genesis we read of the death of Jacob, and the Bible uses highly unusual language to speak of Jacob's approaching demise. 'And Jacob lived in the land of Egypt,' it tells us. Now think about that, for it is most strange, is it not, to speak of life when the Bible means death? But in its paradoxical way, the Bible seeks to teach us that when a man dies, and the death notice appears in the papers, it is really a *life* notice. It says to us: 'Do not think for a moment that a man's countless deeds can be condensed into column inches; a life is not a rag that can be wrung for a few scant lines of newsprint. For this man lived, and this man worked, and this man accomplished something—something weighty and substantial and memorable while he was here.' And Leo Sacks, I can tell you, accomplished a great deal."

It's about time, I think. He's finally going to say something personal about the Captain.

"I confess I never met the deceased," he continues, "but when I talked with Goldie and Edward, they shared with me the joys and the sorrows, the hopes and the dreams—the stuff of which a family life is fashioned—and from their golden memories they made me feel as if I really knew the man. In truth I am here to eulogize a person who does not need me to eulogize him. And why is that? Because Leo Sacks created his own eulogy in the life he led. Leo was first of all a decorated war hero, an officer who served his country not only in World War II but again in the Korean War. Also he was a brilliant businessman—a successful coin dealer who was respected by all who knew him. And what about his generosity, which was legendary, I am told, for Leo always gave a helping hand to anyone who was in need. Yes, this was Leo Sacks: Loving husband, supportive father, dedicated family man, inspirational brother—"

"Inspirational my ass," whispers Gene.

"So many times," continues Melnick, "Goldie told me, she dropped him off at the train station in Valley Stream, one of the multitude of unobtrusive commuters who ride the Long Island

Rail Road every day into the bowels of the city, where he toiled selflessly for his family, confident in the knowledge that he was always able to provide for them the best."

I look over at my uncle, who is rolling his eyes, and I have to suppress a laugh. I don't recall Goldie telling the rabbi any of this crap. My dad hated the LIRR. Riding the train always made him grumpy. He was too antsy to read and he got bored looking at the scenery. Give him his Caddy any day of the week. He needed to be in the driver's seat, weaving in and out of traffic, flooring that powerful V-8 and tailgating like a maniac. That's what I would tell this crowd if I were giving the eulogy. And I'd illustrate it with that joke he once told me: A guy has a heart attack on the street. A priest attends to him and whispers, *It's very bad, son.* He starts to administer last rites but the stricken man waves him away.

Leave me alone, he barks.

But you won't be allowed to enter heaven, pleads the priest.

Father, he says, *I don't care if I go to hell, so long as I don't have to change at Jamaica.*

The clueless Rabbi Melnick, or Rabbi Nudnik as I'm beginning to think of him, is meandering toward a forgettable conclusion with yet another sententious stream of prose: "Although he is now departed from our midst, be consoled that you knew such a man, that such a man was your husband or your father or your brother, and know that his strength will be with you as an eternal memorial, his wisdom as a shining example, and his spirit as a constant beacon, and let us say, Amen."

After announcing the details for forming the motorcade,

Nudnik approaches us, his eyes unnaturally wide with sympathy and concern.

"Thank you for your beautiful speech," says Goldie.

"It went quite well, I thought. I really tried to communicate what an amazing person Leo was. What did you think?" he asks me.

"Rabbi," I tell him, "no eulogy would have been better than that." Judging from the complacent smile that has infiltrated the corners of his mouth, he hasn't the slightest idea I've just insulted him. I have an unholy urge to smack him with a prayer book, so I tell him we'll see him at the cemetery and start to lead my mother away.

"I have something to tell you," she says. "I had a chat with Foxy. Nothing's changed. You can still go to Columbia. I made him promise."

"Okay, Ma, we'll talk about it later."

The aisles are jammed with people edging toward the exits like a crowd leaving a hit Broadway show, and I badly want to be out-side in the fresh air. Nervous and agitated, I look around to see if there's another way out when I notice Irving, the luckless assistant from the coin shop, sitting all by himself and weeping miserably into his gnarled hands. Every thankless workday the Captain crit-icized him mercilessly, hounded and insulted him, called him *shlepper* and *schlimazel* and treated him with undisguised con-tempt. Yet Irving is overcome with grief. His hair is unkempt, his clothes are disheveled; he's a mess. It dawns on me that without Irving as a whipping boy, the Captain would have taken all his frustration out on me. Sobered by gratitude and guilt, I feel some-thing in me shift. I exhale fully and then the floodgates burst and

I'm sobbing for the first time since my father died. Goldie comforts me as we're ushered through a side door into a black limo in which Randi, Cele and Gene are already waiting.

"Thank God it stopped raining," says Cele. While we were in the funeral home the front must have blown through.

"Maybe it's a good omen," says Gene. "Leo was never crazy about a wet track."

Our liveried driver swings the limo into line behind the hearse, which leads the entourage east along Queens Boulevard.

"I can't believe how many people came," says Goldie.

"Some turnout," says Gene, "especially in this weather."

"Everyone seemed to like the service," says Cele.

"I thought the rabbi had a nice voice," says Randi.

"And he didn't go on and on," says Gene.

"Personally," says Goldie, "I thought he was from hunger."

"He certainly wasn't my cup of tea," says Cele.

"Let's face it," says Gene, "he's a kid. He doesn't know anything."

"He was so boring," says Randi. "He could have been talking about anyone."

"What do you expect," I say, "when you get someone *tefillin* at the last minute?" But nobody gets my pun.

"Frankly," says Cele, "I've heard better eulogies for pets."

"Live and learn," says my mom. "That's the last time I ask Hy Finkle for a recommendation."

"You know what I liked about Uncle Leo?" says Randi. "He always gave the best presents. For my birthday once he got me a portable easel and these fancy watercolors. I was just ten, you know, but it wasn't this crappy kid's stuff. All the art supplies were like really professional."

"That's Leo," says Goldie. "Everything has to be the best. And generous? There's no one who spends money like him."

"Very generous," says Cele. "The first time I met him, the four of us went out to dinner and we had a big fight over who was going to pay. I thought I'd end it by putting the bill down my cleavage, but Leo snatched it right out of there. Needless to say, I never fought him for another check."

"Listen to this," I say, and tell the story of the Captain drag-racing that van across Fifty-fifth Street. I even get my mother to smile as I describe the red-faced driver oblivious to the gallons of gas spewing from his tank while the Captain laughs his head off.

"But he has a temper," says Goldie. "If things don't go his way he'll hit the ceiling. Remember when he smashed the binoculars?"

"How could I forget," I say. I turn to my uncle. "What do you remember?"

"I don't know," he says, staring out the window. "I can't think of nothing right now." But the way it comes out suggests he's think-ing of plenty and not saying it. His silence, brooding and palpable, seems to suck the oxygen out of the air, extinguishing conversa-tion. In the ensuing lull I concentrate on reading road signs and monitoring our progress over the lightly trafficked parkways of Queens. Appropriately, our route takes us by Belmont Park so the Captain can bid farewell to his old stomping grounds. Too bad he can't be interred in the Belmont infield, but at least he will be laid to rest close by, at Beth David Cemetery, in a plot that is only a horseshoe's throw from the shedrow where Secretariat is stabled.

The mourners tread gingerly over the wet ground to congregate by the grave, above which the coffin is suspended on a low aluminum scaffold. The scaffold rests on a jarring green carpet of Astroturf, which lines the rectangular rim of the freshly dug pit. The earth has been removed to a steep neighboring mound from which protrudes the long wooden handle of a shovel.

"At least it's clearing," I say. We use our hands like visors, shielding our eyes to observe the sky, a dramatic division of clouds and calm. Scudding eastward, a mass of angry thunderheads darkens Long Island while above us a bright sun promises a mild afternoon.

"Thank God for small favors," says Goldie.

Our attention automatically returns to the coffin, its wooden lid adorned simply with a raised Jewish star carved into the blond oak.

"I'm glad we went with the dark blue, Eddie. Your father always looked so handsome in it." A breeze stirs, fluttering the mourning ribbon pinned to her black dress.

"He looked great, Mom. Very distinguished." But it bothers me that the conservative burial suit is a far cry from the brightly colored clothes he favored. I had lobbied for the fuchsia sportcoat to no avail.

"The paisley tie would have been better."

"I wouldn't worry," I say, patting her hand. "I'm sure he doesn't mind."

Gene sidles up, reeking of pot, a rebellious glint in his eye. He leans over and hums in my ear the "Call to the Post."

"The horses are on the track," he whispers, "and I'm riding high." His breath stinks of whisky.

"Do me a favor, will you? Try not to fall off."

"What are you worried about? Here, have a hit." He offers me a matchbook with the charred end of a roach peeking out.

"Keep it," I say, eyeing him disapprovingly.

"Hey, Rabbi," says Gene, "let's get this show on the road."

"In a minute," says Melnick, who has been riffling through the Rabbinical Assembly Manual as if he were cramming for a test. When he finds a passage of interest, he scans it intently while stroking his beard. "All right," he says, "why don't we begin." He urges the people in the rear to move forward, and waits for the rustling and the whispering to cease. "The saying goes . . . Can you all hear me? I'll speak a little louder. The saying goes that one who is buried on Erev Shabbat is fortunate to share Shabbat with God. And today is not only Erev Shabbat, but Erev Yom Kippur, which means that sundown begins the holiest day of the year. Thus it is our fervent wish that the Eternal God will welcome Leo Jacob Sacks with open arms." Melnick pauses to consult the manual.

"Need any help?" says Gene, getting a laugh at the rabbi's expense.

"I was going to read a psalm . . ." says Melnick, paging feverishly back and forth. He seems far less certain of himself than at the funeral home, as if he had spent all his time writing the eulogy and none preparing the graveside service. "Ah, here it is," he says. "'The earth is the Lord's'—I'm sorry, did I mention this is from the 24th Psalm?"

"Jesus," hisses Gene. "Just read the damn thing."

Melnick looks up at Gene, who motions with his hands as if to say, *Get on with it, will you.* Pausing to collect himself, the rabbi wipes the sweat from his forehead and manages to sweep his hair into an awkwardly plastered crest. I find myself feeling sorry for him, the poor bastard. I doubt they taught him at the seminary how to deal with someone like my uncle. Melnick takes a deep breath and resumes his tedious delivery.

"Who may ascend the mountain of the Lord?" he intones. "Who may stand in His holy place? He who has clean hands and a pure heart, who takes not God's name in vain, swearing falsely."

The last sentence brings me up short, like a steeplechase rider who finds himself sailing over a hedge when his mount refuses to make a jump. A day did not go by when my father didn't curse up a storm. And I'm not sure how clean his hands were, what with all the silver he was smuggling. And God knows his heart could have been purer where his brother was concerned. If there is a heaven, it's possible the Captain's soul may end up in the winner's circle, but I wouldn't exactly call it an odds-on wager.

Having finished the psalm, Melnick cues the gravediggers to lower the coffin, while he recites a prayer in Hebrew, which he dutifully translates: "The dust returns to the earth, as it was, but the spirit returns unto God, who gave it. May the soul of Leo Jacob Sacks be bound up in the bond of life eternal."

The rabbi motions Goldie forward and hands her the shovel with a cupful of topsoil—less even, a demitasse—which she tosses into the grave. I take the shovel from her, plunge it into the pile of dirt, face the open pit and hesitate. I can't shake the impulse to ask the Captain's forgiveness. Sometimes I wished him dead, but it's more than that. I have a lingering suspicion that I caused his heart attack. I certainly contributed to it. Maybe that's why I feel like I'm getting away with murder.

Instead of an apology or a prayer, what comes to me is a poem a college friend used to recite:

Ashes to ashes
Dust to dust
Die we will
But live we must.

I aim the dirt at the Jewish star in the middle of the coffin, where it splatters. Gene relieves me and dumps in a heaping shovelful. Instead of quitting, he heaves in another, and another, load after load into the grave, attacking the mound of earth with surprising ferocity. The gravediggers eye each other and shrug as Melnick stares, panic-stricken, unsure of what to do to make Gene desist.

"Maybe that's enough, Mr. Sacks," he says, but Gene either ignores or does not hear the rabbi's gentle reproof and persists in his manic shoveling. I can see it's up to me to rein him in, but before I can say anything, my aunt beats me to it.

"For the love of God," cries Cele, in that awful screeching voice of hers. "Will you stop, already?"

Gene freezes, staring like a sleepwalker at the fresh shovelful of dirt he is holding. "What the hell," he says, and tosses in one final scoop before surrendering the implement to Melnick, who races through the Mourner's Kaddish as if vying for the *Guinness Book of World Records*, then, still clutching the shovel, wanders off unsteadily among the graves.

Back at Robin Road the mourners gather throughout the house in somber groups of three or four. Few venture out to the patio, even with the unseasonably warm temperature. Goldie holds court in the den while I work the living room. Gene is in the kitchen playing bartender, a job that grants him ample opportunity to ply himself with schnapps, so you can imagine the shape he's in by the time I have to drive him to the city to report to the Men's Detention Center, from where he will be transferred to a federal correctional facility.

I don't particularly want to fight Friday rush-hour traffic, especially with so many people trying to get home for the holiday, but it's a good excuse to get away from the house, where I'm tired of telling people that my father packed more living into his fifty-one years than other people did into ninety. Gene is so blitzed he can't walk straight, but that's okay, he assures me in his slurred and halting delivery, because the jail stinks to high heaven and the only way to deal with it is drunk. I ask him what else he has heard and he says you have to turn in all your clothes for prison fatigues, but before you get dressed they search under your scrotum and in your asshole.

"Too bad you can't take a rain check."

"Too bad is right. Then they throw you in a cell with thirty guys."

"I can't imagine."

"And one toilet."

"Jesus. What about the food? Terrible, right?"

"No, they say the food isn't bad, except the cook uses coffee to color the gravy. Also, you play a shitload of pinochle and—"

"Wait a second. The cook uses coffee?"

"That's what I heard." He downs the last of the half-pint of rye and stares at the empty bottle. "Shit. Oh, and the Black Muslims run the place. They get special food, push people around."

"Sounds like fun."

"Got any suggestions?"

We're stuck in stop-and-go traffic on the Cross Island Parkway, a good place to teach him *As-salamu alaykum* and a few other Arabic phrases I learned from Moose, but before we get to Jamaica Avenue he's out cold. I rouse him an hour later in the West Village across from a gray clapboard building with a bar on the ground floor. Transoms above the pub windows all bear the same white profile of a horse's head against a black background.

"Where the fuck are we?" he says, yawning and scratching his balding scalp.

"The White Horse on Hudson, a few blocks from the jail." The bar is something of a shrine to the memory of Dylan Thomas, the Welsh poet. One November night he downed eighteen whiskies—a house record. Then he fell into a coma and died. "Come on. I'll buy you a drink."

"I don't think I can walk in there yet." Gene has the stupefied air of a beaten boxer who slumps on his stool after a bout. I gaze enviously at the crowd in the front room carousing behind a red neon Guinness sign. I would love a beer, but I probably shouldn't encourage him. The last thing Gene needs is more alcohol.

"We can always hang out in the car."

"Thanks, kid. I can't deal with all the people. Besides," he says, "I have to get rid of this." He holds up the matchbook with the roach.

"Be cool, Gene. There are a lot of people on the street."

"Ah, stop worrying."

"It wouldn't be too good if we got caught."

"What do I fuckin care?" He takes a hit and passes it to me.

"How about some music?" I punch in the Sinatra station. "In honor of the Captain."

We finish the joint listening to a melancholy tune in a minor key: *"When I was seventeen, it was a very good year . . ."*

"What a depressing song," he says.

"You okay, Gene?" He has the foggy look of a man who is well beyond his limit.

"Man, I'm wrecked."

"I can see that." But I'm not sure if he's referring to his advanced state of intoxication or to his reduced circumstances

"You know what I really miss about my job," he says. "Of course I liked being on my own with nobody breathing down my neck. It was great for that. But what I really liked was going out to Coney Island for the annual inspection. See, an elevator inspector has to check every ride at all the parks and fairs around the city, but Coney Island was always the most fun. You picked a nice spring day. You rode the Cyclone, the Jumbo Jet, the Parachute Jump, and the great thing was you were getting paid to do it. I think I even took you one time."

"We went to Coney Island?"

"Sure we did. We went over Easter break. You were about eight. We had lunch at Nathan's. I took you to Steeplechase Park. You had that accident in the bumper cars when you hit your nose on the steering wheel. You must remember that."

"Oh, yeah. That's because you bumped me too hard."

"You know what I remember about you? You were nuts about the subway. You liked to ride in the front car and look out the window at the tracks. That was your big thing, peering into the subway tunnel watching the stations zip by and the signals change. You still do that?"

I look at him like his elevator doesn't go all the way to the top floor.

"Are you kidding me?"

"I'm curious," he says. "What's the coolest thing you remember about the subway?"

"Boy, are you stoned."

"All right, forget it." The way he shakes his head makes me feel as if I've ignored a condemned man's final request.

"I liked the fact that August Belmont financed the original IRT."

"The guy who the Belmont Stakes was named for?"

"No, that was the father. An Austrian Jew named Schonberg who was a banker and a racing fan and changed his name into French to fit in. I'm talking about his son, August Belmont, Jr. Not only did the son finance construction of the subway, he also built Belmont Park."

"Speaking of Belmont," he says, "you going out Columbus Day? Secretariat's running in the Man o' War."

"I'm in mourning, Gene. I can't go anywhere."

"Tell you one thing," he says. "I wouldn't want to be God when Leo realizes he's missing the Man o' War. Talk about pissed."

"Maybe we should get going," I say, glancing at the clock in the dash. Gene doesn't answer. He's picking nervously at the skin around his cuticles, which are scarred with angry patches of red. "Listen, man, it's not going to be that bad. Just keep a low profile and don't talk back."

"That's easy for you to say."

"How about this?" I propose. "After you finish your jail time, why don't we take off for a week?"

"You want to take a vacation somewhere? Just the two of us?"

"We can go fishing. Go up to Lake George—"

"Not Lake George," he says sharply. "I hate that fuckin place."

"Then the Thousand Islands or Lake Champlain. Rent a cabin. Schroon Lake, someplace like that." He doesn't say anything. He just stares through the windshield. "What's the matter, Gene?"

"How could you do that to me? Sleep with Randi?"

"I didn't sleep with her."

"This is me you're talking to. I wasn't born yesterday."

I ought to stonewall him, but he'll know I'm lying. He always does.

"I'm sorry, Gene. It just happened."

"Nothing just happens."

"It was stupid of me. I am sorry."

"After all we've been through, this is how you treat me?" His eyes dismiss me with such disappointment, he reminds me of the Captain. "Listen," he says, "I won't be going on any trips with you when I get out."

"So what are you saying? We're not going to pal around anymore?" When he doesn't answer or look at me, it hits me what I've lost and I have to squeeze shut my eyes until the impulse to cry subsides.

"Whatever you want," I say. "Just tell me one thing. What happened in Lake George between you and the Captain?"

"How do you know something happened?"

"Come on, Gene, I wasn't born yesterday either."

He doesn't say anything for minute, but when he speaks his voice is so soft I have to strain to hear.

"Leo and me were fishing, just the two of us, early in the morning. No one else on the water. We had already caught a couple of fish. But now that I think about it, only I had caught a couple—perch, bass, something like that—and he says, 'Do me a favor will you and hold my wallet for a second, my butt is killing me.' So I'm holding the wallet while he's massaging his butt. But I'm a wiseass kid so I make believe I'm losing my balance and I'm going to fall overboard and I got the wallet in one hand and I'm flailing around with the other. And I ask him, 'If I fell into the lake and I went in one direction and the wallet went in the other, who would you save first?' He says, 'That's easy. Wallets can't swim.' This is how he treats me, my big brother the war hero, after I waited the whole fuckin war for him to come home and spend some time with me. This is what he has the nerve to say?"

People are so fragile, I think. My uncle is bent out of shape over the answer he didn't like to a hypothetical question he posed twenty-five years ago.

"The son of a bitch," he says. "My whole fuckin life . . ."

He sprawls back, his head resting between the door and the seat, his face creased in a tight, bitter smile.

"Come on, Gene," I say, patting him on the shoulder.

"It's funny, right? He cared more for his fuckin wallet than for me."

"We both know the Captain could be a jerk."

"Fuck it," he says, "let's have a drink."

"I'm worried about the time, Gene. I think we should go."

"One drink. What's the big deal?"

"You have to be there in fifteen minutes."

"All right, already. Drive the fuckin car."

The sun is setting over Jersey and the sky beyond the river is all the colors of a bruise. I drop Gene off a block from the jail, where we say goodbye without shaking hands. "See you at the next funeral," he says. As I pull away he's taking a piss against the brick wall of a warehouse. He should make it on time, but you never know with my uncle. I just hope he doesn't return to the White Horse and drink himself to death.

Back on the Island, my mother sedates herself with sitcoms: "Bewitched," "Sanford and Son," "The Odd Couple." The canned laughter might as well be mocking me as I rack my brain searching for an excuse to get me out of the house so that I can go meet Randi, who must have totally spaced out to schedule the abortion on Yom Kippur. When the "Dean Martin Comedy Hour" comes on, Goldie sets up the ironing board and touches up her black dress. No more sitting *shiva*, she reminds me. The mourning period is suspended when it falls on a holiday, so we're going to temple tomorrow to say Kaddish. You would think someone in mourning would want to avoid the crowds at the synagogue, but not Goldie. She spent a fortune on those reserved seats and to waste the money would kill her.

On Saturday I still don't have a clue how I'm going to get away until my mother miraculously declares that she doesn't have the energy to go to synagogue.

"I can't bear to face that mob scene," she says.

"It's perfectly understandable, Ma. Stay home and rest."

"It's more important you go, Eddie. You've got a lot to atone for."

"Gee, thanks, Ma. Do you think I have a chance with all my sins to be inscribed in the Book of Life for another year?"

"I wish I knew what goes through your mind, Eddie. I just don't understand you anymore. When are you going to straighten out?"

"I'm working on it," I tell her as I swipe the car keys off the kitchen counter. "See you in a few hours."

"You can't drive today. It's *yontif.*"

"Ma, who's going to care?"

"It's not respectful, Eddie. You'll have to walk if you want to go."

"We never walk to services."

"Don't argue with me. Your father just died and you're not taking the car. That's all there is to it."

My mother goes to temple three days a year. Either she's suddenly become ultra-Orthodox or grief has made her *meshugge.* I have no choice but to tear out of the house, grab the bus to Hempstead Turnpike, then transfer to another that will drop me at the subway. I should just make it, but I have no room for error. If I'm late, Randi will never forgive me.

The Queens-bound bus eventually arrives at Hillside Avenue in Jamaica. I slip a brass token into the wooden turnstile and hurry down the steps to where the next trainload of people is gathering. Beyond the brightness of the station, the tracks disclose no sign of an approaching train. After checking my watch, and then the scrap of paper with the address of the clinic, I pace the platform, studying the black circular splotches of chewing gum that have been stamped flat onto the dirty concrete until my attention is distracted by a rat scampering brazenly along the rail bed, sniffing here and there at discarded candy wrappers. It bolts away as if startled by an electric shock and I glance down the gloomy tunnel as a silver ribbon of light blossoms along the rails. In a moment the headlights pop into view and the train follows, pushing the stale air before it like the musty breath of a huge subterranean beast.

The ancient subway car that shrieks to a halt in front of me is covered in graffiti. "StAYHiGh," it exhorts in stylized sky-blue letters. The identical spray-painted message has been tagged across the dark green exterior of adjacent cars with the same anarchic flair. Built for the original IND line that opened in 1932, these R-1 "city cars" were innovative in combining the speed of existing IRT units with the larger capacity of the BMT rolling stock. Once they inspired Billy Strayhorn's "Take the A Train," but that was decades ago. They were supposed to have been retired last year, yet here they are, still being pressed into service.

Boarding the dilapidated car—with its dingy rattan seats, old-fashioned overhead fans and metal straps that resemble stirrups—is like stepping into the city's past. The nostalgic effect is enhanced by the lighting, a smattering of bare fifteen-watt bulbs. In the center of each, a gumball-sized nugget of light burns brightly, surrounded by a fading aura of illumination.

The doors close and a thin black man introduces himself, wailing a raucous, otherworldly riff on a beat-up alto sax. "My name is Kadeer and I come from the planet Irkus," he says. "My spaceship has crashed and I need Earth money to repair it before I can return to my galaxy." He circulates through the car collecting a few handouts. "Thank you, Earth people. Tell anyone who asks that Kadeer did it to your ear." For an encore he reprises the same three discordant notes, which suggest the minimalist theme for a low-budget sci-fi flick. The sax is so strident in the narrow confines of the train that I get up and walk into another car.

Immediately I get a negative vibe from a scruffy dude in a combat jacket who is eating ribs from a cardboard box and tossing the gnawed bones onto the floor. Disgruntled vet? Psychiatric outpatient? Poor white trash? The sign above his seat reads, JUST A DROP IN THE BASKET HELPS KEEP NEW YORK CLEAN. An arrow descends from the T in BASKET into an artist's rendering of a trash receptacle. No use stopping here. I'll probably tell him off and end up in a fight. I move on to the next car and sit across from a young Hispanic couple.

A *Daily News* lies discarded on the seat beside me, its boldface headline in a type size usually reserved for reporting the onset of a war. "JUSTICE DEPT. SAYS: SITTING VEEP CAN BE INDICTED." It seems if Agnew is indicted by the grand jury, he can be tried on criminal charges before he leaves office. Without any protections from prosecution, and with indictments for malfeasance pending, Agnew will become a political liability. It means he's on his way out, which is great news. And once Agnew is gone, we can concentrate on dumping Nixon.

Looking up, I notice the young Latina is carefully clipping her boyfriend's nails as the train lurches and sways. I stare at them, transfixed, until she notices and I avert my eyes to study a Morningside Chapels ad. A photo of a much younger Foxy Rosenthal gazes down with an air of kindly compassion. The slogan reads:

"When life is unfair, we care." A bulleted list mentions *chapel and graveside services, complete arrangement*s and *extensive casket selection*. This last item brings to mind an uncomfortable moment at the funeral.

Goldie and I were being given a private viewing. The Captain was laid out immaculately in his blue suit, but other attempts to prettify him seemed off. His tie was knotted too neatly in a full Windsor, his hair parted to the wrong side, his face unnaturally rouged. I had the sentimental idea of enclosing in the coffin the uncashed ticket on Secretariat he had given me at the Belmont Stakes. With Goldie's approval I substituted the crisp two-dollar ticket for the handkerchief he never wore. My mother sat down and I was there alone with the body. I was taken with the urge to touch my father, to feel his stubbly cheek with the flat of my palm as I sometimes used to do when I was a child, to say goodbye with a familiar gesture of affection, but I froze. And as I vacillated the desire vexed and intensified, expanding into a paralysis of longing as poignant and implacable as regret.

I couldn't touch him and I didn't know why.

Did I hate him that much?

A moment's hesitation. A stifled impulse. A bitter memory impossible to set right. And that line from Blake I couldn't get out of my head: *Sooner murder an infant in its cradle than nurse unacted desires.*

I was always hesitant around my father, cowed by his insistence to shape my aspirations. He was always telling me in no uncertain terms what to do. Maybe in death he was doing it one last time, warning me to keep my hands to myself. Maybe that was my final punishment. I wanted to rub his cheek and he wouldn't let me.

One thing for sure, he didn't want me to follow in his footsteps. My father was a gambler who made his bones by luck and accident, a journeyman who handicapped a hundred-to-one shot and hit it big in the coin business. But with my prospects he hedged and played it close to the vest. With Columbia he was backing the odds-on favorite. Betting the predictable chalk. Going with the sure thing. When I had the gall to remind him that I liked to gamble too, that I wanted to experiment as he did until I sussed out my own idea of a worthwhile pursuit, he either treated me dismissively or blew his top. He didn't trust me to find my own way and I despised him for it. Sometimes I hated him so much, I wished he would drop dead, but at least I don't hate him now. Since he died. That's the difference between my uncle and me. Gene will always hate his guts.

I wonder how he's doing in jail, my uncle. Probably trying to stay high, knowing him.

At the next stop, a woman enters, looking dazed and weary, as if she hasn't had a decent meal in a month, but when she goes into her pitch, her voice is surprisingly strong. "Ladies and gentlemen," she shouts, "what's the greatest city in the world? Generosity. I was kicked out of my apartment and now I have to ride the trains. I don't steal and I don't do drugs. I'm just trying to get something to eat. A penny, a nickel, a dime—anything will help. Please be generous." I like her spiel, so I give her a buck. Instead of thanking me, she asks if I can spare another.

Jesus, lady, who do I look like, my father? I escape to the next car, wondering if people in Amsterdam are so aggressive. As soon as I graduate, I'll see for myself. There'll be plenty of time when I get back to pursue a livelihood, but at least I won't have to please someone else. *It's not what you want to do, but what you want to do next,* the woman at Jamaica Bay had said. And what I want to do next is something that intrigues me. I may not know what it is, but I have a good idea where to find it. It's waiting for me somewhere in the city, like a rare old penny in a pocketful of change, and one of these days, if I keep looking...

The front of the train beckons and I weave my way toward it, lights flickering. The glass to which I press my forehead is so old it's embedded with chicken wire. I mold my hands to the side of my face and look out. The contours of the dark world resolve into recognizable shapes. A yellow block signal turns green, giving us the go sign. Gathering speed, the wheel trucks skip out a comforting percussive rhythm like a heartbeat. Down the tunnel the lights are green and the straightaway is clear. The headlights cast their narrow beams. The rails gleam and dim. The steel supports flash by like a fresh deck of cards being shuffled.

ACKNOWLEDGMENTS

I wish to thank several friends who have read the manuscript at various stages of progress and offered suggestions and encouragement. A shout-out to Rich Rosenblatt, David Ruck, Jane Schwartz, Victor Aboulaffia, Linda Johanson, Josh Goldbas, Dennis Paoli, Jack Tuchman, Miriam Lieberman and Mark Saltzman. Thanks also to Lenny Messer for his useful recollections, and to William Rothlein, the great rememberer, who continually inspired me with vivid descriptions of his wild exploits.

Many people were invaluable in researching aspects of the story. I am indebted to the following: Janet S. Rapaport, the effervescent U.S. Customs Public Affairs Officer for New York and New Jersey, for facilitating interviews with alacrity; Ralph Hackney, Port Director at Alexandria Bay, NY; Mike Bridgeman, Resident Special Agent in Charge in the Office of Investigation, Rouses Point, NY; and Robert L. Guthrie, retired supervisory special agent at the Office of Investigation, Ogdensburg, NY. Thank you to Joe Pavone, Interim US Attorney for the Northern District of NY; Becky Martin, Assistant US Attorney for the Southern District of NY; and Celeste Koeleveld, Chief of Criminal Division, US Attorney's Office for the Southern

District. Thanks also to Paul Daigle, Deputy Clerk for the Burlington, VT, branch of the U.S. District Court; Gary Jarvis, Sheriff of St. Lawrence County, NY. Thanks to Eileen McHugh and Lynn Palmieri of the Cayuga Museum, Auburn, NY; Donna Dutton, City Historian of Watertown, NY; Fred Rollins and Amber Hills of the Jefferson County, NY, Historical Society; John Russell, manager of the Woodford Hotel in Watertown from 1958 to 1973; and Jack Scordo, Esq., of Watertown for his recollections of Fred Exley.

I am grateful to several people from the world of horseracing: John Lee, former Director of Broadcasting, New York Racing Association (NY__ __ _____ ___ _____ ___ ___ ___ _____ B_b Duncan, S   former
b   ;eum of
F